When Henry VIII came to Dinner

(And other guests...)

Paul Wreyford

Chiselbury

Published by Chiselbury Publishing, a division of Woodstock Leasor Limited, 14 Devonia Road, London N1 8JH

www.chiselbury.com

ISBN: 978-1-916556-20-1

Cover design by Jeremy Leasor www.jeremyleasor.com

The Guests

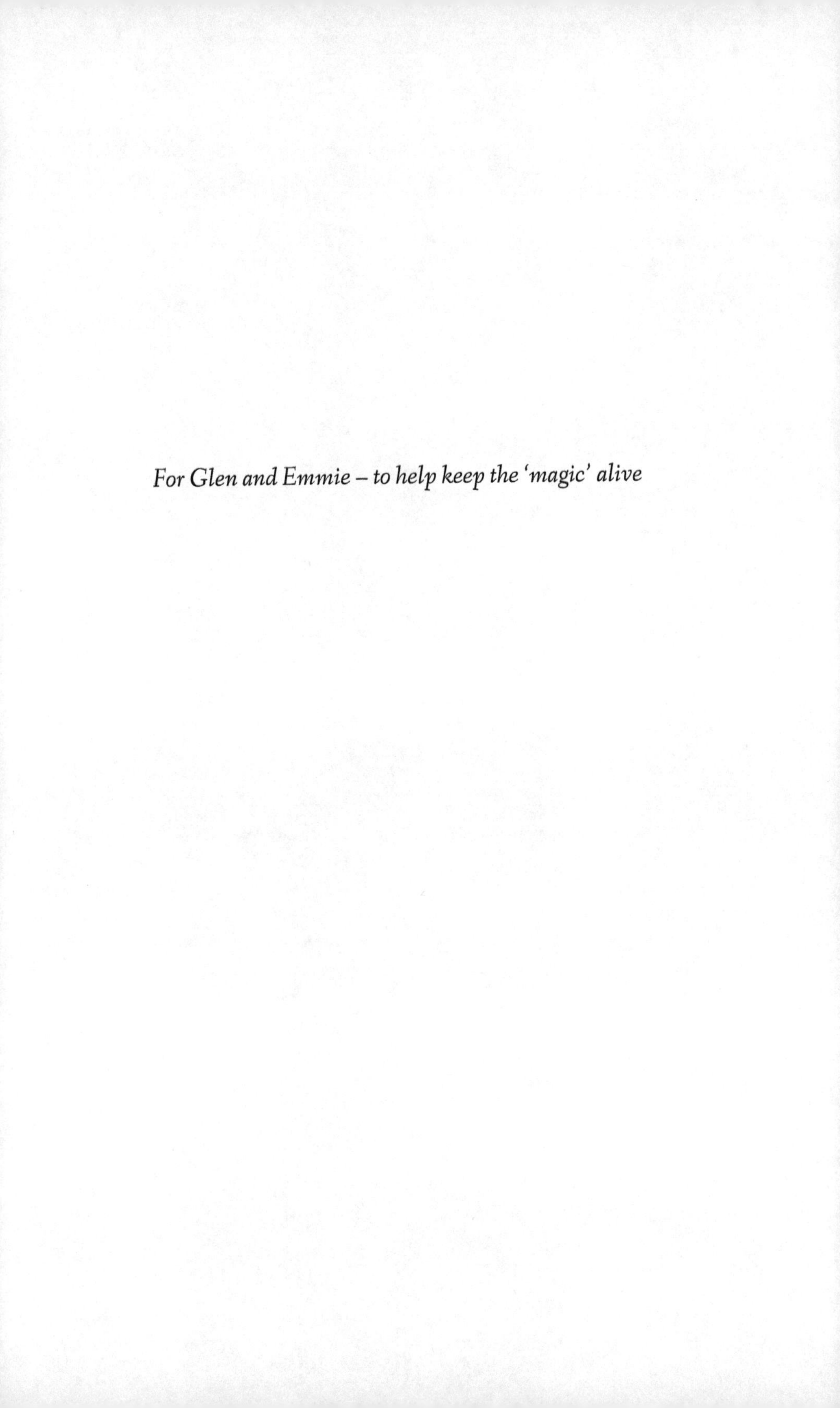

For Glen and Emmie – to help keep the 'magic' alive

Chapter 1
Henry VIII

"I think we're going to need more than *one* bargain bucket!" I shrieked, as my eyes fixed upon the imposing figure making his way down the garden path. "He *really* is enormous – and he's not alone!"[1]

The doorbell sounded, and I instinctively withdrew to a position even further behind the living room curtain from which I had been peering.

"Do you want plates?" Dad shouted from the kitchen, my fretful announcement seemingly having not reached his ears. "Or do you want to eat the chicken straight out of the bucket?"

I gulped. It was not the first time that I had been struck by the thought that a king might expect a bit more than a takeaway for dinner.

The doorbell sounded once more. It sounded different this time, as though the presser was using more force than before. Even though I dared not steal another glance from behind the curtain, I knew that it wasn't *him* pressing it – of course such a menial task would be left to one of his entourage. Besides, the bell might have germs on it.[2]

The doorbell sounded again, this time the presser had not left so long a pause.

I stumbled towards the hallway.

"I'm sure these buckets are getting smaller every time," I heard Dad remark from the kitchen. "In my day, they were..."

I didn't hear the rest. The few seconds after I had gingerly opened the front door were a blur.

He was not the first to enter the house. Two of his broad-shouldered attendants who could have been mistaken for bouncers from a Tudor nightclub (though I don't suppose they had nightclubs in the 16th century) marched straight past me. One made his way upstairs and one headed into the living room.

A third attendant entered and closed the front door behind him. He stopped and started to examine me with his eyes. I returned a sheepish smile. I did at this moment think about engaging in some sort of small talk: should I inquire whether last year's stag-hunting season had proved to be successful; or whether he thought the latest doublet was less itchy than normal? But, by the time I *had* thought about it, the third attendant had finished his examination of me and had also headed off, in the direction of the kitchen, leaving me alone in the hallway.

He remained outside. The front door was still closed, so I couldn't see him, but I knew he wasn't alone, as I could hear more voices.

At last the first attendant came down the stairs.

"It's all clear up there – there's only a *few* rooms," he said with a sneer to the second attendant, who had re-emerged from the living room at the same time.

"Looks like they're dining in *here*," the second attendant replied, his lip curling as he did so. "It's...*small*."

I felt obliged to respond with an apologetic smile.[3]

The third attendant returned from the kitchen.

"Just a simple-looking cook in there," he nodded, joining the others in the hallway, which was now almost at full capacity. "Where are the rest of them?" he continued with suspicion, his eyes falling back on me.

"*Rest of them?*" I responded, even though I knew what he was getting at, having refrained from the temptation of informing him that Mum was out shopping.

"The staff?" he replied impatiently.

I shrugged my shoulders. "It's their day off."

I instantly regretted my flippant remark, but the third attendant believed me to be in earnest. He shook his head. "So there are only *two* of you here?" he deduced. "*Two* of you? And where's your master himself?"

"My what?"

"The host of this party? Is he not even here to greet my..."

He stopped. I shrugged my shoulders once more and I knew from the look of incredulity on his face that it had finally dawned on him that the host was standing before him. He turned his head towards the kitchen, but his expression never changed, and I knew that he was thinking about the *simple-looking* man who would be serving us. Then he turned his head towards the front door and grinned. I knew what that grin meant; that he didn't fancy our chances of our heads still being attached to our torsos by the end of the day.[4]

"What's going on?" a voice from outside thundered. I had no doubt it was *his* voice. "Is it safe to enter?" he added, this time with a hint of anxiety in his tone.

One of the three attendants puffed out his cheeks and let out a lungful of air, before squeezing himself past the now half-open door. I tried in vain to get a glimpse of my renowned guest before the door closed completely again.

"Was there a lot of traffic?" I nervously asked the two attendants that were left standing beside me. "Did you get through the road-works OK? Those temporary lights take forever to change," I continued to babble. At this point, I would have liked to have informed you that I was a bit more comfortable talking about traffic hold-ups than stags or doublets, but *comfortable* was the last word I would have used to describe myself at this particular moment.

Suddenly, the front door swung open and Henry VIII – the most famous monarch England has ever had – was standing there, bearing down on me. Only a few gaps of daylight were detectable behind his giant frame that had almost succeeded in taking up the entire doorway.

I bowed. I didn't know what else to do.

"Thank you for coming...Your Majesty," I added cautiously. "Would His Majesty like to hang his robe up?"

I looked to the bannister. Blast! Dad had left his coat and bobble hat there. Henry stepped inside without answering or even acknowledging me. I wasn't sure that was because he had also mistaken me for a servant, or whether it was because he considered *everyone* to be his servant.

"I hope you'll be warm enough," I started, observing that only those famous white tights (or hose, to give them their proper name) were all that covered his legs from the knees down. "Dad *does* turn the thermostat up a few degrees when we have visitors, but do let me know if it's not warm enough for you."

I opened the living room door for Henry to enter. I swear he lowered his head slightly, though I don't think it would have quite hit the top of the door frame, even if he had been wearing his crown. And, much to my relief, he didn't get stuck in the doorway, though the fringes of his black, ermine-lined robe *did* brush both sides of the frame as he entered.

The table was set for only two people and, not for the first time, I wondered whether I would have to accommodate Henry's *entire* royal court.

"Would you like to sit here, Your Majesty? The sun from the window will warm your back," I suggested. Not that there was any sun, but I just kept thinking he might be a bit chilly in *those* tights.

I pulled his chair from under the table, beating one of his attendants to the job. Henry sat down. Yes, the chair stood firm! However, the battle wasn't over, for he had not yet put his fat legs into the position where they were supposed to be – *under* the table. I was not totally sure how the tricky manoeuvre was accomplished, as two of his attendants had rushed to his aid and momentarily blocked my view of the king, but there was a lot of tutting and grunting, and, when Henry was in view again, now sitting facing me at the other end of the table, he did look a little pinkish. I feared his thighs had been so forcibly wedged in; that any sudden movement on their part might cause the table to rise.

I now took my seat, having, of course, politely waited for my guest to have taken his. I pretended to have as much difficulty getting my legs under the table as he did, but I was not very convincing.[5]

Just one attendant stayed in the room with us, much to my relief. He stood to attention.

Without any further delay, I started to gush: "It's a great honour to have you here, Your Majesty. I have to say that you look just like all those pictures in the history books."

Henry was not listening to me, which was perhaps fortunate. I got the impression that he thought it was not his duty to do so. He fingered the knife and fork in front of him, before picking up his empty wine glass, sniffing the rim of it.

"Forgive me," I apologised. "You must think me very rude...Dad!" I yelled. "You forgot the wine...Dad!"

Henry still didn't look at me. In fact, he had barely looked at me since his entrance. He was more interested in his surroundings, a look of curiosity seemingly permanently etched on his bloated face.

My father entered with a box of wine. "Your Majesty," Dad bowed, his eye immediately set on the king. "It is an honour to be in your presence. Permit me to serve...I hope Your Majesty does not feel *disesteemed* by being served wine from a box?"

Wow! Where did that word come from? Not from Dad's *Daily Mirror*, that's for sure. I was surprised and impressed by my father. He had started well.

"A box works out a bit cheaper than buying individual bottles, you see," Dad went on to explain. I groaned. Well, it *had* started well.

I don't think Henry felt *disesteemed,* but rather intrigued, even amused, as he watched Dad do battle with the plastic tap on the wine box. Positioning the box so that the tap overhung the edge of the table, Dad filled Henry's glass, failing to notice the fact that he had left a droplet of wine clinging to the tap. I didn't have long to wait... for the moment when that droplet chose to detach itself from the tap and fall onto the carpet. Yes, I notice things like that and, make no mistake; Mum would have done so as well if she had been present!

Henry didn't express any gratitude as the glass of wine was placed in front of him. I also got the impression it was another thing that kings did not need to do. Dad made up for it, though.

"Thank you, Your Majesty, thank you," he enthused, putting himself into reverse gear, mindful that it was rude to turn your back on a monarch. "May I again express our *indebtedness* to you for gracing our humble abode?"

I sighed, as Dad continued to back away in the direction of the door, occasionally bowing his head, all the while offering compliments in that voice he only usually used for when he answered the phone.

Dad fumbled for the door knob – his back still to the door – and took several seconds to locate it.

"Oh!" he said sharply. "I nearly forgot. I have prepared a little *hors d'oeuvre*. Please help yourself, Your Majesty."

Dad was smiling profusely, having no doubt surprised himself with his pronunciation, now pointing towards a glass bowl that sat in the middle of the table, the contents covered by a tea towel (our Whipsnade Zoo tea towel). Dad returned to the table and whipped the tea towel off to reveal what was in the bowl – lettuce.

I groaned. Henry raised his eyebrows, before turning to his attendant, a wry smile on his face.

It was the attendant who spoke on behalf of his master.

"His Majesty does not do vegetables."

Not a good start.

I looked at the lettuce and started to prod it with a fork. "I think there might be some cherry tomatoes under here," I submitted. "Do you like tomatoes? Technically, they're a fruit...aren't they?"

At least Henry appeared to have a sense of humour.

"I don't do *fruit* either," he informed me, a grin on his face.

"Nor me," I smiled. "All this rubbish about needing to eat 'five a day'; just open a pack of Starburst, I say. Perhaps we should move on to the next course?" I suggested.

My father had already departed the room muttering something about 'Opal Fruits' (whatever they were).

"Dad!" I yelled once more. "We're ready for the next course."

I could sense that Henry was beginning to relax. He lifted his wine glass to his lips and downed half of its contents...before coughing them up again!

His attendant was beside him in an instant.

"Your Majesty!" the alarmed attendant shrieked. "What have you done to him?" he added, turning towards me accusingly. Fortunately, Henry was not choking and did not need the thump on the back that the attendant feared he might be obliged to give.

"Sugar!" Henry roared, banging the empty glass down on the table. Well, it was definitely empty *after* it hit the table, a splash of red wine now visible on the white tablecloth. At least it wasn't the carpet this time.

"It's OK," I assured everyone. "Don't worry; it's only an old tablecloth. Well, no, I don't mean old...it's our best one, of course...we would only use our best one for you..."

"Sugar!" Henry roared again.

That's not the word Dad usually uttered when he was angry.

"Sugar!" Henry growled for a third time. "Bring me some sugar!"

"Dad!" I yelled again.

Dad heard me this time. He appeared in a flash and it was not long before a bowl of sugar was placed before the monarch. Henry picked the teaspoon out of the bowl before pouring most of the sugar into his empty glass. He then held the glass aloft. Dad had hastily left the room on this occasion, so it was the attendant who was obliged to fill the glass of sugar with wine.

Henry offered me a stern look. "I hope your ale is kinder on the taste buds than your wine, my friend."

I assured him it was; secretly hoping that Dad had had the foresight to put a few tins of beer in the fridge.[6]

I felt a swift change of subject was in order. "I hope I am addressing you in the proper fashion, *Your Majesty*. Is that how I should address a king?"

Henry nodded. "It is, but you can call me Hal."

Dad popped his head around the door. "Are you a Paul Simon fan as well? *If I'll be your bodyguard*," Dad sang incorrectly, losing no chance to share his love of eighties' music. Henry frowned. Like me, he was from a different era and didn't get Dad's joke.

"Bodyguard?" the monarch smirked, eyeing my father with disdain. "*You'll* be my bodyguard? I don't think so, my friend. I prefer my bodyguards to have a bit more meat on them. Talking of meat... are we going to get any?"

My deflated Dad got the hint and this time retreated with a nod, rather than a bow.

Despite his reputation – and lack of meat to date – Henry seemed jovial enough, but I decided that I would probably not call him 'Hal' and would stick with 'Your Majesty'.[7] I put his good mood down to the fact that we were observing one of his favourite pastimes – eating. Well, I say eating, but, as Henry himself had pointed out, we hadn't actually started to do that just yet...the lettuce, needless to say, remaining untouched. And I did fear that unless the next course was to his liking, Henry might not be so convivial towards us.

Henry raised his glass and downed its contents. His attendant knew the drill and was quick (he was becoming adept at using the tap) to refill the glass with wine...and the remaining sugar.

"You have an unusual palace, my friend," Henry said, casting his eye around the room. "You must give me a tour. I must say, that is a particularly unusual tapestry over yonder."

He had spotted our Mickey Mouse beach towel that was draped over the back of a chair.[8]

Dad at last came in with the food.

"I think you're going to like this," I said, as the red-and-white cardboard bucket was placed in the middle of the table, next to the untouched salad bowl.

"I think this meal is very *you*," I continued. "Would you like me to serve?"

Henry looked perplexed. He was studying an image on the bucket.

"Who is the gentleman?" he inquired, seemingly put out that it was not his own image.

"His name is Colonel Sanders," I replied.

"He's a military man," Dad mocked, as he was leaving the room.

Henry nodded thoughtfully. "Not heard of him, but I'll bear him in mind if I need any further help in suppressing those damned Scots. It'll be better than leaving it to the missus to see them off. Don't get me wrong, Cath did all right last time, but I didn't hear the end of it!"

I smiled politely, but had no idea what he was talking about.[9]

"Now," I started to explain, as I took the lid off our bargain bucket; "there are pieces of breast and legs in here. You can eat with your hands if you like. I think you'd prefer to do that, wouldn't you? And I somehow get the feeling you'd prefer to have a drumstick!" Yes, I *had* seen him feasting in all those films and television dramas!

Henry did not reply, but looked on with interest as I placed two chicken drumsticks onto his plate (yes, Dad had felt we needed plates). I then took a packet of fries out of the bucket and pushed it towards him.

"These are what we call chips or fries," I revealed. "They're just cut and sliced potatoes really. You do eat potatoes, don't you? Wasn't it Sir Walter Raleigh who brought them to England? Oh, hold on a minute, he might have come *after* you? Anyway, I think you'll like them."

Henry looked to his attendant. It was a signal. The attendant picked up one of the fries and popped it into his mouth. He shrugged his shoulders as a response. Presumably assured that his attendant was not about to keel over, Henry was happy to try one himself.

"The chicken might taste a bit different to what you're used to," I smiled, "but it's finger-lickin' good!"

Henry started to eat, though gorge would have been a more apt description; the king lifting the paper packet and tipping the fries into his mouth in one go. I thought it only polite to do the same (well, at least try to). Needless to say, we didn't need the cutlery.

"I thought you might have brought somebody with you," I suggested, in an attempt to start a conversation. "I mean a lady friend," I added, catching sight of one of his male attendants pacing up and down the front garden path.

"A woman? I didn't want to spoil my appetite!" Henry quipped. At least I think he was quipping.

"Of course," I continued, pushing another packet of fries in the direction of my guest, "you might have had a job choosing *which* lady to bring?"

Henry looked up; his lips smeared with grease from the chicken. For a moment I wondered if my comment had caused him offence.

I tried to remedy the situation. "I meant your wives, not the..."

Henry studied me closely. "My mistresses?" he smiled, feeling the need to complete my sentence.[10]

The smile that I returned was a little more abashed than his.

Henry seemed undaunted by my questioning and showed no sign of embarrassment. He was more concerned about his stomach. He turned his eyes to the chicken drumstick in his hand, the flesh now gone, just the bone remaining.

"Go on!" I urged him. "Throw it over your shoulder!"

To my disappointment, he did not oblige.

"You have small chickens here," he went on, now a rueful smile on his face. "Are you sure this isn't the leg of a sparrow?"

Surprisingly – and to complete my disappointment – Henry placed the fleshless drumstick onto his plate.[11]

I wondered which wife Henry was on at the moment and came to the conclusion it was his final one. He had seen better days, for sure, and it looked like he was at the point in his life when he wouldn't be seeing too many more!

"And what about you?" Henry asked; now a playful grin on his face. "Do you have many lady friends?"

I dithered. "Just one or two," I lied, feeling the need to do so. Henry winked at me and I blushed.

I pushed the cardboard bucket closer to the king.

"Help yourself to some more chicken. There's plenty more from where that came from," I lied...again.

Henry did so. He took a bite from another drumstick, not waiting to clear his mouth before speaking.

"Which one would I bring?" he mused, going back to my original question. Clearly, his love life was not a sensitive subject to him. "Anne," he concluded.

I nodded thoughtfully. "I thought you might say that. They did say that Anne Boleyn was very beautiful."

"No, not that Anne," he spat out. "Anne of Cleves, of course."

"But wasn't she...wasn't she *the*...?"

I stopped myself from saying the word 'ugly'.

"That's right," Henry interrupted. "To say that she wasn't much of a looker would be an understatement – she was hideous!"

I think I was meant to return a smile, but that would have proved difficult due to the fact that my mouth remained wide open. I didn't know how to respond and ended up unconvincingly mumbling something about how good it was that he went for personality rather than looks.

Henry started to laugh and raised his arms. "I'm jesting with you, my friend – of course I wouldn't choose Anne of Cleves to join me.

Good grief, man, I got rid of her quicker than you can eat these thin potato things of yours!"[12]

"Why did you marry her, then?" I felt the need to ask, pushing my uneaten second packet of fries his way.

"Cromwell!" Henry barked. "I never forgave him for that. Of course, I got my own back on him – in the end![13] None of it was my idea; it was all his doing – he arranged, or should I say *manipulated*, the wedding; told me that it was a perfect match. What he had omitted to tell me was that my bride looked like a mare!"[14]

I immediately realised he was talking about a horse and not a dignitary who opened summer fetes.

"I suppose it was my own fault," the king reflected ruefully; "to judge someone from their portrait. I should have known that she'd be nothing like it in the flesh. I mean, it wasn't like that picture over there..." He pointed to a framed photograph of my mother on the mantlepiece. "The artist has been very honest in that picture, hasn't he?" Henry went on. "I mean; no-one would dream of marrying a hag like that, would they?"

As I said earlier, it was a good job Mum wasn't here! I forced a smile. Actually, I didn't have to force it. I wondered if Dad was earwigging on the other side of the door. "Yes, no-one would dream of marrying someone who looked like that, would they?" I mischievously repeated, raising my voice as I did so.

"So how would you rate her out of ten, then?" I readdressed Henry, with an uncharacteristic wink of the eye, now feeling confident that someone who seemed to have a weakness when it came to the fairer sex would relish a bit more 'man talk'. "I mean Anne of Cleves...not my mother," I felt the need to add. "Was she really as bad as you say, or just a plain Jane?"

The smile on Henry's face evaporated in an instant. He glared at me.

"What are you saying about my Jane?"

I hesitated. "I didn't mean *your* Jane."

Henry resumed a state of calm.

"There has only ever really been one lady in my life," he said.

I wanted to dispute that fact, and inform him that even the toddler next door probably knew that Henry VIII had no less than *six* wives, but I dared not rile him again.

"Jane, my dear Jane," he said with a melancholy smile.

I knew he was talking about Jane Seymour, of course. There were plenty of Catherines and Annes, but only one Jane. I quickly tried to place her in my mind. Which one was she? The one who gave him a son, of course! What was her fate? I muttered the rhyme under my breath: divorced, beheaded, died...divorced, beheaded, survived...but what number was she?[15]

"I need to relieve myself," Henry announced suddenly, flicking his head in the direction of his attendant, who rushed to his side, ready to begin the operation of freeing his master from the table and chair.

"You have a garderobe?" the attendant inquired on behalf of the king, as he got to work attempting to prise Henry's legs from under the table.

"A what?" I responded, having risen from my seat and grabbed hold of the wine box for fear a sudden jolt of the table would send it crashing to the carpet.

"If not, a chamber pot will suffice," the attendant continued. "In fact, that might be the better option," he muttered under his breath, as Henry puffed and panted, putting all his concentration into the job of standing up. "Yes, a chamber pot will do," the attendant went on. "His Majesty cares not."

But I did, fearing they might still find a use for the salad bowl!

"Yes, we have a *bathroom*," I declared, making my way to the door of the living room.

Of course, I had to wait there a while before Henry reached me. We then made our way to the foot of the stairs where another of the attendants was sitting. He wasn't expecting us and got to his feet quickly.

"It's up there, first door on the right," I pointed. Henry looked up the stairs and then scowled at me. At first I thought he was taking offence at my lack of manners in not leading the way, but a cough from one of the attendants, and his despairing eyes, told me that we could have done with Grandma's stairlift.[16]

With the help of his attendant and the bannister, Henry somehow managed to scale his personal Everest, but he was panting profusely when he reached the landing. I opened the bathroom door for him.

"Sometimes you have to hold the lever down for a couple of seconds to get it to flush," I felt the need to explain. He and his attendant looked at me with puzzled faces. "Don't suppose you know what a flush is?" I said.

Henry lifted up his arm and smiled.

"Indeed I do, my friend – and I do hope there will be time for cards after our repast is over."

I giggled. A royal flush! Dad would have appreciated the joke if he had been up here with us. Dad was fond of *toilet* humour.

Henry entered the bathroom and, much to my surprise, was followed by his attendant.

I walked down the stairs, thinking it best not to loiter outside.

"Do they always go to the loo together?" I asked the other attendant left at the foot of the stairs.

"Of course," he replied. "Who do you think de-robes him?"

"You mean pulls down his trousers!"

Of course, I had forgotten that Henry didn't wear trousers and recalled those white tights – but somehow that image made it even worse.[17]

I made my way to the kitchen.

"You all right, Dad?" I inquired. "It's going well, I think."

"Do you think he'd like Victoria sponge for dessert," Dad responded, "Victoria being his family and all that?"

I closed the door and shook my head.

It was a good 15 minutes before Henry returned to the living room.

He still looked out of breath as he retook his seat, but made no attempt to place his legs under the table this time. I should point out that what I meant was that he looked still out of breath from his ascent of our stairs and not from what he might have been doing in our bathroom. And it was a good job that I didn't point that fact out to my father who, as I said, was particularly fond of toilet humour!

"May I ask what the next course is, friend?" Henry inquired. "The starter was very...interesting."

I involuntarily made a whimpering sound. Starter? Next course?

"I can't remember what the next course is," I lied. "Why don't we let Cook surprise us? Just out of interest, how many courses do you normally have?"

Henry screwed up his face. "I don't know – a couple of dozen?"

I winced in return. Oh dear!

"So what does a typical course consist of, then?" I probed, now in mind that we would need to raid a few of our cupboards.

Henry reeled them off, each one a dagger to my heart: pork, lamb, chicken, beef, game, rabbit, swan, peacock, seagull...

I think there was more to come, but I held up my hand and he stopped.

"Don't worry," I said. "I'm sure Cook has knocked up those delights, and many more."

I did for one moment think about Whiskers in his hutch at the bottom of the garden, but it was only for a moment...honestly.[18]

"What about some music?" I suggested; looking towards the CD player, hoping it might take his mind off food that we didn't have. "I know that you're a bit of a musician yourself," I went on. "Dad has *Greensleeves* on a James Galway compilation. You wrote that, didn't you?"

I started to hum the tune, and Henry seemed to recognise it.

"Is it true that Anne Boleyn inspired *Greensleeves*?" I continued to question my guest. "And I have to ask you, or my friends will never forgive me, is it *really* true that she was prone to having a runny nose and...well...that she didn't carry handkerchiefs?"

I stopped. No, of course it *wasn't* true.[19]

Something had caught Henry's eye. "I can see that you have a very unusual harpsichord," he said, lifting a chunky finger in the direction of Mum's electronic keyboard at the back of the room. "Mine is very different," he added.

I didn't doubt it. I plugged it in. "It's all yours if you want to play something."

He did want to, even though it meant he would have to get up again. He waddled over and I pointed to the piano stool to make it clear to him that this was what he was supposed to sit on. Like a concert pianist about to give a recital, he pushed his robe away from his bottom as he sat on the velvet stool, so that it dangled down onto the carpet – the robe that is, even though his fat bottom might have done so as well! I was praying the stool was as strong as the dining table chair.

He pressed a key, then another, and then one more, before shaking his head in disgust.

"Is this a jest?" he exclaimed, turning sharply to face me. "I have never heard an instrument so out of tune in my life. Bring me something else; bring me your bagpipes."

"My bagpipes?" I stopped and started to stroke my chin. "Now, where have I put *them*?"

"A lute?" Henry suggested, noticing that I had not so much hesitated, but stalled. "Come, you must surely have at least a lute in your possession?" he queried. "How do you woo the ladies if you haven't got a lute?"

An image of my father serenading my mother with a lute flashed into my head. "There might be a recorder in the house," I offered tentatively.

"One?" Henry replied aghast. "You only have *one*? I have 78, my friend – and 78 flutes too."

"And 76 trombones?" I suggested cheekily, but then quickly regretted having done so.[20]

Much to my relief, the king had turned his attention to another framed photograph that was in view from his new vantage point at the keyboard – this time of my grandmother.

"Your portraits are all very strange," he mused, "strange in that your artist does not choose to flatter his subjects. They are almost life-like – brilliant, I have to admit, but why does your painter include the wrinkles and warts? You should have him pressed for the insult!"

"Pressed?"

Henry got up from the stool and limped back to his seat at the table.

"You're right, perhaps pressing *has* had its day," he nodded. "Indeed, there are far more imaginative ways to punish miscreants these days. By the way, what do you think of Skevington's Daughter?"

I shook my head. "Can't say I know her? Is she one of your mistresses?"

Henry laughed. "Crouch down," he ordered, "and tuck your knees in so that they're almost touching your head. Go on, man," he roared, irked by my hesitation.

I was instructed to adopt what I can only describe as a sort of foetal position. I don't think I could have quite appreciated what the victim of this strange torture would have actually experienced, because I only succeeded in maintaining the said position for some 20 seconds. Yes, I got up because I was feeling uncomfortable, not in the physical sense, but because I was sure that Dad would choose this moment to return to the room, and the last thing I wanted to do was to give him even the momentary pleasure of thinking – if he saw me bent over, red-faced and wheezing – that I had failed to make it upstairs to the bathroom to release my bowels! As I have already stated on at least two occasions, Dad liked his toilet humour.

To be honest, I hadn't been expecting to play party games, especially not this one.

"You win!" I declared, after unfurling my body. "Can we play pass the parcel instead?"[21]

Then I remembered that Henry liked to play cards. I reached for the sideboard draw and pulled out a pack.

"Now this is more like it," Henry beamed, helpfully clearing the table by simply removing the tablecloth with one mighty yank, having not bothered to firstly remove the items upon it. I looked at the upturned empty bargain bucket and the *not* empty salad bowl on the floor – though it was empty now! It was not the same as throwing a half-eaten drumstick over his shoulder, but this was more like the playful Henry that I had been expecting.

"You know Primero?" he asked.[22]

I shook my head. "Is he a Shakespeare character?"

Henry looked confused and I realised I had got my historical dates muddled again.

"How about pontoon?" I suggested.

As I started to deal the cards, Henry's attendant pulled out a money bag and gave it to his master. He in turn emptied some coins onto the table.

I put my hand in my pocket and retrieved a few coppers. We would be playing for big money – all of seven pence on my part. Henry looked impressed.

And so we played pontoon, and I won the first game. Needless to say, I didn't win the second...or third...or fourth. The eye of the attendant had caught me after my initial triumph and it told me in no uncertain terms that it was not in my best interest to win those second...and third...and fourth games."[23]

As Henry gleefully scooped up the last of my coins, he stopped to stare at the image of Elizabeth II on a two-pence piece.

"Who's the pretty lass?" he inquired.

I smiled. "Your great, great, great...never mind. Can I see *your* picture?"

Henry seemed reluctant to pass me a coin. At first I thought it was because he didn't trust me to return it, but he seemed embarrassed by it.

"The silver comes off too easily these days," he admitted hurriedly, "and when it does, it makes a fine mess of my face."

"They call him Old Coppernose," the attendant, much to my surprise, butted in, a cheeky smile on his face.[24] He probably wished he had not pushed his luck. Henry was in a good mood, but not that good a mood!

"And anyone who calls me that to my face will be introduced to Skevington's Daughter for real!" Henry snarled, thumping his fist on the table.

The attendant straightened up, his face resuming a look of solemnity.

"There's a game on tonight," I chirped, keen to quickly change the subject, pointing my head in the direction of the television. "It's your local team as well – Hampton & Richmond Borough. It's the FA Cup. They're 100-1 to beat Liverpool. Fancy a bet?"

I thought that might grab his attention.

"It's football," I continued, not sure if he even knew what I was talking about; "that game where they kick the pig's bladder around."[25]

Henry sniffed. "Is there no jousting? I prefer a good joust."[26]

"We've moved on from that," I assured him, "but you can bet on anything these days – I mean *anything*: whether it will be a white Christmas or whether the royal baby will be called Louis."

"Louis?" he spat. "A *French* name! Never!"

I smiled. "I'll get my dad to put a bet on for you, if you like. He likes a flutter too. What do you fancy? You like tennis, don't you? How about naming the next Wimbledon champion?"

Henry stroked his ginger and grey beard. "I *bet* you that I could eat an entire cow," he declared.

I sighed. He probably could – and all we had left was a Victoria sponge.[27]

"So, when will the other guests get here?" Henry inquired all of a sudden. "When's this party *really* going to get going?"

"Party?"

"Is this it?" a downhearted Henry responded. "I did fear that might be the case. It's not the biggest palace, and I did wonder where your grand hall for entertaining might be."

"Your other attendant is in the only hall we have," I admitted.

Henry leant back in his chair and started to reminisce.

"I once entertained the King of France – you wouldn't even fit his wardrobe in this room. Now that was what I call a party: 30,000 fish and 5,000 chickens!"

"Was it fancy dress?"

"No, my friend – that was what we consumed...not to mention 25,000 litres of ale."

Henry stopped and looked at me.

"So, shall we step outside to fight?" he inquired casually.

"Sorry?"

"Well, there isn't much room to fight in here," he reminded me. "And if there are no other guests, we might as well get on with it."

I hesitated and he continued to study me with curious eyes.

"Are you going to fight me, or not?" he persisted.

Henry might have been well past his prime and barely able to stand up, but I still wouldn't have fancied my chances. Was he serious? Was he really asking me to join him outside?[28]

Dad had entered the room, and for once his timing was perfect, as the announcement that he was about to make soon put all thoughts of our duel to the back of Henry's mind.

"Sorry to bother you, Your Majesty," he started, with a bow, "but I thought you'd be ready for the final course. Please accept my apologies, but the Victoria sponge was out of date, though I've found a couple of ice lollies."

He held them aloft.

Henry looked at me confused. "Did your man say *final* course? Is that it?"

I nodded regretfully.

Dad shrugged his shoulders. "So you won't be wanting these, then?" he asked, still holding the ice lollies aloft.

I gritted my teeth. "No thanks, Dad."

My somewhat disgruntled father left the room. He had long given up going into reverse.

"I'm sorry," I said, turning to Henry. "If you're still hungry, I can offer you a bowl of cereal or something."

He looked interested, but didn't know what I meant.

"Cereal?" I repeated. "You know; something you might have when you get up first thing in the morning, though I'm guessing you don't eat a bowl of Frosties for breakfast?"

"I have meat for breakfast," Henry declared, a hint of sarcasm in his voice, though I didn't doubt he was telling the truth.

"And for lunch?" I asked.

"Meat."

I smiled. "I don't suppose I need to ask what you have for afternoon tea?"

"You want to sort out your cook," Henry growled. "He's committed an act of insubordination! No more meat in your palace? It's an outrage. He should be punished."

I agreed. "Do you have any ideas? Skevington's Daughter, perhaps?"

Henry shook his head. "Boil him alive in his own pot. That's what we did to the cook who poisoned the Bishop of Rochester's guests."

I grinned. "I'll probably give my cook a second chance, if it's all right with you."[29]

Henry shook his head. "You're too lenient, my friend. You can't let those beneath you get away with it. They will stab you in the back before you know it. Never trust a soul and never turn your back on anyone, that's my adage. And if I can be so bold, I have to admit I'm already a little concerned for your safety. My attendant tells me that there isn't even a lock on your chamber door?"

I shrugged my shoulders.

"Does that mean you brick up your chamber door every night instead?" Henry inquired. "That's what I do. You can't be too careful," he added, flashing a suspicious look in the direction of his attendant.[30]

I sneezed. "I beg your pardon," I said, pulling a tissue from my pocket. "Shame Anne Boleyn isn't here," I added, wiping my nose, but not the smirk off my face.

Henry looked disturbed. "You are ill?" he queried, a mixture of suspicion and fear in his voice.

I shook my head. "It's probably hay fever – it's getting to that time of year."

"A fever?" Henry persisted. "When did it come on? Why did you get me to come here if you're sick?"

"I'm not sick. I just sneezed."

Henry rose from his chair, quicker than he had done so all day.

"It is time to depart," he announced, edging further away from me. "No food. No party. And now you are showing symptoms of the pox. It has been interesting, my friend, but I am disappointed that I probably leave with your germs rather than with a full stomach!"

I rose from the table and followed Henry towards the front door, he keener than ever to make a quick (well, quick for him) exit for fear I might pass on 'the pox'.[31]

"Did you hear that noise?" he said, suddenly turning to his attendant and patting his rumbling stomach. "It's crying. Make haste to the palace...and let's get some proper food inside us."

I watched as Henry and his attendants made their way down the garden path.

"If I can be so bold," I called after him, "there's a Burger *King* on the edge of town."

Henry never turned around, but lifted his arm in the air, a token act of acknowledgement.

"But if you order a Whopper," I added, raising my voice, "you might want to ask them to take out the lettuce..."

Chapter 2
Napoleon

We had a problem: our cat was called Napoleon.

We had another problem (though it was only a problem because of the first problem): the *real* Napoleon was coming to dinner and, as Dad kept reminding me, the 'little corporal' didn't like cats! Needless to say, he would probably be even less amused to discover this particular feline actually shared his name.[1]

And there was another problem (which was again only a problem because of the other problems): we couldn't find Napoleon...I mean the *cat* Napoleon.

That is why we were now in the back garden shaking a tin of cat biscuits.

"Napoleon!" Dad shouted for the umpteenth time. "Napoleon! Where are you? We've got your favourites...the pilchard-flavoured ones."

"It's no good," I sighed. "He's going to have to stay out there now. We haven't got time for this. He'll be here any minute." I meant the *real* Napoleon, this time.

"OK," Dad nodded, lifting his hands in submission. "Be it on your head. All I'm saying is that Napoleon Bonaparte is not the sort of guy you want to upset. Let's just say that he's got a bit of a reputation. And I don't think he'll be too thrilled if our Napoleon chooses this particular day to be unusually sociable – and decides he wants to meet his namesake."

Dad was right. And I feared for our pet as well – what if our hot-headed, feline-hating guest decided to bring his sword with him?

Another problem (but again linked to the other problems, though, in truth, you could say that not even the first problem would have been a problem if it were not for the *other* 'problems') was that the front and back doors were fitted with cat flaps. And that was now our most-pressing concern: if we didn't know the whereabouts of our elusive moggy, how could we stop him from wandering in at will and causing our visitor much anguish? No, it would have been better if we could have found him, and shut him in a room upstairs – I'm now talking about the cat, of course!

"I can tape up the cat flaps?" Dad suggested. "And close all the windows? He won't be able to get in then."

"What if he's already inside and we've just missed him?" I pointed out. "You *have* checked upstairs as well?"

"Yes," Dad assured me. "I even checked the bathroom to see if he was taking a shower!"

The doorbell sounded.

"It's too late." Dad started to panic. "Remember," he added, nodding in the direction of the front door, "don't mention his height either. He's a bit touchy about that subject as well."[2]

I headed for the door, but Dad pushed in front of me.

"Actually, son, I think you'd better let me handle this," he declared. "I think I'm a bit more experienced in diplomacy and dealing with difficult people. We want to make a good first impression."

I groaned. "He's probably a very nice guy. Don't you think we're over-reacting a bit?"

Dad puffed out his cheeks and put his hand on the door handle.

"First impressions will be crucial, son," he assured me. "It's important we don't get off on the wrong foot."

And so it was Dad who opened the front door and had the first look at Napoleon Bonaparte. Dad went to shake the emperor's hand, but was still holding the tin of cat biscuits in his right hand and had to transfer them to his left.

"Sorry – they're just biscuits," he informed our guest, noticing Napoleon was focusing on *them*, rather than on his outstretched hand. "Biscuits for humans, of course...not for cats," Dad added. "No cats here," he continued to mumble, giving the tin a shake. The lid was off and a suspicious Napoleon bent forward to sniff the contents. He immediately reeled back in disgust.

"I know they whiff a bit," Dad admitted, "but they taste better than they smell."

I cringed as Dad popped one into his mouth and started to chew. "Yes, definitely for human consumption and not for cats," he went on. "They're just smaller than normal biscuits...but still for humans...and not necessarily *small* humans..."

He stopped (finally) and smiled apologetically. If my dad had possessed a tail, it would have been firmly between his legs as he retreated back to the kitchen without another word.

A somewhat dazed Napoleon turned his attention to me. He stood immaculately dressed in full military uniform, just like in the pictures that were so familiar to me. And just like in the pictures, one hand was neatly tucked inside his waistcoat.

"Come in," I beckoned him, "and please mind the step." I stopped and thought about what I had just said. Then I panicked. "Not that it's a *big* step and that you're too *small*..." I stopped again. I had seemingly caught Dad's foot-'in'-mouth disease.

Napoleon entered and handed me his coat, which I draped over the bannister, and then his bicorne, that famous two-cornered hat of his, which I placed on the bottom stair, not really knowing what to do with it. He was immediately attracted to a painting on the wall, a coastal scene. He nodded his head approvingly and took out a tiny notebook and pencil, as though he were a debt collector valuing the contents of our home. He ignored me.

"You like art?" I inquired, as I ushered him into the living room.[3]

He never answered my question.

"Please take a seat. Can I offer you an aperitif?" I continued, hoping to impress our guest with my knowledge of French.

Napoleon declined. After taking his seat on our sofa, he removed a little shell box from his waistcoat and started to sniff its contents.

"Is that a snuff box?" I asked; a hint of alarm in my voice. "Better put that away before Dad sees it. He'll mistake it for drugs!"

Napoleon looked at me with bemusement, but did as I asked. And that surprised me. Perhaps he wasn't as fierce as people portrayed him?

"Dad...I mean my servant...is working on the dinner now," I started. "Would you like to talk or play a game in the meantime?"

Napoleon shrugged his shoulders. He had still not said a word, and so I thought the game idea might work better than the talking!

"I know just the game for you," I said, opening a door on the sideboard. "Have you ever played *Risk* before? It's a board game – a game of strategy and conquest," I added, reading off the side of the box.

I proceeded to lay the contents onto the coffee table which stood between us; I myself sitting in the armchair opposite my guest. "The idea is to conquer a continent or the entire world," I began, pointing to a map of the globe on the board. "These are your armies," I went on, pulling out a bag full of small plastic figures. "What colour do you want to be, black?"

Napoleon; now with a keen interest in the proceedings, shook his head vigorously.

"No, not black – no army of mine will ever wear black," he snarled, at last breaking his silence. "Les Bleus! Les Bleus!" he shouted, clenching his fist.[4] He then rubbed his hands together. This sudden release of emotion caught me by surprise, but clearly the idea of pitting his wits against me had filled him with excitement.

"I like the look of this entertainment, sir," he eagerly assured me. "Now, pray tell me how we go about conquering the world? I have my eye on Asia, you see. I have a cousin whose birthday is coming up and need to find a present for him."[5]

I held up my hands. "No! You mustn't *tell* me what countries you're going to conquer – the other player isn't supposed to know. We have to deal the cards to see what your mission will be."

He nodded thoughtfully. "Yes, the element of surprise; I understand what you're getting at."

I handed him a card and he immediately threw it onto the table in disgust. "I've *already* conquered Europe," he stormed. "I want Asia now!"

I lifted my hands up again, this time in submission. "OK. That's fine. You do what you want," I conceded, putting the relevant card in front of him.

"Indeed I will," he replied, a look of defiance on his face. "Do we have weapons?"

I handed him the dice.

Dad entered the room. "Is everything all right?" He stopped. "Oh no, you're not playing *that* game are you?" Dad was positioned behind the seated Napoleon and he made a point of establishing eye contact with me before whispering: "Just let him win!"

It was a couple of hours before we concluded. I had suggested on a couple of occasions that we could stop and call it a draw, but each time Napoleon had merely replied: "Surrender? Never!"

In the end, I took Dad's advice and decided that there should be only one winner – and that winner wasn't going to be me. However, from the moment I had decided on that stance, it was just typical that I seemed incapable of throwing less than a four on the die. And every time I reluctantly picked off one of his armies, the act was met with a little grunt of dissatisfaction from my irritated opponent. When the battle was finally over, Napoleon offered a smile of contentment and, much to my surprise, leant over the coffee table and affectionately pinched me on the cheek. I wondered if he had celebrated all his past victories in that manner.[6]

"Do you play chess?" he asked suddenly. I shook my head, pretending I had no idea what he was talking about. I had had enough of playing games. And his smugness was making me abhor him.

He tutted. "Huh! You English are such bad losers."

"Maybe that's because we're not *used* to losing," I said with a somewhat conceited smile on my face. I should have stopped there. And I don't know what possessed me to start singing the ABBA song: "*Waterloo...Waterloo...*" (I only knew the tune and not the lyrics).

Napoleon glared at me. Yes, I should have definitely stopped there!

"You English are all the same," he hissed. "You only ever remember that insignificant little place in Belgium."

I boldly shook my head. "Actually, we won at Trafalgar as well!"[7]

I'm sorry to say that I was enjoying the process of winding him up.

"What about all my *triumphs*?" Napoleon chirped. "I am the greatest military commander the world has ever seen. You know of Alexander the Great...Hannibal...Julius Caesar, yes?"

I replied with a nod.

"Well, let me tell you," Napoleon boasted, "I gained more victories than all of them put together."[8]

Dad re-entered the room. "Everything OK?" he inquired. "I heard raised voices," he added, looking accusingly at me. "I see you've finished your game. Who won?"

Napoleon sank into the sofa and crossed his legs.

"I did," he said defiantly, but, as he leant back, I noticed a couple of blue plastic figures fall from his pocket. "You've been cheating!" I exclaimed.[9]

"Dinner is served," a concerned Dad shouted, even though it wasn't. "Please make your way to the table."

Dinner – when it *was* finally served – did not start well. The soup was too cold and Napoleon twice ordered his to be taken away and made hotter. I heard Dad boil the kettle after the second refusal and this time he returned with a cup-a-soup. Napoleon didn't seem to mind. In fact, he seemed to enjoy putting his rather effeminate hands around the mug to keep them warm.[10]

The emperor did not eat much of the main course and chose to use his hands, rather than a knife and fork. It was a good job Dad and I had decided against feeding him spaghetti Bolognese!

Napoleon never once looked at me during the meal. He kept the answers to my questions to a minimum, concentrating on the business of eating. I was just a mere distraction to him.

Dessert was Napoleon pastry.

"I thought it the most appropriate thing," Dad beamed as he brought it in.[11] "And perhaps you would like to finish your meal with a...*Napoleon* brandy?"

Dad made a point of laughing at his own joke (well, no-one else did), before stopping suddenly. "Actually, I hope you don't," he admitted. "To be honest, I don't have any Napoleon brandy; couldn't find any at Tesco."

Napoleon ignored my dithering father and took out the little shell box once more. Dad looked at it suspiciously. "It's not drugs," I whispered; "it's a snuff box, I think."

But I was wrong. It was full of...liquorice.[12]

"It helps my digestion," Napoleon explained.

Dad looked concerned. "You have indigestion?"

"Well, he did eat his dinner a bit quickly!" I snapped, glancing at my watch.[13]

Dad looked at me with alarm, believing I should have been offering our guest some sympathy, rather than accusing him of wolfing down his food. But, as you have probably gathered, I was not too enamoured with the 'little corporal' and had been further riled by this latest act; the contempt in his voice convincing me that he was implying that the meal had not been to his satisfaction and had, in fact, been the very *cause* of that indigestion.

I should also add that the manners of Napoleon, or lack of them, were also a source of irritation to me. It wasn't the fact that he had eaten with his hands that annoyed me, but the fact that he had not once said thank you. Dad had worked hard on this one.

"Perhaps you would have preferred beef to chicken?" I teased Napoleon; "Beef *Wellington* perhaps?"

Napoleon thumped his fist upon the table, immediately wiping the smirk from my face. "Do not mention that name again," he barked. "If you do, sir, I swear I will run my sword through you."[14]

I reluctantly apologised. Well, I wasn't that reluctant to do so, as I felt it would have probably been to my disadvantage if I hadn't.

"We may have some pills that will help your indigestion," I suggested, a contrived hint of sympathy now in my voice. "I'm sure they'll be more effective than liquorice."

"Pills!" Napoleon said dismissively. "No, I must decline. I swear I will never take another – they never do what they're supposed to do." [15]

Napoleon placed his hand back in his waistcoat.

I nodded in reflection. "So it *is* true?" I mused. "They said you always put your hand in your waistcoat because you were holding your aching tummy – though Dad said it was because you never wear a belt and that you needed to hold your trousers up!"

Napoleon flashed me a look of stupefaction, and I instantly ascertained that I (and certainly Dad) may not have been quite correct.[16]

Napoleon didn't seem to want to talk about his stomach and seemed more intent on satisfying his competitive urge.

"Enough of this," he declared. "It's time to see what you're really made of. Where is your chessboard, sir?" he asked impatiently. "The English must play chess, yes?"

I nodded dumbly.

"It is only right, sir," he went on, "that I give you another chance to restore your honour...a chance for you English to get your own back."

"We did – at Waterloo," I reminded him.

He tutted again. "Waterloo! Waterloo! Is that all you can say? What about Toulon! Toulon!" he taunted me.

"What about it?" I asked, not having any idea why that place in France could be used to taunt me.

"Ah!" Napoleon nodded; a smug smile emerging on his face. "Yes, I thought so, you English conveniently forget about that embarrassment, don't you? Why would you want to remember it? Of course, Toulon was the making of me."[17]

I tried to recall the little knowledge I had of Napoleonic history, but the only name of a battle that kept coming to mind was... Waterloo.

Napoleon sneered at me and – as if he could read my mind – started to sing. "*Waterloo...Waterloo...*" I realised he was trying to mimic my rendition of the ABBA song that I had belted out a little bit earlier, but it was a different tune and sounded nothing like even my version, let alone the real one.[18]

He stopped. "Yes, let me remind you of the one fact that people seem to forget about Waterloo, my friend."

For one moment I thought he was talking about the song, and that he was going to tell me that it won the Eurovision Song Contest, though, of course, that would have probably been the one fact that people *did* know about it!

"Yes," he continued, "you English keep harping on about Waterloo as if you did something incredible..."

I smiled and that made him pause. "Well, wasn't it?" I attempted to explain. "It must have been *incredible* if we managed to outfox the greatest military genius that has ever lived..."

I think Napoleon liked that bit; at least he nodded in agreement.

"Well, if that is the case," I continued; "we did pretty well to beat you, then, didn't we? And it has gone down in history as one of England's greatest victories on the battlefield, hasn't it?"

Napoleon couldn't really argue with that. Actually, he could.

"We? We? We?" he chanted.

At first I thought he was saying 'oui' because he was in agreement with me, and then – for one moment – I thought he might have needed the toilet, but he soon cleared up any doubts.

"When you say *we,* I think you are talking about *you*, as in the English, yes?" He paused. "You say that it was one of *England's* greatest victories? I think you are doing a little disservice to your allies."

"OK," I nodded. "We probably got a bit of help from some other countries. Perhaps I should say it was a *British* triumph, instead of an English one."

Napoleon was shaking his head.

"No, sir," he went on, "you had almost the whole of Europe on your side! It was hardly a fair fight. The only reason I lost was because my army was outnumbered. Your army was bigger than my army!"

I wanted to assure him that size wasn't everything, but wisely thought better of it.[19]

"And that wasn't the only reason I lost," Napoleon continued mournfully; "the rain didn't help either."

"Sorry? You're blaming the weather now?"

"The battleground was a quagmire."

"It was the same for both sides," I was quick to inform him, thinking that he reminded me of a certain football manager who was also quick with his excuses after a heavy loss.

Napoleon grunted. "I had to delay the attack – until the ground had dried out a bit."

"I thought you were fighting – not playing cricket," I quipped.[20] "Anyway," I added, "whether we outnumbered you or not, we still won. You still met your Waterloo at Waterloo, as they say!"

Napoleon started to shake his head again. Goodness me, he was a stubborn fellow! Now what?

"Actually, I never set foot in the town of Waterloo," he stated. "The battle was fought three miles from there."[21]

I didn't even attempt to argue that point.

"Anyway, enough of this talking," Napoleon ordered, making his way to his seat on the sofa. "Where is this chessboard, sir? Anyone would think you were trying to wriggle your way out of the fight."

I went to the sideboard. Dad had been listening at the door and had now entered the room. He had a tin of peaches in his hand.

"I found these. Would anyone like some?"

Napoleon smiled. "And that is another thing you English can thank me for," he said, pointing to the tin.

Dad went on the defence. "No, actually it was *me* that bought them – from Tesco."

Napoleon shook his head, but didn't get the chance to explain.[22]

"What are you looking for?" Dad turned to me.

"The chessboard," I replied.

"It's not in there," Dad responded. "I think it's behind the sofa. I'll get it."

Napoleon started to chomp on some liquorice as Dad went to the back of the sofa. It was a good job my father was now behind our guest. It meant only I saw the look of horror on Dad's face. Something was wrong – very wrong.

"What is it?" I mouthed.

"Napoleon!" Dad mouthed back.

I looked at my guest. Napoleon raised his head and his eyes met mine. He snarled at me, revealing his black-stained teeth, before refocusing on the contents of his little shell box. As he pulled out another lace of liquorice, I turned my head towards my flustered parent, a look of confusion on my face.

Dad was now pointing at something behind the sofa, something out of my view. He mouthed the name of our guest again. I still didn't get it. Dad mouthed the name for a third time...still nothing from me. And so Dad was forced to begin a game of charades. He bent his arms and rested his chin on the back of his hands, turning his fingers towards the ground, before ludicrously licking the air with his tongue. My dazed expression convinced him that I still had no idea what he was doing.

But then I got it! Well, it was the meow that came from his lips that now left me in no doubt as to what he had found behind the sofa: the cat! Unfortunately, our guest also heard the meow and turned around sharply.

Dad smiled and let out a howl; then he roared like a lion and neighed like a horse. “I like to do impressions of animals,” he declared unconvincingly to our guest. “Is that something you enjoy?”

Napoleon stared at Dad, a look of incomprehension on his face.

I tried to change the subject.

“Was there a lot of traffic when you came today?” I inquired of our guest. “Did you come by car? Or do you still prefer travelling on horseback?”

It worked. The moody emperor turned his attention away from Dad.

“Traffic!” he spat out, as though it were a swearword. “Is it any wonder there is traffic chaos? You foolish English still drive on the wrong side of the road!”[23]

He stopped and turned his head, his suspicious eyes refocusing on Dad, who was still hovering behind the sofa. “Your valet is a strange man,” he concluded, still studying him intently. “Is he going to get the chessboard or not?” Napoleon paused and added: “Or is he going to start hooting like an owl next?”

I looked at Dad.

He returned a guilt-ridden smile.

“There’s *something* on it,” Dad announced, keeping his eyes on me. Oh no! He was trying to tell me that our cat had deemed the chessboard as good a place as any to have a nap on!

“We could play another game?” I suggested hopefully to Napoleon. “I can get the Xbox? Are you familiar with *Call of Duty*?”

The emperor shook his head. “We are playing *chess*, sir. Shall I get it myself?”

To our amazement and alarm, Napoleon rose from the sofa.

"No!" Dad screamed. "*You* can't get it."

"Why not?"

"You won't be able to reach it."

Whoops! That was perhaps not the best lie to offer to someone who was supposedly a little bit sensitive about his lack of inches.

Napoleon pointed his finger at Dad and showed his teeth again – those same hideous, black teeth.

My father winced when he caught sight of them. "He should have got a few replacements while he was at Waterloo," Dad winked at me.[24]

I had no idea what he was talking about and Napoleon was too flustered to have even noticed that a joke had been made at his expense.

"Shall I run my sword through him, or shall you?" Napoleon growled, turning to me. I must stress that it was Napoleon growling this time – and not Dad doing more animal noises.

And I should at this moment also point out that Napoleon *had* brought his sword, in case you were wondering. And it was now in his hand and pointing at Dad!

My father shrieked and disappeared behind the sofa. For one moment I feared he was going to re-emerge with our cat in his hands. After all, if it were true that Napoleon was scared of cats...our moggy might make a very good weapon!

Napoleon shook his head.

"Coward!" he roared, Dad still being out of view behind the sofa. "You English are all cowards! You're nothing better than dogs."

I politely agreed. At least he didn't say cats.

I knew it was up to me to act. I needed to change the subject again, to divert the attention from Dad, who had now started to creep from behind the sofa towards the living room door – on all fours. But Napoleon spotted him.

"What is he now – a monkey?"

"Are you going anywhere nice on holiday this summer?" I blurted out, in a last-gasp attempt to diffuse the situation. "I know you like travelling. Have you any more of your tours planned? I've always fancied a trip to Russia..."

"Don't talk to me about that dreadful place," Napoleon interrupted, now waving the sword in my direction. "Let me assure you, sir, you would not like Russia. Do you know how cold it gets there?"

He had a point. I was about to suggest two weeks in Tenerife might be a better option, but he seemed keen to continue to talk about his last trip to Russia – even though he had told *me* not to. At least my plan had worked, his attention now drawn away from my retreating father.

"Russia was top of my list as well once," he said, replacing his sword in his scabbard and retaking his seat. He reeled off a whole host of countries that he had conquered, as though he were reading from his shopping list, before stopping when he came to cabbages, I mean Russia. And from his tone of voice – and not through my knowledge of Napoleonic history – I realised that his sojourn into that particular country had not been a good one.

"Oh well," I sympathised with him, "you can't win them all. Anyway, did you really need another country; isn't your empire big enough already?"

Napoleon shook his head.

"It can never be too big," he declared.

I shrugged my shoulders. "But they say small is beautiful..."

I honestly wasn't deliberately goading him and must stress that I had *inadvertently* brought up the subject of size again, though, fortunately, Napoleon was too deep in thought to notice anyway.

"No-one would have been able to stop me," he went on. "I had it all planned, but I came up against an adversary even more deadly than the Russians...the weather."

I groaned. He was blaming the weather again! This time it was snow and ice that apparently thwarted his troops.

"I lost most of my army – that's why Europe started to turn on me. They wouldn't have dared do so if I hadn't have been outnumbered," he reflected.[25]

"So maybe Russia is out for your hols this year," I concluded, offering a sympathetic smile.

"Sir," Napoleon responded, "I tell you; I will never set foot in that abominable place ever again."

I nodded. "I know how you feel...Dad made a similar vow after visiting Farnborough! No, I think you definitely want somewhere in the sun," I continued. "By the way, have you ever been to a place where the weather *hasn't* been a problem?"

"Egypt!" Napoleon smiled. "I like Egypt. I have very fond memories of that trip, though I was a lot younger when I went there."

I pictured Napoleon as a child playing in the sand with his bucket and spade, but he wasn't talking about a family holiday. No, his army had accompanied him on that 'vacation' as well.

"And I had about 150 savants with me," he added.

"Wow!" I gasped. "That's a lot of people to cut your toenails."

"Savants! Not servants," Napoleon corrected me; "scientists, scholars and engineers – to survey the topography and culture of the country. You know we found the Rosetta?"

I shook my head. "Were you looking for her?"

"The Rosetta Stone," he tutted.[26]

Napoleon seemed disturbed by the fact that I had no knowledge of this.

"You English are fools," he repeated, shaking his head. "I do not just conquer countries – I embrace them, indulge myself in them...in their culture, their art. I like to call my conquests expeditions of discovery. All you English think I did in Cairo was get my men to use the Sphinx as target practice for our cannons!"

"So it was *you* who broke its nose?" I exclaimed. "That was taking it a bit far, wasn't it? I mean...just because you don't like cats."[27]

I stopped, reminded of the fact that our cat was *still* behind the sofa.

Dad had managed to leave the room and I continued to ramble

on, hoping Napoleon would forget the incident the longer I kept him talking about holiday plans.

"You could go island hopping," I giggled. "Elba...St Helena..."[28]

Napoleon stared at me.

"How about a trip home to Corsica?" I suggested.

This idea seemed more to his taste. He nodded in agreement and started to reminisce about his homeland.[29] He seemed happy to talk and I was happy to listen, buoyed by his improvement of mood, almost for one moment forgetting about Dad – and the cat.

So it was probably a good time for our pet to remind us that he had been asleep behind the sofa. I stress the word 'been' – because he wasn't sleeping now. Without needing to turn my head, I could make out something black sauntering towards the living room door. I tried to keep my guest talking, hoping it wouldn't catch his eye too. I thought we were going to get away with it, but our darling moggy decided to stop before he reached the door. Unaware there was a volatile guest in the room who was scared stiff of cats (actually, he was probably all too aware), he nonchalantly started to have a stretch – and then a wash. Now seated, he lifted one leg in the air as cats do, and started to lick his fur without a care in the world. It was almost as if he were sticking two fingers up at us – or one leg at least! If the emperor had turned his head now, he would have come face to face with his worst nightmare. Fortunately, Napoleon (the human) seemed to like talking about himself and I tried to keep my eyes on his, so that his own eyes would remain on mine and not stray to the middle of the room.

As he spoke, I heard the voice of Dad again. I didn't dare look in the direction of my father, but I knew he was in the hallway, behind the half-open door, trying to entice our cat towards him. The aroma of pilchards also convinced me of that fact.

I tried to concentrate on Napoleon, but it was one of those moments when even though someone is talking to you, your focus and ear is trained on a conversation elsewhere in the room. And all I could hear at this particular moment was Dad.

"Napoleon," I heard him whisper, "come on, come to Daddy!"

And the whispers, as Dad became more frustrated, seemed to be getting louder. Then he lost it. "Napoleon!" Dad *shouted*.

I looked up. The cat looked up. And, worst of all, Napoleon Bonaparte himself looked up. As he did, Dad was in the process of throwing a towel over our cat and, in no time, he had our pet (towel still covering him) in his arms.

"It's that infernal valet of yours again!" Napoleon roared, rising to his feet once more. "Now he's calling my name, goading me as if I were an animal! I won't stand for it any longer!"

Dad was off with the cat. I had to come clean – well, sort of. "No," I offered, sensing Napoleon was about to give chase, "Dad – I mean my valet – was calling our pet. Our pet...*hamster*! That's it. It was just our hamster under the towel."

"A hamster?" Napoleon quizzed me.

I wondered if he knew what a hamster was. "They're like mice," I explained; "little sandy-coloured things."

"That creature under the towel was black," Napoleon sneered; "and was bigger than a mouse, sir!"

"Well, they *can* be black...and size isn't really important, anyway, is it? I mean, whether you're big or small...who cares about size?"

I didn't know if Napoleon was getting angrier because he knew I was lying to him, or because he thought I was mocking his stature again.

"Of course," I went on, "it might have been the dog. Definitely not a cat...we don't have cats...horrible things; scary things!"

Napoleon was red in the face. "You have a *dog* named... Napoleon?" he scowled.[30]

"That's it!" I smiled. "It's named in your honour – just like the pastry, and the brandy..."

"And the wars," he added.

"Wars? Which ones?" I asked.

He shook his head. "The Wars of the Roses, of course!"

"Really?"

"No! The Napoleonic Wars!" he bawled.

I blushed. "Sorry."

"So let me get this straight, sir. There is a dog in this house and it is named after *me*?"

I nodded. "It's just a dog – a nice animal, not a horrible animal... not something like a pig," I assured him. "We wouldn't dream of using your name for a disgusting animal like that. That would be illegal, anyway, wouldn't it – in France at least."[31]

Oh dear. I'm not sure my knowledge of useless trivia had helped the matter.

Napoleon was still on his feet. For one moment, I thought he was going to reach for his sword again. Instead, he pulled out his little shell box. I was getting the impression that his liquorice was his comfort food.

"It has not been a good day, sir, I have to be honest," he started, trying to assume a state of calm, "but then I knew it wouldn't be. It's Friday, you see. They are never good days. And what is the date today, sir? It's not the 13th by any chance, is it?"

"It's the first day of December," I replied. "Don't forget to put up your advent calendar!"

"I thought so," he continued, ignoring my quip. "Tomorrow will be a better day, you'll see. In fact, it will be the best day of the year. It's my lucky day."

Napoleon crossed himself and headed for the door.[32]

"And it is your lucky day today, sir," he went on, "lucky that I haven't run a sword through you or your incompetent and insolent valet. I am willing to oversee all your failings and put it down to the fact that you are English, after all. I should have expected nothing more. Now I shall take my leave before I..."

"Thank you," I interrupted, not wanting to know what would have come after the 'before'.

We met Dad in the hallway. The cat was nowhere to be seen.

Napoleon avoided eye contact with my father. He coughed. "I need to use your..."

"It's upstairs," Dad butted in. "I'll show you to it."

"Do not trouble yourself," Napoleon snarled. "I'd rather not follow an imbecile – an English imbecile."

My father nodded in empathy. As Napoleon headed up the stairs, Dad shouted: "Can you go easy on the loo roll? We're running a bit *short*..."

I don't think Dad meant it, but it was that word again. And it stopped Napoleon in his tracks. He stood on the tenth step, his back still turned to us. "It's first on the right," Dad went on. Napoleon must have thought about it, but he only *tapped* the sword in his scabbard and continued up to the bathroom.

"I'm glad he's going," Dad turned to me. "I knew he was a bit touchy, but he really hasn't got much of a sense of humour, has he? I thought we handled it quite well on the whole."

"At least he hasn't run a sword through us," I added. "By the way," I inquired, "where did the cat go?" Dad didn't have time to answer. There was a scream from the bathroom upstairs. Oh no! That's where he went.

The terrified emperor hastily descended the stairs, his sword drawn. At first we feared the sword was meant for us, but we quickly realised that Napoleon had drawn it in the bathroom – to defend himself from the creature lurking there.[33]

"What is it?" I questioned him, knowing full well what it was that our guest had confronted. Strangely, I had a vision of our cat taking a shower at the moment when Napoleon had entered the room. I almost wanted to smile.

"It's horrible," Napoleon wailed, fear now in his voice, a shadow of the man who had ascended the stairs moments earlier. "It was looking at me...so *black*...and so...*big*."

Napoleon returned his sword to his scabbard. He hurriedly reached for his coat and bicorne, failing to notice that it was now out of shape, he having trodden on it when he had descended the stairs in terror. He opened the front door himself. We were too stunned to move.

"I hate them!" he continued to sob. "And I tell you, sir," he said, looking me in the eye, "...that was the biggest spider I've ever seen!"

And with that he took his leave. I flashed Dad a smile and then watched the 'little corporal' head down the garden path. He stomped straight past our cat. In fact, he didn't even give him a second glance.[34]

Chapter 3
William Shakespeare

"Knock, knock," Dad giggled, lifting his head from his book.

I sighed. "Who's there?"

"It's Shakespeare."

"Shakespeare who?"

I waited for my father to deliver the punchline. It never came.

"I mean, it's Shakespeare," Dad explained excitedly, "that's where all those knock-knock jokes started from. It's a scene from *Macbeth*!"[1]

I faked a yawn and continued to lay the table.

Dad didn't take the hint and went on. "I didn't know he was responsible for so much of what we say nowadays...for goodness' sake!"

"What is it?" I turned sharply, thinking Dad had dropped *The Complete Works of William Shakespeare* onto his foot.

"That's *his* phrase as well," Dad grinned, tapping his Smartphone, having now abandoned the book. "The world's my oyster... tower of strength...one fell swoop... they're all his, you know."[2]

I nodded in appreciation and went back to laying the table.

"Do you think he's going to speak like he writes?" Dad mused.

"Sorry?"

"You know," Dad persisted, "if he sees a light outside, is he going to say something like...but soft, what light from yonder window breaks?"

I shook my head. "I don't know...I wait with bated breath," I added sarcastically.

"That's one of *his* as well," Dad yelled, rising from the sofa. "This is going to be fun!"

I have to admit, Dad was more excited about meeting the Bard than I. You see, Dad was an actor. Well, I say an actor – he was a member of the local operatic society and had a string of credits to his name: a waiter in *Hello, Dolly*; a mute in *Camelot* and a dead soldier in *Oh! What a Lovely War*. As Shakespeare might have put it himself: all the world's a stage...and one man in his time plays many parts. That's Dad, even if they're only...*little* parts!

The doorbell sounded.

My father looked disappointed. I think he wanted Shakespeare to knock twice, so that Dad could have shouted back: "Who's there?"

Dad beat me to the door and opened it.

The famous playwright stood alone, a smile on his face. Dad gawped at him.

There was a pause.

"Can I come in?" Shakespeare suggested to my star-struck father.

Dad nodded. "My apologies; thou art most welcome. I hope our humble abode wilt be to thy satisfaction."

Oh no! It was going to be a long evening.

Dad showed Shakespeare into the living room and to his seat at the table. I waited for Dad to head to the kitchen, but he didn't. He hovered. Dad had a tendency to hover – and to babble. What I was not expecting was his determination to continue to talk to our guest as though he were communicating to a foreigner and not a fellow Englishman.

"Be seated, thou art most welcome," Dad repeated, now beginning to sound more like Yoda. "Tis an honour to have you here, or should I say..." He stopped and looked to his Smartphone. "Yes, it is a honorificabilitudinitatibus to have you here." He grinned, his pronunciation not as clear as the word is written on this page. He looked to see if our guest was impressed by his knowledge of the word, but Shakespeare wasn't listening – and who could blame him. The playwright was too busy casting his eye around the unfamiliar furnishings and trappings of our living room. Dad felt the need to explain to me. "It's his longest word – a hapax legomenon," he winked. "It can be found in *Love's Labour's Lost*, it says here," he added, nodding towards the Smartphone in his hand.

"What's it mean?" I asked.

Dad shook his head, believing its meaning to be an irrelevance.[3]

Shakespeare was now studying a jug of water on the table and had started to sniff it.

"Shall I pour you a glass?" I offered.

"Or would thou like something stronger?" Dad intervened. "What be thy poison?"

"Indeed it *is* poison," Shakespeare remarked, gingerly pushing the jug away with one fingertip. "If I'm not mistaken, that's water in there," he concluded.

Both Dad and I looked at our guest for an explanation.

"Do you *drink* this?" Shakespeare obliged. "You drink *water*? You must have strong stomachs, my friends. I must admit, I thought at first this was your chamber pot! Of course, you might as well take a swig from that anyway, if you're going to touch this stuff. Really?" He went on, still flabbergasted. "You really drink...*water*?"

I shrugged my shoulders.

"I suppose that's up to you," Shakespeare continued, "but I think I'll stick with the beer, thank you."[4]

Dad glanced towards me. Oh no! That glance told me that Dad may have forgotten the said beer.

"You have no beer or ale?" Shakespeare responded; having himself translated *that* glance.

"Don't worry," I assured him, "the supermarket's just down the road. Dad will pop out and get some, won't you, Dad," I insisted, seeing it as my chance to rid the room of my overbearing parent. "You can trust Dad – he knows a good beer when he sees one."

Shakespeare nodded. "So did my father," he pointed out.[5] "But why does he need to pop down the road? Doesn't your maid or good lady produce ale or beer for you?"

Dad smiled at the idea before making his exit.

Shakespeare looked nonplussed. "I don't get it. Looking about me, I wouldn't put you down as being of a poor situation; that you have no means of producing your *own* ale. Of course, please accept my apologies, I had no idea you had no other choice but to drink... *water*."[6]

Now even I was also starting to view the jug of water with suspicion.

Shakespeare spotted the book that my father had been reading. Well, I say reading; actually, no-one in our household had ever read that particular book. *The Complete Works* was one of those books that Dad had acquired merely to impress guests, and it had sat next to *War and Peace* on the bookshelf since the day it had been obtained from the charity shop. And, like *War and Peace*, the pages had remained unturned and would have remained unturned if it had not been for the fact that the author himself was joining us for dinner.

"I expect you recognise it," I smiled, as Shakespeare started to thumb through the pages. "It's got all your plays in there."

Shakespeare shook his head. "No, my friend, not all. Where is *Cardenio*? *Love's Labour's Won*? There are only 37 plays in here."[7]

"So you did write more?" I nodded thoughtfully. "They said you did, though some said that not all of them were yours." I hesitated. "In fact, some people say that you were not really the author, and that William Shakespeare didn't actually write the plays of...William Shakespeare, if you get what I mean?"[8]

Shakespeare looked at me with interest.

"What I mean," I continued, "is that some people reckon they're all a bit too good for...how do I put this...an uneducated man...a man that didn't go to university? You didn't, did you? That's what Dad told me...I mean, didn't go to university...I'm not saying I believe you didn't write them..."[9]

Shakespeare closed the book and pushed it along the table towards me. I got the impression he was simmering. I felt like I was digging a hole, and it was getting bigger.

"It's just what other people say," I attempted to clarify. "I don't believe it myself."

"And who do they say wrote them, if I didn't?" Shakespeare hissed.

"I can't remember now," I waffled. "Dad looked it up this morning – he's just got a Smartphone and he's on it all day at the moment. Think one of them was Christopher Marlowe. He's the only one that I'd heard of."[10]

Shakespeare stared at me.

"Kit Marlowe? You think he wrote my plays? Is that because he went to university and I didn't?"

I lifted my hands in defence. "Not at all," I replied apologetically, in no doubt that I had touched a raw nerve. "My dad didn't go to university either...it doesn't mean that you're..." I stopped. "OK, my dad is probably a bad example. Look, it's not my idea – I'm sure you *did* write all those plays – these are just conspiracy theories – and I'm happy to change the subject if you'd prefer. I'm not trying to pick a fight with you...that's the last thing I would want to do."

Shakespeare frowned. "And that's the last thing that poor Kit *did* do..."[11]

My guest had resumed a state of calm and now looked at me, straight in the eye.

"Look, I'll be honest with you," he said, nodding his head in the direction of the book. "I'll tell you exactly how it was..."

I was about to get the solution to a mystery that had puzzled scholars for centuries...when Dad re-entered the room.

"That was a bit of a wild-goose chase," he tittered, knowing full well he was quoting another of our guest's sayings. "The supermarket was closed, but I managed to get a couple of bottles from next door."

I smiled and looked at Shakespeare. "Straight from *his* barrel," I joked. "Our neighbour *does* have his own brewery."

Dad looked at me in bemusement.

"Anyway," Dad went on, still wearing his coat, a bottle of beer in his hand. "You doth permit me to pour?"

Shakespeare bobbed his head and Dad did the honours.

The Bard picked up his glass and sniffed its contents. He then gave it a shake, just like a wine connoisseur (or maybe his father) would have done, and I marvelled at how he did so without making a mess, the beer reaching the very top of the rim of the glass but not spilling over. The contents seemed to be to his satisfaction.

"Have I missed anything exciting?" Dad chirped, turning towards me. "Don't forget to ask him about Anne Hathaway. He was her toy boy," Dad whispered, with a wink of his eye.[12]

I shook my head. "Why don't you take a seat, Dad," I offered, my father having already done so, now three of us sitting at the table.

Dad turned to our guest. "Tell me, Will...oh, you don't mind me shortening your name, do you?"

"No, if that is your *will*," Shakespeare responded with more than a hint of sarcasm.

My father smiled awkwardly. "Anyway, what's in a name?" he pondered. "A rose by any other name would smell as sweet!"

Shakespeare didn't seem that impressed by my father's knowledge of his work – or his apparent infatuation with him – and merely returned a token smile.

Dad went on. "They call you the Bard of Avon as well, don't they?" He stopped and turned to me again. "I called your mother the *lard* of Avon...when she worked as an Avon rep before you came along...she was carrying a few extra pounds at the time." He paused to explain. "You know...Avon...the cosmetics firm?"

He didn't need to explain the joke. The reason I was goggling at my father was because I couldn't believe he would dare call my mother anything of the sort.

Shakespeare put his glass to his lips as Dad continued to witter.

"Did you know that our guest can't spell?" Dad nodded, again directing his question at me, with another wink. "Isn't that right, Will?"

Oh no! Where was this leading? By the way, I should point out that I hadn't actually noticed the moment when Dad had abandoned speaking 'Shakespearian'.

"It's true," Dad persevered; a cheeky grin on his face, "though the joke works better if it comes from *his* lips. Tell him, Will."

The Bard shook his head in bewilderment, and Dad had to mouth the exact words he wished our guest to say.

Shakespeare – under further duress from my father – finally complied. "I am a weakish speller," he mumbled.

Now it was my turn to return a look of bemusement.

"It's an anagram," Dad laughed, "of his name – William Shakespeare. It's amazing what you can pick up on the internet, isn't it?" As I had said, Dad had spent a long time playing with his new toy. And he was holding his Smartphone in his hand now. "Hear me as I will speak," Dad continued, looking at the screen for confirmation. "That's another anagram of his name." He paused. "One more, I think...here it is...I'll make a wise phrase."

I shook my head. I doubted that very much. I mean, I doubted that *Dad* could 'make a wise phrase'. He was good at talking nonsense, though.

"I was just asking Mr Shakespeare whether all of those plays were his work," I said to Dad, eager to reconvene the conversation we were having before my blundering parent had re-entered the room.

Dad just returned a smile, preferring to lead the conversation elsewhere.

"Do you know there are 80 variations of your name?" he said, now turning to Shakespeare, his eyes still focused on the information his Smartphone was providing. "It says here that you signed your name in different ways – never spelt it the same way? You *are* a weakish speller!"[13]

I groaned. I had surely missed my chance to discover whether Shakespeare was the author of all those 37 plays, and failed to solve one of the greatest mysteries of English literature.

"Perhaps our guest would like to talk about something a bit more...less trivial," I suggested to Dad. "We could ask him about the lost years."

"The lost years?" Dad quizzed me. "Where did they go?" he added, turning to Shakespeare with a grin on his face. "Did you find them?"[14]

I sighed. "It's all right, Dad – you just carry on..."

And Dad did. He was having a whale of a time. He had now got up and opened a drawer, pulling out a small red book. "It's my Gideon Bible from school," he said. "Will will know..." He stopped. "That sounds funny...*William* will know what I'm talking about. You translated it, didn't you, Will?"

I looked up at the same time as our guest did. I have to admit, Dad had gained our interest this time.

"The 46th psalm – you left your signature on it, didn't you, Will?" Dad elaborated, turning to me before continuing. "That's right. If you go to the 46th psalm in the King James Bible you will see that the 46th word is 'shake'." He paused, a look of conceit on his face. "And if you look at the 46th word from the end of the 46th psalm you will read the word 'spear'. Is that not right, Mr *shake...spear*? And I do believe you were 46 at the time the translation went to print?"[15]

I must admit I was amazed. Dad had surpassed himself this time, or at least the internet had.

Shakespeare remained tight-lipped. "You can check it for yourself," Dad informed me, sliding the Bible across the table.

I picked it up and looked at the cover. "It's not the King James' version," I was sorry to inform him, "and it's only the New Testament. The Book of Psalms is in the Old!"

I realised that Dad's Bible was another book – like our copy of *The Complete Works* – that had not been read very often.

Dinner was uneventful. My bumbling father continued to hover and we were only left alone when Dad had to clear the plates or bring out the next course. We finished with cheese, and Dad had great pleasure in bringing out the cheese knife, the said item clasped in his clenched fist.

"Is this a dagger which I see before thee," he wailed theatrically, "the handle toward my hand?"

"No, Dad," I groaned. "It's a cheese knife, so if you wouldn't mind putting it next to the cheese."

Shakespeare ate the cheese with gusto and washed it down with another beer. He had a hearty appetite and preferred to eat than talk. I thought it quite odd that a man of words was rather short on words, though with Dad around, he didn't have much chance to impress us with his words!

"And now for the after-dinner entertainment," Dad announced. "Could you be so good as to make your way to your seats in the auditorium."

Dad ushered us to the sofa. I had no idea what he was up to now.

Then I got it. Dad had a DVD in his hand – not any DVD, but a DVD of his operatic society's production of *Beauty and the Beast*. Dad had played a pitchfork-bearing villager.

"I'm not sure Mr Shakespeare will appreciate or understand a pantomime," I pleaded with Dad.

"Nonsense," Dad reassured me. "I am a man of the theatre myself you see, Will," he said, turning to his fellow thespian.

Shakespeare looked impressed. "A fellow player? Bless you, my friend – you are a man after my own heart."[16]

"Is that another of your phrases?" my father asked, only this time receiving a blank expression in return. "Never mind," Dad went on, as only Dad could, now reaching for the remote control.

"What the dickens is this?" Shakespeare asked, shaking his head in disbelief, as Dad switched on the television.

"It's called a TV," I started to explain. "Hold on, didn't Dickens come after you? He was Victorian!"

Dad had reached for his Smartphone again, as Shakespeare remained transfixed, his eyes rooted to the flashing TV screen. "Oh! That *is* one of yours," Dad muttered to himself. "It has absolutely nothing to do with Charles Dickens," he informed me, his voice a whisper for fear he might disturb our guest, who was watching intently an advert for biscuits.

"They're Hobnobs," Dad revealed, finally lifting his head from the Smartphone. "They're good for dunking in your tea."

Shakespeare shook his head and attempted to convince us that the word 'hobnob' had nothing to do with biscuits. And we couldn't really argue – apparently it was one of *his* again!

And so we watched *Beauty and the Beast* – all of it.

The pantomime dame was the first character to appear on stage, even before the curtain had gone up, her (or his) welcome including an appeal to the audience to switch off all mobile devices. I felt an explanation might be in order: not about mobile devices, but as to why a 20-stone Scotsman was wearing make-up and a spotted pink and yellow dress!

"So it's a male playing a woman," Shakespeare responded with indifference, shrugging his shoulders. "What's so strange about that? Who else is going to play the part of a woman?"[17]

However, Shakespeare was definitely in need of an explanation when the curtain rose and a beaming Belle came onto the stage. The Bard shook his head in amazement.

"I have to hand it to them," he said, vigorously clapping his hands, "I would have sworn on my life that that chap was a woman."

"She is one," I confirmed. "At least I think she is. That's Faye from down the road."

Shakespeare rose from the sofa.

"A woman? A woman on stage!" he cried, shaking his head in astonishment. "I don't understand. What's a woman doing on the stage?"

"It's normal," I said. "Look, there are lots of them," I added, pointing out others in the chorus. "Didn't you have any women actors in your plays?"

"Of course not," Shakespeare responded. "The boys play the female roles."

My father looked puzzled.

"What about *Twelfth Night*?" Dad inquired. "I saw that play at the Octagon a few months back. Doesn't the plot involve a woman disguising herself as a man?"

Shakespeare nodded, without taking his eyes off the screen.

"So in your time," Dad cogitated, "the audience would see a man pretending to be a woman pretending to be a man?"

Our guest felt no need to respond, keen not to miss a line of the show. At one point, Gaston forgot one of *his* lines and started to giggle. Shakespeare shook his head disapprovingly and started to boo, before reaching for the bowl of fruit on the coffee table before us. He picked up an apple and lobbed it at the television!

"What are you doing?" Dad screamed. "You'll break it."

Shakespeare looked concerned. I wasn't sure if that look was in response to the said apple simply rebounding off the screen onto the carpet instead of hitting the tiny animated figures, or whether he was just surprised that we were not joining him in attempting to ridicule the fool who had forgotten his line.

I tried to discreetly remove the bowl of fruit from the coffee table, but Shakespeare noticed and flashed me a look of disapproval. Clearly, he believed it had been put there for the sole purpose of propelling its contents at the cast.[18]

Dad came on stage about an hour into the production.

"That's me!" he pointed out. "Wait for my line."

The said line was delivered.

"What do you think, Will – from one actor to another – was I good?"

Shakespeare didn't answer the question or ask one, but his expression told us that he probably wanted to ask more than one:

such as how Dad could be in two places at the same time, or how he was able to shrink to just a few inches in height and appear inside a flat screen?

"What did you think of the set?" Dad felt the need to probe. "I had a hand in that as well."

Shakespeare nodded approvingly.

"That set was one of our best," Dad added. "It only took about a year to construct."

Shakespeare shrugged his shoulders, still not averting his eyes from the television screen. "A year? We built an entire playhouse in less time than that," he said.

"He means a theatre," I felt the need to explain to my father, before he had the chance to crow over the fact that he had once assembled a Wendy house in the bottom of our garden in two days (even though B&Q said the job should have taken no more than two hours).[19]

"Let's see what's on the box now," Dad said, reaching for the remote control again and switching from DVD to TV mode.

"Where is *the* box?" Shakespeare inquired, pulling out a small drawstring bag full of coins. "Where do I pay?"

Dad lifted up his hands. "Put your money away, my friend, that performance was on the house."[20]

Shakespeare had no time to argue, or to look for a box *on top of our house*. The sound of an explosion made him shudder. He returned his eyes to the television screen. Dad had found a war film on one of the channels. The sound of machinegun fire and further explosions kept our guest mesmerised for several minutes, before he started to enthusiastically clap his hands, as an unfortunate soldier was somersaulted through the air.

"This might be a bit violent for him?" I suggested to my father. "See if *Strictly Come Dancing* is on."

Dad coughed and turned to me. "Too violent? You have the master of gore sitting next to you. This is the author of *Titus Andronicus*!" he added, placing his hand on Shakespeare's shoulder.

I *had* heard of that particular play, but needed Dad to elaborate. Needless to say, he took much delight in doing so, informing me that the play contained no less than 14 deaths, with throats being slit; tongues being cut out; hands being severed and two sons being served up to their mother in a pie.

After he had finished, Dad turned to Shakespeare and nudged him in the ribs. "Hope you didn't find any fingernails in your steak and kidney pie tonight!"

Shakespeare was too entranced in the film to respond and Dad was alone in laughing at his own joke.

I shook my head.

"You might be right," I conceded, still contemplating the horrors of *Titus Andronicus*. "In fact, he might enjoy an episode of *EastEnders*!"

Dad was back on his Smartphone. "I'm just trying to find the bit in *King Lear* when they gouge out that man's eyes. Yes, here it is...out, vile jelly," Dad quoted, roaring with laughter. "No, son," he continued, "Mr Shakespeare's plays are not for the fainthearted. Did you know that there are more than 20 different ways to die in his plays: poisoning, decapitation, snakebite, hanging...being eaten by a bear?"

Shakespeare remained motionless, still bewitched by the television, though Dad was keen to involve him in the conversation.

"You didn't mind a bit of blood on stage, did you, Will?" my father grinned, nudging him in the ribs again. "Still, what's another beheading to you lot? I suppose it was just a bit of harmless fun compared to all those *real* executions."

Shakespeare smiled politely, but still did not avert his eyes from the screen.

"It looks so real," he pondered, continuing to shake his head in disbelief.

"I expect the special effects have moved on a bit since your time," Dad smiled. "Don't suppose you had anything like that at the Globe?"[21]

Shakespeare winced as another grenade attack catapulted a

group of soldiers into a river. "Those men; will they be all right? It looks so *real*," our guest repeated again, still not convinced it was a performance.

I did my best to allay his fears. "They'll be fine. Everyone gets up again – just like they did in your day."

Shakespeare shook his head.

"That is not true, my friend," he corrected me. "Not everyone *did* get up. I know how dangerous it can be on stage and many have suffered injuries on their way to hell."

"Sorry?"

"When the trapdoor is opened and they plummet to the depths of the Underworld. Of course, they're supposed to fall on bundles of hay, but sometimes we forget..."

He stopped and grinned, as though he were reminded of one particular incident.

"And it's not always easy reaching heaven either, my friend," he went on. "Some of the wires used to carry us there are not always strong enough for the job – and we have some rather overweight players," he laughed. "I need not tell you what fate befell them ten feet in the air!"

A cannon in the war film was fired.

"Ah!" Shakespeare continued. "We have those as well. Yes, one inadvertently set fire to our theatre, you know."

"Of course," I interrupted, "the Globe burnt down, didn't it?"

"We rebuilt it," Shakespeare was quick to point out.

"So did Sam Wanamaker," Dad smiled. "No, I don't suppose you'd know him. Did anyone die in the fire?"

Shakespeare shook his head. "I don't think so. Someone's breeches were alight, but there is always plenty of ale on hand."[22]

"You were lucky that there were no casualties," I said.

"Or unlucky that there was a fire in the first place," Dad surmised. "What was the play...*Macbeth*?" Dad paused. "Tell me, I've often wondered...if it's unlucky to say the word 'Macbeth' on stage, what do you actors do when you're performing that particular production?"

Shakespeare flashed my father a look of bafflement, before the television caught his eye again, a wounded soldier now clutching his stomach, his hands smeared with blood. Our guest looked horrified.

"He'll be fine," I again attempted to reassure the playwright. "It's not real – honest."

Shakespeare was not convinced. "Now *that* does look real to me," he insisted. "You see, I knew of a street entertainer who had to stab himself with a knife. He had a bag of pigs' blood under his shirt, of course, but one day the fool got so drunk...he forgot the bag."

Shakespeare smiled and I tried without success to gauge from that smile whether he was telling the truth or not.

"Have *you* ever been hurt on stage?" I inquired.

"It's the groundlings you have to watch," he replied. "It's not just fruit they throw at us from the pit."[23]

Dad butted in. "They're called stinkards in the summer," he helpfully added.

It didn't take me long to think of the reason why.

I took the remote control and changed the channel. We started to watch a documentary on the work of a veterinary practice. Now I had to explain that no-one was acting and it was for *real*.

"Have we missed the fighting?" Shakespeare asked, as a dog was being bandaged. "Are they starting with the cockfighting instead?" he added, as a hen was having its claws clipped. "Will there be bears later on?"[24]

I tried to explain that that form of entertainment had long been abolished.

"Our shows are a bit more sedate these days," I smiled. "Actually, they're not," I added, thinking of *Britain's Got Talent*.

I thought it best to change the channel again. It was a mistake. *Paddington* was on.

"No," I insisted, "there's no bear-baiting in this one either!"

I changed the channel again. Brad Pitt and Nicole Kidman were being cheered as they walked into a cinema via a red carpet.

"They are from the royal court?" Shakespeare questioned.

"No. They're actors," I informed him. Not for the first time, he shook his head in bewilderment.[25]

Dad had left the room after I had snatched the remote control from him, and I had assumed he was sulking, but he had now returned with a script. I groaned, but I should have expected it.

"You'll like this, Will," Dad said, handing it to our guest. "It's our next production – *West Side Story*."

Shakespeare took the script and started to flick through the pages.

"You have a big part, my friend!" he concluded, the script now balancing in the palm of his hand as if he were weighing it.

Dad shook his head sorrowfully. "No, just four lines, I'm afraid."

"Then this is an outrage!" Shakespeare declared.

Dad nodded. "Yes, you're right! It *is* an outrage! It's Mrs Hall that's wrong. She said I was past playing Riff – but I keep telling her that they can do a lot with make-up these days."

Shakespeare pushed the script into Dad's midriff. "You'd better hide this," he whispered, glancing behind him, for fear someone may be hiding behind the sofa (someone other than Napoleon – I mean our cat Napoleon). "I don't understand why you're in possession of a script of an entire production," Shakespeare mused, "a *complete* script with *every* line on it? You'd better guard this well, my friend," he instructed my father, his voice still muted.

"It's OK, we've got plenty of copies," Dad assured him.

"Copies?"

"Well, what I mean is that it's easy to print another off if someone loses one," Dad explained.

The Bard continued to shake his head in disbelief.

"But what if your rivals get hold of one of these *copies*?" a distressed Shakespeare continued to probe. "It'll be all over London in no time."

Dad shrugged his shoulders. "That's OK. It's been performed hundreds of times anyway."

"Hundreds of times? The *same* play?"

"Well, yes. What's unusual about that? *The Mousetrap* has been on for more than 70 years," Dad pointed out. "It's all right – I won't spoil the end and tell you who did it!"

Shakespeare tossed his head back. "I imagine everyone knows who *did it*...whatever it is they did...though you'd have thought they would have caught the mouse by now! Is that really true...70 years?" Shakespeare reflected. "The audience must know *every* line. The groundlings would throw more than apples at us if we did the same play every day for 70 years!"[26]

"Anyway," Dad persisted, "*West Side Story* is probably performed every day – somewhere in the world."

"In the world?" Shakespeare gasped. "The same play is being performed all over the *world*?"

Dad nodded. "And you should take it as a compliment, Will; that we're performing something that is down to you in a way."

"Me?"

"Well, yes, in a way, *West Side Story* is *your* work."

"My work?"

"Yes, you might recognise the plot," he continued, handing Shakespeare the script again. "It's based on your *Romeo and Juliet*, only it's now the Jets and the Sharks, rather than the Montagues and the Capulets."

Shakespeare was on his feet again.

"You have copied *my* work?"

"Not I," Dad smiled. "I think Laurents, Bernstein and Sondheim should take some of the credit."

Shakespeare was not amused.

"There is foul play at work here," he barked. And, yes, that was one of his phrases. "I don't understand it," he continued; "none of our actors receive the complete script. We'd never dream of making an entire copy. How did you get hold of it?" Shakespeare stopped. "Hold on," he added, suddenly glancing towards *The Complete Works* on the table. "You've copied *all* of my work!"

Dad didn't know what to say, so he said something that only made the situation worse.

"But every house in the country probably has a copy of your plays," he announced, "only most people are more likely to use the book as a doorstop than read it."

"*Every* house?" Shakespeare cried. "What do you mean by that? Are you saying you're not the only one with a copy? And what do you mean *use it as a doorstop*? Are you implying that my work is not fit for any other purpose?"[27]

Dad returned a repentant smile. "I thought you'd be pleased that your work is accessible to everyone – let me show you," he added, moving his Smartphone closer to Shakespeare.

I shook my head. I didn't think our guest was quite ready for the World Wide Web just yet.

"Anyway," Dad continued, deciding to give up on that latest venture, "*West Side Story* is a lot different from *Romeo and Juliet* – it's got songs in it."

"Songs?"

Dad started to sing a number from the show.

Shakespeare grimaced. "There is singing? It's not supposed to be a play of merriment. It's not a comedy, my friend...it's a tragedy!"

Dad stopped. "No, that's the *Bee Gees*. I'm singing *I Feel Pretty*."

I could almost hear Shakespeare grinding his teeth.

"These plagiarists – whatever their names – have made a laughing stock out of me." Yes, that was another one of his phrases. "They have no right to play fast and loose with me." And another one. "I'll give them a bunch of fives, if I see them!" That probably isn't one.

Dad protested: "No, they made a really good job of it, actually. The songs break it up a bit. It's a long time to be sitting there."

"A long time? Are you implying that my audiences get bored?" a suspicious Shakespeare probed.

"Well, I don't mean that *Romeo and Juliet* is boring, or even that long, but some of your plays can get a bit heavy, can't they? *Hamlet* could do with a few songs here and there. You have to admit, that one is a *bit* lengthy."

"Lengthy?" Shakespeare objected. "You have never been to a mystery play before, my friend."

"Yes, I have," Dad assured him. "I love *An Inspector Calls*."

I butted in. "He's talking about those religious plays, Dad. I think they literally went on for *days*."

Shakespeare nodded. "Forty days, my friend. That's how long *The Acts of the Apostles* lasted. Forty days!"

Dad puffed out his cheeks.

"I must admit, I might have struggled learning my lines for that one!" he said.[28]

Shakespeare started to head for the door. "I think it is time for me to take my leave," he said. "I am a little distressed and aggrieved that you seem unable to appreciate my work."

Dad was about to contest that point, but Shakespeare lifted his hand to stop him. The Bard was about to deliver his grand soliloquy before the final curtain and did not wish to be interrupted.

"I am sorry that my work is too long for you, and makes for a better doorstop. You are not the first unable to appreciate it and I shall take no offence. I think of Robert Greene whenever I am insulted. You don't know him?"[29]

We shook our heads. That seemed to please Shakespeare.

"He was a university wit...I should say *twit*," our guest explained, producing a smile of conceit. "He wanted people to believe an actor like me couldn't write as well as a university-educated playwright like him. Greene by name and green by nature – yes, *green* with envy, no doubt. He was a green-eyed monster...yes, that is one of my phrases...but good riddance to him...that's another. I beg you not to be small-minded like him, my friends...be not afraid of greatness."

"And that's another, I guess?" I chipped in. Shakespeare nodded.

Dad puffed out his chest this time. "Some are born great, some achieve greatness, and some have greatness thrust upon them."

"And what do you mean by that?" Shakespeare asked warily.

"I don't know," Dad admitted. "You wrote it!"

Shakespeare exhaled deeply, before opening the front door. "Farewell, my friends. As I also once said...the rest is silence."

Actually, the rest was not silence. Dad was determined not to let our guest leave feeling unappreciated.

"Wait," my father pleaded, and, as Shakespeare halted on the doorstep, Dad started to rave. "I don't want it to end like this, Will. I think I may have offended you; I didn't mean to. I've got a habit of putting my foot in it sometimes. I often wish the ground would swallow me up – or perhaps one of your trapdoors could?" He paused. "Look, I'm your biggest fan. You don't know how much I love you..."

I groaned. Our front doorstep was not quite a balcony in Verona, but Dad was doing his best to recreate a scene from a Shakespeare tragedy.

"All right, I *like* you," Dad felt the need to clarify, after my groan convinced him that he was probably laying it on a bit too thickly. "As you yourself said, Will," Dad continued to gush; "the course of true love never did run smooth."

Shakespeare remained unimpressed.

"Please," Dad urged him, "you've enjoyed yourself really, haven't you? I wouldn't want you to leave with a bitter taste in the mouth. Was that one of yours? Look, it's been a good day...hasn't it?"

The Bard turned to Dad and announced sadly: "We have seen better days..."

I had no need to ask if that was another of *his*.

Dad was about to speak again, but Shakespeare raised his hand to stop him. He then smiled and affectionately patted Dad on the back, giving my father the assurance that our guest did not feel aversion to him – merely pity, though Dad seemed happy with that.

My father turned to me as we watched Shakespeare make his

way down the garden path. "All's well that ends well, then," Dad smiled. I sighed.

It had started to rain, as the greatest playwright of all time headed into the night.

Dad looked thoughtful for a split second, before grinning: "When shall we three meet again...in thunder, lightning, or in rain?"

Judging by that parting look on William Shakespeare's face (and who knows or cares if the following is one of his phrases), I would hazard a guess...never.

Chapter 4
Cleopatra

"Sign here, please."

The courier standing on our doorstep was not a patient man. He thrust a digital notebook into my midriff. "You don't need a pen – just use your fingertip," he instructed me.

"Dad!" I yelled. "There's a delivery. Shall I sign for it?"

"What?" Dad called from the kitchen. "Who is it?"

The courier was joined by his colleague. "What's the matter? It's the right address, isn't it? Where do you want it?" he queried, directing his final question at me.

At last my apron-clad father, tea towel draped over one shoulder, joined me at the front door.

"Sorry," he smiled, rubbing flour from his hands; "I was busy making hieroglyph biscuits. We've got an important guest coming soon."

"Were you expecting a delivery?" I asked my father.

He nodded and took the digital notebook from me, before focusing on the biggest courier of the two.

"Where do I sign?"

"Just there, mate."

"Have you got a pen?" Dad asked.

"You just use your fingertip," I and now *two* impatient couriers responded in unison.

Dad handed back the digital notebook, oblivious to the fact that he had left white fingerprints on it. He started to look for the package. One of the couriers nodded towards their van. "It's in the back – where do you want it?"

Dad looked confused.

"We'll bring it in for you," the other courier attempted to explain. "Which room?"

Still Dad looked confused.

The two men went to the back of the van and between them lifted out a cardboard box – a big cardboard box.

"I only ordered a DVD," Dad said, scratching his head. "It must be a long film."

The box was the size of a washing machine, and I did wonder if Dad had finally lost patience with our temperamental old one. In fact, even now we were expecting the arrival of a plumber to fix it, not for the first time. However, the fact that Dad did not choose the kitchen for the unboxing assured me that he had not lost *so much* patience to have been persuaded to burrow into his wallet to buy a new one.

"I wonder what it is?" he pondered, running his finger along the box, which now sat in the middle of the living room. "I don't think your mum has ordered anything this big, and I don't remember doing so either. It's a mystery."

Dad continued to contemplate what might be inside. "I can't even begin to guess what it might be," he said, shaking his head. "Of course, they do use a lot of unnecessary packaging these days. It probably *is* my DVD."

I looked at him doubtfully.

"No, I really don't know," he went on. "I'm completely at a loss. Suppose we better open it."

At last! I did think that would be the best way of finding out what was in the box.

Dad started to pick at the tape.

"I'll get the scissors," I offered, making my way to the kitchen, leaving my dad to continue picking, both the tape and his brain. "It could be a present from Aunt Martha?" he called out. "She does..."

Dad never finished his sentence. He was interrupted by a loud bang, and then the only sound that came from his mouth was a... scream.

I dashed back into the living room. Standing upright in the now open box, white polystyrene packing chips strewn all over the carpet, was a thing. And that was all it was to me at first – a *thing*. The 'thing' had arms and it was using them to rip off sheets of bubble wrap that had been tightly wrapped around its body to form a cocoon. I felt for one moment that I was confronting a monster in an episode of *Dr Who*. The 'monster' – though we could now see quite clearly that it was of human form – continued to struggle to free itself from the bubble wrap. We were too stunned to help it.

Dad was kneeling on the floor, his back to me, so I couldn't see his face. I would have liked to have done so, just to see his expression; to see that expression change when he realised the 'thing' or 'monster' was, in fact, a woman. Of course, by the time she had freed herself from the final sheet of bubble wrap, we were both already aware that we were in the presence of Cleopatra VII Thea Philopator, to give our guest her full name.[1]

"I'm not sure that was a good idea," she declared, before exhaling through pursed lips.

We watched in silence as Cleopatra delicately raised a finger to wipe a bead of sweat from close to the bridge of her nose, being careful not to smudge the trademark black lines she had painted under her eyes. Her long, kohl-painted eyelashes were fluttering as she did so.[2] She offered her hand, her bangles dangling loosely from her wrist. We didn't take it. She sighed. "Is someone going to help me out of this box, or not?"

Dad was up in a flash. He took her outstretched hand and she stepped out of the box, before rubbing herself down to remove any remnants of packaging. "Show me to your bathroom," she ordered, seeing no need for any introductions.

"Of course," I answered immediately. "Please follow me. I expect you'd like to freshen up. That was some arrival!"

Dad stood motionless, still staring, as I led our guest upstairs.

"I would like to take a bath," Cleopatra announced, much to my surprise. "My servants will be arriving soon – you can send them up. Now, where do I bathe?"

I had already opened the bathroom door and it was obvious our bath was not quite as impressive as the one she was used to.

"In *there*?" she inquired. "It's rather small."

I looked at it, praying that Dad had not been the last to use it. He tended to clip his toenails in the bath.

"It will have to do. Fill it," she commanded.

"You can do it yourself," I suggested. That, of course, was not the reaction she would have got from her servants and she looked at me confused. I was not, of course, being rude.

"What I mean," I attempted to explain; "is that you can fill the bath up at *your* leisure, by turning those taps."

Cleopatra looked impressed and seemed more than satisfied with the arrangement, even excited at the prospect.

"There's some bubble bath if you want it," I said, nodding towards an array of plastic bottles.

I made my way downstairs. Dad was clearing the debris from our living room.

"You better watch her, son," he warned. "She's a famous seductress, that one. Men fall for her charms – that's how she gets her own way. Just be careful."

I shrugged my shoulders.

Dad headed for the kitchen. "I better put the oven on. Let me know if you can't handle her," he added, closing the door behind him.

Suddenly, there was a scream, only it wasn't Dad this time. It came from upstairs. I raced to the bathroom and stopped at the closed door.

"Are you OK?" I yelled. "Is everything all right in there?"

"There's something disgusting in the bath!" Cleopatra informed me.

Oh no! Perhaps she *had* found Dad's toenail clippings.

No, I was wrong.

"It's coming out of the taps," she attempted to enlighten me. "It's vile."

I hesitated. "What does it look like?"

"It's wet," she shouted. "It hasn't any colour – it looks a bit like... water."

I stopped and smiled. "That's probably because it *is* water," I returned sarcastically. "Dad says the water is a bit hard here, but it's OK."

"What?" Cleopatra wailed. "You expect me to bathe in water...in filthy, unhygienic...*water*?"

"Not another one!" I muttered to myself, thinking of our previous guest. "Don't worry, it's fine," I assured her. "We all bathe in it, even the king and queen do. I mean...*our* king and queen."

Cleopatra was not convinced. "Your queen bathes in water?" she continued to bellow. "Well, this queen doesn't! Bring me the milk of an ass."

"Sorry?"

"Now!" Cleopatra ordered.[3]

I headed downstairs and went to the kitchen.

"What milk did you buy, Dad?" I asked, opening the fridge.

"The usual," he said; "semi-skimmed, why?"

"And that has come from a cow, not a donkey, I guess?"

Dad nodded in response. It was a good job he didn't *really* listen to me when I spoke to him, or he wouldn't have answered my questions so succinctly and without passing comment.

"I'm just going to borrow the milk for a minute," I said, removing the plastic bottle from the fridge. "Is this all we've got?" I inquired, looking hopelessly at the four-pint bottle that was now only half full.

"There might be another pint or two in the freezer, but it'll take a while to defrost."

I puffed out my cheeks and headed despondently up the stairs.

"I've got your milk," I called to our guest. "Shall I leave it outside the door?"

"Bring it in," Cleopatra said firmly.

I gingerly opened the bathroom door and pushed the bottle in. "I'll leave it here."

"Bring it in!" she growled.

I feared that she may have been in a state of undress and half covered my eyes as I entered, but through my fingers I caught a flash of cerise and I realised she was donned in my mother's bathrobe. I lowered my hand.

"Is that it?" she asked, looking dubiously at the milk. "Is that all you've got?"

"How much do you need?" I queried.

"About 700 asses," she replied with a stare.[4]

I sighed. "Will you excuse me? I think my dad might be calling me from downstairs."

I left the bottle and closed the door behind me.

The doorbell had sounded and Dad was showing two women in.

He heard me coming down the stairs.

"This is Iras and Charmion," Dad beamed.[5]

The maids who had arrived to attend to their queen were carrying a basket between them. I led them to the bathroom.

"You didn't come by donkey by any chance?" I asked.

They returned a polite smile, which made me presume that they hadn't. "She's in there," I added, pointing to the bathroom door. "Good luck!"

And so I was left to wait. I sat on the landing outside the bathroom, my back propped against the wall, popping bubbles on the discarded bubble wrap to pass the time. Dad eventually joined me.

He sat close to me and took a sheet of bubble wrap. And we waited some more – and some more after that.

"She's a woman, son," Dad kept pointing out. "Look here," he said, tapping his Smartphone. "It's estimated that the average woman spends one year, seven months and 15 days of her life getting ready!" Dad fidgeted, before adding: "But I do hope she's not going to be too much longer. I need the toilet!"

Suddenly, the bathroom door opened. It was Charmion. She popped her head around the door.

"My queen needs a pot."

"So do I!" Dad snapped, crossing his legs.

"It's actually already in the bathroom," I attempted to explain; "the toilet that is. It's that ceramic thing with water in it."

Dad smiled. "You better tell her what the toilet paper is used for – otherwise she'll be wrapping it around herself pretending to be a mummy!"

Charmion disappeared, but quickly re-emerged, once again poking her head out from behind the door.

"Yes, I've found it, but it's full of dirty water."

Oh no! Had Dad forgotten to flush again?

"And it's fixed to the ground," Charmion went on. "How do I get rid of the dirty water?"

"Push down the little lever. That will do it."

Charmion disappeared behind the door again. She returned after finally flushing the toilet, but looked just as confused.

"It's still got water in it," she moaned. "My queen can't use that. If her urine goes in there – it'll get dirty!"

"That's the point," I explained. "It doesn't matter if the water gets dirty – it gets flushed away and refills again."

"I didn't mean the water," Charmion snarled. "I meant the *urine*!"

I looked at Dad and he looked at me.

"Is that a problem?" I inquired. "Does it matter if the *urine* gets dirty? Was there something you wanted it for?"

Charmion nodded. "Well, of course there is – my queen is cleaning her teeth."

"What!" Dad roared. "She cleans her teeth with her pee?"

"Don't be silly," Charmion responded. "We use toothpaste...the urine is for rinsing out her mouth afterwards."

She stopped and looked down at us, studying our perplexed expressions. "It's all right," she said; "she doesn't swallow it. It's just a mouthwash."

Our expressions didn't change.

"Caesar swears by it," she continued, "and everyone in Rome does it..."

Dad smiled. "And when in Rome..."[6]

"Anyway, what's in *your* toothpaste?" she questioned us with disdain. "My queen took the liberty of using some of it...and she didn't like the taste...which is even more reason why she needs to wash her mouth out."

I had no idea what ingredients were in our toothpaste, and so answered her by inquiring as to what was normally in hers.

"Egg shells...ashes from oxen hooves...nothing unusual," Charmion replied nonchalantly.

"Anyway," Dad sounded, "if she wants some urine to wash her mouth out...let me in! I've been holding this in for so long, I'll probably be able to provide you with at least a gallon!"

"Is your queen nearly...ready?" I tentatively inquired.

"She hasn't started on her make-up yet," Charmion responded aggressively.

I sighed.

"Anyway, when are *you* getting ready?" Charmion abruptly turned, looking down at my still seated father, eyeing the hole in his jeans with contempt.

I giggled. She obviously didn't know Dad. He didn't dress for dinner, even when he went out for dinner.

"Suppose I'd better go and put *my* make-up on, then," he grinned, nudging me in the ribs, but remaining seated.

"Yes, I think you better," Charmion said in earnest. She flicked her head in the direction of the bathroom cabinet and added: "You certainly have some interesting make-up and perfumes in here."

I felt the need to clarify that it all belonged to my mother. To my surprise, Charmion was just as surprised by *my* comment.

"Your father doesn't wear make-up?" she queried. "Why not?"

Dad grinned. "Because I'm beautiful already!" And he pouted, before blowing a kiss in the direction of the confused maid.[7]

"Does it always take her this long to get ready?" I asked Charmion, keen to move on.

"No, but today is a special occasion, isn't it?" she informed me.

"Is it?"

Charmion tutted. "Even if you and your father do not wish to make an impression – my queen certainly wants to look her best for her wedding ceremony."

The door closed. I looked at Dad, and he looked at me. "Wedding?" we uttered in unison, before spending the next couple of minutes in silent reflection. It was Dad who cautiously knocked on the bathroom door, remaining seated as he did so, merely swinging his arm, his back still propped against the wall.

"This *wedding*," he started, "is it taking place here – in our house?"

"Yes," a voice from the other side of the door sounded.

Dad nodded thoughtfully. "OK. That's fine. Are we expecting lots of guests?"

"It'll be a private ceremony," the voice sounded again, "but no doubt the whole of Rome will want to come to the party afterwards."

Dad looked at me and hurriedly got to his feet. "I better open another bag of pasta!"[8]

He was about to go down the stairs, but hesitated, before knocking on the bathroom door again.

"One more thing, just to clarify, when you say the *whole of Rome;* do you mean...well, the *whole of Rome*?"

"If it's any consolation," the voice sounded once more, "I know of at least one person who won't be coming – her husband."

We could hear giggling from behind the door.

My father scratched his head. "You mean the man she's about to marry...isn't coming to the wedding?"

This time Charmion opened the door and popped her head out.

"I mean her *other* husband." The door closed again.

"How many husbands has she got?" Dad went on, forgetting to knock this time.

"Only the one at the moment," Charmion replied, opening the door again to deliver her response.

"At the *moment*?" Dad gasped. "How many husbands does she normally have?"

Charmion shrugged her shoulders. "Two or three? Who's counting?"

However, the maid seemed to have aroused her own curiosity and started to do what appeared to be just that, focusing intently on her fingers as she did so. "Let's see," she muttered to herself, "when she was married to that brother, she..."

We both heard the word 'brother' – but it was Dad who beat me to it.

"Brother!" he interrupted Charmion with a squeal. "How can she be married to her brother? A brother *isn't* a husband," he added.

"Oh, yes it is!" I informed my father, handing him his Smartphone. "You might want to read this."

Charmion closed the door and Dad started to read.

"So her first husband was her ten-year-old brother?" he concluded, turning to face me, an incredulous expression on his face.

"That's right," I smiled.

"And she later married another brother...who was about 12, according to this?"

"That's right," I continued to smile, retaking the Smartphone from my father in order to finish the story myself. "And then she married Julius Caesar," I went on, "while still married to brother number two. And Caesar was also married...so there were two husbands and two wives between them...if you get what I mean?"

Actually, I wasn't sure even I got what I meant.

"And there's more," I added, reading from the Smartphone. "Of course, you know Caesar got assassinated, well, guess what...she married *again...*"[9]

The bathroom door opened and I was interrupted.

Charmion emerged. "The mirror is rather small in there," she complained. "Do you have a bigger one?"

"You can use our dressing table," Dad offered. "It's in there," he said, pointing to the master bedroom. "And feel free to help yourself to my wife's perfume. I think one of them is even named after your queen. I assume your queen does wear perfume, doesn't she?"

Charmion smiled and that smile informed us that my father might just as well have asked me if my mother liked chocolate.[10]

Cleopatra finally appeared from the bathroom, still donned in Mum's cerise bathrobe.

"Your Highness," Dad bowed. "I hope all is to your satisfaction. I would like to congratulate you on your impending wedding." There was more than a hint of sarcasm in his voice.

Cleopatra ignored my father and followed Charmion into the bedroom. This time the other maid remained outside with us.

I took my 'seat' on the landing and reached for the bubble wrap. Dad joined me again, seemingly having forgotten that he was responsible for catering for the *whole of Rome.* And, much to my surprise, Iras joined us as well. She smiled as she started to pop some bubbles.

"So where are her brothers...husbands, whatever you want to call them?" I quizzed her, feeling the need to start a conversation.

Iras grinned. "They're dead."

"Dead? I thought her brothers were younger than her? What happened to them?"

Iras paused and took a deep breath. "Well, I'll start with little Ptolemy, her first husband...and second cousin...and brother-in-law... and..."

"Sorry? He was her brother *and* brother-in-law?"

Iras nodded. "Their father was Ptolemy XII. He was also my queen's uncle...great uncle...father-in-law...think that's right...oh, and her husband."

"What? So her *dad* was really Cleopatra's first husband, then?" my father finally concluded after a minute of stupefied reflection.

Iras continued to nod.

Dad vigorously rubbed the palms of his hands over his eyes. I thought his head was going to explode. I reached for the Smartphone, hoping it might reveal whether Iras had become a bit confused herself over some of the family relationships.

"Don't even bother," Dad turned to me. "Let's just take her word for it."[11]

"Anyway," I addressed Iras, "what happened to little Ptolemy?"

"It got a bit territorial," the maid continued. "They didn't like sharing, you see."

"Children don't," Dad agreed, looking accusingly at me. "He didn't, anyway. Woe betide anyone who touched his Stretch Armstrong...or fuzzy-felts."

I groaned.

"It wasn't toys they were arguing over – it was the throne," Iras attempted to explain. "Cleopatra and Ptolemy didn't want to share it when their father died. So Ptolemy turned to Caesar for assistance. He sent Caesar a gift to win him over."

"That's nice," Dad remarked, "some of his Lego or something cuddly?"

"The head of Pompey."

"Oh!"

"Only Caesar was not impressed with the gift," Iras revealed, shaking her head.[12]

My father started to nod his. "Well, Lego would have been the more sensible option, if you ask me. You can't go far wrong with Lego. It would have been more useful – he could have built Rome with it!" Dad quipped.

"So after that, my queen and Caesar teamed up instead," the maid went on.[13]

"What happened to Ptolemy?" I asked.

"There was a battle and he died fleeing from the Romans."

I tried to picture poor, little Ptolemy attempting to ward off the Romans with his toy sword and shield.

"He drowned," Iras elaborated, "because he was unable to swim with all that armour on."

Perhaps his sword and shield were not made from foam, after all![14]

"And what about brother number two, the second little Ptolemy?" I asked. "What happened to him?"

"Ptolemy XIV? He ate something that disagreed with him."

Her smile left us in no doubt that Cleopatra had been the cause of that too.[15]

"So none of her brothers will be coming to this wedding – they're all dead?" I attempted to clarify. "Has she any sisters? Did she marry any of...*them*?"

"Don't be so ridiculous; of course not. Yes, she had sisters."

"Had? They're dead as well, then?" I surmised.

"Yes. Well, they asked for it. I mean, her little sister Arsinoe was a real pain in the...anyway, my queen saw her off in the end."

"I assume Cleo didn't like sharing with her either!"[16]

Iras nodded. "That's right. To be fair, my queen didn't mind sharing the throne – just not with her brothers and sisters. Of course, she had no problem making another husband co-ruler of Egypt."

"You mean Caesar?"

"No, not that husband...their son. Cleopatra and Caesar had a son, you see..."

"So she married her *son* as well?" Dad exclaimed.

Iras smiled. "Yes, sorry, I forgot *that* husband. Anyway, her son is called Caesarion."

Dad looked at me proudly. "My son was by caesarean as well."

Iras never heard my father, and left us to join her fellow maid and queen in the master bedroom.[17]

I shook my head and turned to the Smartphone. "I wonder if this Caesarion will be coming to the wedding. It says here he died after Cleopatra...at least she didn't have anything to do with *his* death; says here he was killed by his teacher!"

"That's drastic," Dad grinned. "I only got detention if I didn't do *my* homework."[18]

"So who is her *current* husband?" Dad contemplated. "Is Caesar dead yet, I mean at this moment in time, in our time...I mean, today, here and now?"

Dad had a look of confusion on his face that suggested he didn't know what he meant, but we both knew what he was getting at.

"Has she got on to Mark Antony?" I added. "He was the final one. Perhaps he's the one she's marrying today?"

We never had the chance to think more of it. The bedroom door opened.

Charmion emerged.

"There's a fly in the room," she announced. "Where are your slaves?"

"I'll go and summon one," Dad smiled, as he rose and headed for the stairs, believing it to be a good moment to return to the kitchen.

"What do you need a slave for?" I asked.

"To get rid of the flies, of course," Charmion explained. "I'm assuming you have some honey?"[19]

Dad headed down the stairs. "I'll get a rolled-up newspaper," he said. "Are you sure it's a fly? Hope it's not a wasp – because wasps have a nasty sting. Very painful – not as deadly as a bite from an asp, of course," he added, with a cheeky grin.[20]

It was another hour before we heard from anyone in the bedroom.

Dad joined me on the landing at regular intervals, but was in the kitchen when Charmion finally opened the door again.

"My queen would like to know if you will both be joining her for prayers?" she asked me.

I hesitated and Charmion repeated her question.

"You worship the gods, don't you?" she added.

I shook my head. "Not really."

Charmion looked confused. "We saw the stone statues when we arrived – on the grass. Are they not your gods?"

Now I understood.

"They're garden gnomes," I smiled. "We don't really worship them. They're just...well, I don't really know what they're..."

"They don't bring you good fortune, then?" Charmion interrupted.

I shook my head.[21]

"And what about that furry idol on the bed in there?" she persisted. I never had time to answer. She had retreated into the bedroom and then re-emerged with Mum's childhood cuddly toy parrot.

"That's Horace," I smiled warmly.

"I thought so," Charmion responded, to my surprise. "I said to Iras that it was *meant* to be him – though we've both never seen him depicted quite like this. It's the eye that gave it away, though."

I looked to his eyes, one of which was badly scratched.

"He's a bit old now," I felt the need to explain, "but Mum will never part with him. She loves him...not sure she worships him, though," I added doubtfully. "Anyway, I think I'll just see if Dad wants some help with the dinner."[22]

I headed for the stairs, but stopped. "I don't suppose your queen is nearly...ready?" I inquired hopefully.

Charmion never answered my question, but asked one herself, though not before glancing behind her to ensure she was not being observed. "You have plenty of beer, yes?" she whispered.

I was taken aback somewhat. "Beer?"

Charmion put her finger to her lips to inform me that this was not a conversation she wanted to share with anyone other than me.

"Let me tell you a secret," she went on, her voice still muted. "My queen likes a drink or two...or three...or four...or five..."

I nodded in an attempt to assure her that she had no need to carry on – I got the point.

"She likes a few drinks at the club; she goes there with her husband and some other members," Charmion continued, briefly turning to check that she was still not being observed. "Do you know of the club? Perhaps your father has frequented it?"

I shook my head. "I doubt it...not unless you're talking about the *Red Lion*."[23]

Charmion went back into the bedroom and I was allowed to continue down the stairs.

"One more thing," Charmion added, popping her head around the door again. "Your father might wish to cover his head for the ceremony."

I shrugged my shoulders and headed for the kitchen. I wondered if she had noticed his dandruff.

"What's she talking about?" Dad cogitated, as we stared at his Smartphone, examining some pictures of Ancient Egyptians.

"Most of the men are bald...so that doesn't seem to be the problem," I quipped, affectionately ruffling my fingers through Dad's receding hair.[24]

"Does she mean she wants me to wear one of those pointy cones on my head?" Dad suggested. "They do seem to be all the rage in Ancient Egypt."

I nodded. "I don't know, it's possible, and I certainly don't think she means for you to put on your bobble hat!"

"Type in 'Egyptian head cone'," Dad directed me. "There might be some for sale on eBay."

I didn't know if Dad was serious or not. "It doesn't matter," I conceded. "We can't wait for it to be delivered anyway – we haven't got time."

"Don't bet on it," Dad said, lifting his head towards the ceiling. "She could be hours yet!"

I left Dad and went to the living room to read my magazine.

It was another hour (only an hour) before Charmion *finally* came down and found me.

"My queen is ready," she stated. "You better both stand over there," she added, pointing to a space on the carpet. "Is your father ready? He will have his head covered, yes?"

"Dad!" I called. "You better come in. The wedding's going to start."

I thought it odd that the bridegroom had not yet arrived, but assumed they were doing it the other way around – maybe it was the bride who waited for the groom to walk down the aisle in Ancient Egypt?

I put my hand over my mouth and gasped as Dad made his entrance. Yes, it *was* my father and not a unicorn, as Dad had stuck an upturned ice-cream cone on the top of his head, a piece of string under his chin to hold it in place. It looked like the school bully had plonked it on his head, and I expected to see some cream running down his face. Anyway, I was left in no doubt that there had been no ceremonial Egyptian head gear for sale on eBay, after all!

Dad looked ridiculous and he knew it. He had a cheeky smile on his face. I just shook my head and hoped Cleopatra would see the funny side of it.

As Dad and I stood beside each other, I started to wonder who was going to perform the ceremony. Would a priest be arriving? There was still no sign of the bridegroom.

We never heard Cleopatra coming down the stairs, but we got a whiff of the fact, quite literally. Yes, I was left in no doubt that she *had* discovered my mother's perfumes![25]

I gasped again as the queen entered the living room. We were stunned by her appearance. Yes, her make-up was sensational...her jewellery dazzling...her gold dress mesmerising...but that wasn't what left us reeling. It was the pointy *beard* that did that!

Dad lowered his ice-cream cone and placed it under his chin, so that it too became a 'pointy beard'.

He winked at me, before addressing Cleopatra.

"I must say that you look incredible, Your Highness," he offered. "I have not seen a beard like that since Jimmy Hill introduced *Match of the Day*."

My Dad was old. I had no idea who Jimmy Hill was either, the remark meaning as much to me as it did to Cleopatra and her maids.[26]

Charmion approached Dad. "Do you have a wedding gift for my queen?"

He hesitated. For one moment, I thought he was going to rush upstairs to raid Mum's jewellery box.

"I assume you haven't set up a wedding gift list at John Lewis?" Dad inquired hopefully. "Anything in particular you need for your palace?"

Charmion was not amused. She held out her hand.

I had to act quickly and went towards a drawer.

"Here it is, our wedding gift," I said, handing a small enamel badge to Charmion. "It attaches to your clothes by this pin." I started to show her how it was done and, between us, we attached it to the dress of Cleopatra. The queen looked satisfied with the gift. I was sorry to lose it, but it did give me pleasure to think that Cleopatra VII would be getting married wearing a Watford FC badge!

"And *your* gift?" Charmion demanded, turning to Dad. Oh! They wanted a gift from *both* of us.

Dad reached into his pocket. He pulled out a 5p coin and handed it to Charmion, once he had removed some bits of fluff and tissue from it.

Cleopatra looked interested. "Is it *very* valuable?"

Dad nodded.

Charmion handed it to Cleopatra.

The queen held the coin aloft.

"I suppose that is the face of *your* ruler?" she contemplated. "We shall have to do something about that, but I accept your gift."[27]

I bet Dad was relieved to hear that, but was probably thinking that he could have got away with giving her a penny instead!

"I already have a fortune, of course," Cleopatra felt the need to inform us, in case we hadn't guessed by the amount of gold on her attire, "but I spend a fortune every day."

"So does your mum," Dad smiled, his joke accompanied by another wink in my direction.

Cleopatra focused her eyes on my father.

"And I bet you that I can consume a fortune before you can say Tutankhamun is a fat prince with orange hair," the queen said to him, a mischievous grin on her face. At first we didn't realise that she *really* did want him to repeat her words. "Go on, say it," she persisted.

And so Dad obliged. As he did, she popped the coin into her mouth and swallowed it.[28]

"Good job I didn't give her a £2 coin," a perplexed Dad turned to me. "Or even the car!" he added, fiddling with his keys in his pocket. "Actually, that reminds me, our car's named after you, Your Highness," he pointed out. "It's a Renault *Clio*!"

Charmion moved forward in an attempt to prevent my babbling parent from babbling any longer. "Are you ready? My queen is waiting."

"Are we starting?" Dad asked. "So where's the groom? I can't see anyone walking down the aisle?" he added, looking out of the window along the garden path. "Hope the postman doesn't come now, but I don't think he walks like an Egyptian!"

"What is a groom?" Cleopatra inquired, rubbing her beard thoughtfully.

"The doomed prisoner!" Dad teased. I gave Cleopatra the truthful answer.

She started to laugh. Her maids started to laugh.

"*You're* the groom," Charmion said suddenly, nodding at Dad, a smug smile on her face. "Didn't we mention that?"

No. I think we would have remembered that fact.

Dad – after giving out a little shriek – started to laugh; it was a nervous cackle, actually.

"Let me get this right," he started, "your queen thinks she is going to marry...me? It's a bit presumptuous of her, isn't it? I mean, I haven't even proposed to her."

Charmion smiled. "Well, she is proposing to you..."

I nudged Dad in the ribs and showed him the date on my watch.

"It's February the 29th today – it's a leap year!"[29]

"Look," Dad went on, his right eye starting to twitch, "don't get me wrong, your queen is very beautiful and all that – but I think there's been a misunderstanding...I'm already married, you see."

That, of course, was the wrong answer to give to someone who was *also* already married, and who didn't seem to mind sharing husbands, even if she didn't like sharing thrones.

"This is a joke, of course," I put forward. "You wouldn't want to marry Dad. If you think those toenails in the bath are his worst habit..."

It was Charmion who attempted to explain what was going on. "My queen likes the look of this kingdom that you reside in. It would be beneficial to have an ally here."

Dad gulped. "Look, as I said, your queen is a very lovely lady and I'm flattered, but her track record is not great, is it? All the other husbands have come to a rather sticky end by the sound of it."

Dad's Smartphone suddenly started to play a tune – it was his ringtone, not *Here comes the Bride*.

He looked at the screen and then to me. "It's your mother!" he said, slapping his forehead. "How am I going to explain this one?"

My father didn't say much on the phone. He kept his answers to a minimum, though that was nothing unusual when it came to conversing with my mother.

"That was my *wife*," he informed Cleopatra when the conversation had ended. "And she's on her way, right now! And even if your husbands aren't a tad jealous of the other husbands, I do not want to be the one to have to explain to my wife that *I'm* about to get another one...I mean, another *wife*!"

Cleopatra flashed Dad a playful smile. "I didn't say that my husband wasn't a jealous man."

She waltzed towards my father and affectionately stroked his face.

"So he *is* a jealous man?" a nervous Dad attempted to clarify, straightening his back, as his bride-to-be continued to caress his cheek. "And can I assume that he doesn't approve of you getting married today?" my father continued to probe.

"He doesn't know," Cleopatra smiled mischievously. That, of course, explained why he wouldn't be attending the wedding – he didn't know anything about it!

"I think you all better go," Dad insisted, backing away from his temptress, "before my wife gets in," he added, as Cleopatra attempted to snuggle up to my father once more. "She'll probably kill you if she discovers what you're up to," he felt the need to elaborate.

The warning went unheeded. Cleopatra was having too much fun teasing my increasingly flustered parent. "Your wife sounds like a feisty lady...I like the sound of her."

Dad shook his head. "You will not like the sound of her when she finds you this close to me!"

There was a knock on the front door. During the commotion, no-one had noticed anyone come up the aisle...I mean, the garden path.

"Oh no! It's her!" Dad howled. "That was quick! I don't know how we're going to explain this."

Dad had been backing away from Cleopatra, but now had nowhere else to go, sinking into the armchair that had prevented further escape. As I headed for the front door, Cleopatra plonked herself on his lap. I couldn't help but smile.

I opened the door. It wasn't Mum...or the postman. The man gave me his name and I left him on the doorstep and re-entered the room.

"There's a man at the door. He wants to speak to you, Dad. Says his name's Mark...or it may have been Antony?"

"That's *him*!" Cleopatra squawked. "That's *my* husband! I'll kill the traitor who told him about this!"

Cleopatra was off Dad's lap in a second, a look of alarm on *her* face now.

"Is there another way out of here?" she turned to me hastily. "He'll kill me – and your father – if he finds out what's going on."

I nodded. "You better come with me."

"I guess the wedding's off, then," my relieved Dad muttered under his breath, still seated in the armchair.

I guided a frantic Cleopatra and her maids towards the kitchen.

"This way – please excuse the mess, but you'll be exiting through the tradesman's entrance."

I opened the back door and pointed towards the far end of the garden.

"Thank you for coming," I said. "Don't forget to close the gate after you."

I smiled; I felt like I was the butler delivering the final line of a bedroom farce.

And that was that. They were gone. Cleopatra's exit had been as dramatic as her entrance.

I walked calmly back to the front door and showed the man into the hallway. A dazed Dad was still sprawled in the armchair. The man had now given me his card and I prepared to read it to my father, the newcomer having followed me into the living room.

"*Mark and Tony – for all your plumbing needs*," I read aloud with a grin, before lifting my head to view the man's grease-stained overalls. "I think he's here to fix the washing machine."

Chapter 5
Christopher Columbus

You can find almost anything in our loft. Dad thought so, at any rate. Well, at least until he started *looking* for something in our loft.

"What are you searching for, anyway?" I called from the landing.

"An American flag!" Dad bellowed from among the rafters and beams.

As I said, my father really did believe he could find *anything* up there.

I scratched my head. The question that immediately came to mind was why Dad had got it into his head that we might be storing an American flag in our loft, and, strangely, that was even before I got around to wondering why Dad *wanted to find* an American flag in our loft!

"I'm sure we have one somewhere," my father continued to shout. "We bought it when some friends from New York were staying with us, while the Super Bowl was on."

I groaned. Yes, that was the sort of thing Dad would do.

"It's no use," he went on. "I've looked everywhere. I did find this, though."

He threw a piece of white material from the open hatch. It landed on my head.

"Do you remember it?" he asked, now peering down at me from his *lofty* (please excuse the pun) position.

It was a T-shirt – a very small one. I started to unfurl it.

"You used to wear it all the time," my father informed me with a grin; "couldn't get it off you, and you used to cry when Mum had to wash it."

I held *aloft* (yes, another pun) the source of his merriment, in two hands, so that I could make out the now fading image of Mickey Mouse emblazoned on it. I forced a smile and chucked it back up, as Dad started his descent of the loft ladder. "Oh well, suppose I'll just have to use my pants instead," he conceded.

"Sorry?"

Dad disappeared into the master bedroom. When he emerged, he was holding up a pair of boxer shorts, forcefully stretching them to test the elastic.

He turned to me. "What do you reckon? Will these do?"

"I suppose so – no-one will see them anyway," I felt the need to point out, at least I *hoped* no-one would see them!

"I'm not going to *wear* them," Dad corrected me. "I mean to use them as a flag."

I should at this point inform you that the boxer shorts were in the design of the stars and stripes of America, or it wouldn't have made a lot of sense. Actually, it still didn't make a lot of sense!

"A flag?" I queried. "You're going to make a flag out of your boxer shorts?"

"Why not?" Dad replied. "I must admit, though, I did think about wearing them today, for *his* sake. I haven't worn them for yonks."

"I'm not surprised," I smiled. "So they were bought in honour of your New York friends as well, then?"

Dad shook his head. "I said 'yonks' – not 'Yanks'."

I sighed, as my father now put the boxer shorts to his nose.

"I think I last wore them for Independence Day a few years back," he speculated. "Anyway, they'll have to do."

Of course, they didn't *do*. Dad spent more than an hour trying to fix his boxer shorts to a pole, and another hour trying to work out how to actually make them flutter in the absence of a breeze.

In the end, he gave up, instead fixing a makeshift washing line across our front lawn. Two pegs eventually held his boxer shorts – I mean flag – to the string. I didn't know what was more embarrassing: seeing my Dad's stars-and-stripes pants fluttering on the line, or giving the impression to our neighbours that we might be American!

Still, no doubt Christopher Columbus would appreciate the gesture.[1]

I looked at my watch. Actually, he should have been here by now.

"Will you be playing the American national anthem when he arrives?" I asked my father, more than a tint of sarcasm in my voice, as I placed the palm of my hand over my heart.

Dad joined me in the living room. He was holding a CD. "Found this in the loft as well," he informed me. "I thought he might like some Disney music instead. How about...*A Whole New World*?"

I smiled. Actually, that was quite a good joke for Dad.[2]

"And I've got some Disney DVDs here that you used to watch," he continued. "It'll at least show him that the settlers did something constructive after he left them in the New World."[3]

At last the doorbell sounded.

"I'll get it," I insisted. "You put the kettle on and bring out some biscuits...or should I say *cookies*."

Columbus was not dressed as I imagined he would be. He handed me his thick fur coat and a hat made from iron. He also removed a sword and an axe from his belt, leaning the weapons against the hallway radiator.

"It's a great honour to have you," I started, ushering him into the living room. "I've always wanted to meet you – the man who discovered America. Did you like Dad's pants?" I quizzed him, nodding my head in the direction of the front garden. "They're flying in your honour."

I received a polite smile in return, though I knew Columbus had no idea what I was talking about.

"Of course, the Americans today think pants are their trousers," I continued to waffle. "In fact, I bet the natives you came across when you landed weren't wearing trousers or pants...or very much at all."

Not only did Columbus not dress in the manner I expected him to, he didn't look like the man in my history books either. His hair was very long and reached well below his shoulders. On account of my wittering, it was several moments before Columbus spoke. He stroked his bushy beard (something else I hadn't been expecting) as he muttered something about the weather.

And not only did Columbus not dress as I thought he would, or look as I thought he would, he also didn't speak as I thought he would. I struggled to place his accent.

As he started to relate stories of his travels, Dad entered the room, holding a bowl of crisps.

"I've brought in some *potato chips*," he said with his worst American accent. I could see that he too was taken aback by the fact that our guest looked more like a heavy metal star than an explorer.

"Hope you had a good journey," Dad said, composing himself. "At least the weather held off – you were lucky," he added, pointing out some menacing clouds outside.

Columbus nodded in agreement. "That is indeed what they call me."

"Do they?" I inquired. "Is it a nickname? Are you always lucky? We had a cat called Lucky. Shall we call you Lucky or Christopher – though neither sound very Spanish?"

Our guest looked confused.

It was Dad who corrected me on his nationality.

"Of course," I apologised, "you're not Spanish, but Italian! And it wouldn't be Christopher...how about we call you Cristo?"[4]

Our guest still looked confused.

"My name is Leif Erikson," he stated, "but you can call me Leif the Lucky if you prefer."

"That is *very* different to Christopher Columbus," I mused.

"Christopher Columbus? Who's he?" the man asked, now offering me another hint that it might not be Columbus standing in our living room, after all.

I studied our visitor closely.

"You're *not* Christopher Columbus then, are you?" I finally concluded. "So I don't have the man who discovered America in my living room," I added, failing to hide my disappointment.

"My name is Leif Erikson," the man repeated. "I am the son of Erik the Red."

I now realised why Christopher Columbus was dressed as a heavy metal star; he *wasn't* Christopher Columbus. And, actually, he wasn't a heavy metal star either...he was a Viking.

I nodded as I refocused on the hat still in my hands. Of course, the rivets, and the fact that it was made out of iron, should have told me it was a helmet, not a hat. If it had had horns on it, I might have been a bit quicker to have realised it belonged to a Norseman.[5]

"What is this America you keep talking about?" the man queried, before I even had a chance to question why a Norseman – and not Columbus – was in our living room. "Is it a place?" he guessed.

Dad reached for the globe that he had purposely placed behind the sofa. Actually, it was an inflated novelty beach ball, but it had all the countries on it, or at least the main ones. "Catch!" he said, tossing it in the direction of our visitor. He caught it first time.

"It's the world," Dad informed Leif – as we should now call our unexpected arrival. My father started to sing: "*He's got the whole world in his hands...he's got the whole world in his hands...he's got the whole...*" He only stopped when he realised the lyrics were a bit repetitive.

Leif studied the globe closely.

"This is the...*world*?" he returned, a grin appearing on his face. "I don't think so, my friend," he went on, now laughing raucously. "The world is not shaped like a snowball!" he added, when he finally caught his breath, thrusting the beach ball into my stomach. Ouch! Round or not, it was a good job the 'world' was only made of plastic![6]

"Anyway, *this* is America," I pointed out, my finger resting on a mass of yellow on the globe. "It's a pretty big place, as you can see."

This time Leif nodded.

"Ah! I see," he said. "I think you mean Vinland."

"No, it's America," I corrected him. "Finland is...well, it's up your way, isn't it?"

Leif shook his head. "No, not Finland...I said Vinland. That place you point to is Vinland, I tell you – and I discovered it."

"You must be getting confused," I politely explained. "A man called Christopher Columbus discovered America...or *Vinland.* It's a well-known fact."[7]

Leif shook his head. "No, I discovered it. There was no-one called Columbus living there when I landed."

My father took the beach ball from me. "Did you discover *this* place?" Dad patronised, his finger hovering. He stopped. "Where is Finland, son?" he asked, turning to face me. I pointed somewhere in the direction of northern Europe. As I said, it was not a very accurate map of the world – it was a beach ball, after all.

Leif continued to shake his head. He was getting more and more frustrated.

"It is Vinland," he insisted, returning his chunky finger to the mass of yellow.

"It's America," Dad responded.

"Vinland."

"America."

"Vinland."

"Hold on!" Dad declared, turning abruptly to me, keen not to act out a scene from a pantomime, despite his fondness of amateur dramatics. "Could it be possible that it was called Vinland before Columbus discovered it?"

I returned a look of bewilderment. "And who would have given it the name Vinland if that was the case," I mocked him; "the man who *discovered* it, perhaps?"

Dad nodded dumbly, but then realised what I was implying. "I see," he admitted, "Columbus wouldn't have been the first to discover it then, would he?"

"He wasn't!" Leif interrupted. "I was the first to set foot in Vinland...or whatever you want to call it and, during my entire time there, I never met a soul by the name of Columbus."[8]

"Finland does sound a lot like Vinland," Dad persisted.

"It is *Vinland*!" Leif stormed. He was getting angry now, really angry.

I held up my hands.

"Let's call it Vinland," I conceded, nodding to Dad, having suddenly remembered the sword and axe in our hallway.

Leif nodded and resumed a state of calm. "Thank you. I know it is not Finland," he started, "because it was I who named it *Vin*...land, after all the grapes there. And, of course, there was a reason I chose *that* name. You see, I hoped the name might tempt a few more to come and settle there. You see, my people like wine very much. I hoped it might encourage them to follow me to this new land of plenty...plenty of wine," he added, licking his lips.

Dad nodded. "He has a point. A name's important...no wonder the *Nag's Head* is always empty!"[9]

"My father, Erik the Red, used the same tactic," Leif continued. "He was exiled and found this big island covered with snow and ice, so he named it..."

"Iceland!" Dad interrupted with fervour.

Leif shook his head. "No, Iceland was his home country, but let me tell you, it couldn't have been any easier enticing people to a desolate place like Iceland either."

"That surprises me," Dad responded, a smirk appearing on his face; "they normally only have to make their sausages cheaper than Tesco!"

I had guessed the punchline long before Dad delivered it, though Leif, of course, had no idea what we were giggling about.

"No," he sought to elaborate, "this new island my father discovered also had snow and ice – people didn't want more of the same...so he called it Greenland."

"Not Redland?" Dad suggested. "He could have named it after himself."

"No, your father was something of a PR genius," I admitted to our visitor; "Greenland does sound a lot more appealing."

However, as I offered my praise, I did wonder what those who followed Erik the Red all the way to the 'promised land' would have wanted to *do* with Erik the Red...when they discovered that there wasn't even a dandelion in sight!"[10]

"Anyway," Leif went on defiantly, "there it is; take it or leave it, my friends: I was the man who discovered..." He paused. "Vinland."

There was a ping from Dad's Smartphone. He took it from his pocket and peered at the screen.

"It's a tweet," he announced, looking up at our visitor.

I twitched, knowing full well that my father was contemplating another joke at the expense of the man in our living room, having – unlike me – seemingly forgotten the sword and axe in our hallway.

"It's from Columbus," my father explained with a wink, having failed to successfully interpret my nervous reaction. "He's left Bridge Street and heading towards...Iceland."

"Well, he has a long way to go," Leif felt the need to inform us.

I smiled. He didn't get the joke the first time around, so I refrained from contradicting him or offering an explanation.

Leif snatched his helmet from my hand and made his way to the hallway. "I'll leave you to this Columbus, then," he said, turning to look at us for the final time. "Besides, I have better things to do than to listen to fools like you," he pointed out, nodding at the beach ball, which was now in Dad's hands. "I suppose this Columbus of yours also thinks the world is round?"

Leif was still shaking his head and spitting out obscenities as he headed down the garden path.

"He was a bit feisty," Dad reflected, as we watched him depart. "I get the feeling he had an axe to grind with someone."

"I'm just glad he didn't decide to grind it in here!" I sighed.[11]

Columbus finally arrived another hour after Leif had left us. At least this man on our doorstep was *definitely* Christopher Columbus; that I had no doubt, as he handed me an oddly-shaped black hat. However, he was much taller than I expected and he had a nose like the beak of an eagle.[12]

"Come and sit down, and rest your weary feet," I proposed, showing him into the living room. "You must be tired. Tell us about your journey. Was it a difficult one?"

Columbus sank into the armchair that I offered him. He sighed. "Yes, a very difficult and hazardous one, my friend."[13]

"I'm surprised you travelled alone," I observed, briefly glancing out of the window, as if I might see a ship docked in our street. "I thought you would have had a crew?"

Columbus took a deep breath, kicking off his shoes and stretching out his long legs, which were donned in white tights. "I did when I set off, but their hearts were not in it. All that my men could say every hour of the day was...*are we there yet?* No, I'm afraid they didn't have the stomach to see it through."

Dad flashed an accusing glance in my direction; he clearly felt it was a good time to remind *me* of my own protestations as a young child during those long car journeys on holidays to Cornwall.

"What happened to your crew, then?" I asked, noticing from the corner of my eye that Dad was taking a seat at the table, my father presumably as gripped by the story as I.

"Mutiny!" Columbus snarled, clenching his fist and hitting it against the arm of his chair. "Dirty mutineers, the lot of them..."

"They tried to kill you?"

"Not exactly, but they abandoned me...tempted by riches beyond your imagination."

"Riches?"

"Yes, of course, there were temptations in every land we passed, but the final place was like no other we had seen before. They all abandoned me for it, every one of them."

Columbus paused and I took it as an opportunity to offer him a potato chip. He didn't even notice the bowl I floated in front of that *nose* of his, his eyes being fixed on one corner of the room, though his vague expression assured me that he was not focused on anything in particular.

"They decided *that* was the place for them, and nothing I could say would stop them jumping ship," he went on. "Yes, the temptation was too great...but I shouldn't have been surprised." He paused once more, his eyes still rooted to the corner of the room, but when he spoke again; his voice betrayed a sense of wonder. "Believe me," he said, "even I haven't seen treasures like that anywhere before on my travels."

"Were you not tempted to follow your crew?" I suggested. "Why didn't you just go with them – to have a share of this treasure?"

This question finally roused him from his trance. He raised his head and looked at me sternly.

"Have you not heard of a siren, my friend?"

Dad grinned from the table. "Too right we have, my car alarm's always going off!"

Columbus continued oblivious to my father's quip.

"They were everywhere," he went on, "beautiful and beguiling women (and men), standing behind huge sheets of glass, trying to lure us in, enticing us to sample their wares. Everything you could want was there: gold...spices...strange silks, just like yours," he added, nodding at my clothes. "So much treasure to hand, but guarded by... *sirens*."

I turned to Dad and smiled. "We know this land he speaks of – I think he might have found the indoor shopping centre!"

Columbus ignored me and continued to mutter in a feverish manner, again as though he were talking to himself and no other. "I can't imagine what fate has befallen my men – lured to something worse than death, perhaps?"

He could be right – that was how I felt when I had to go shopping with Mum!

"I'm sure they'll be fine," I assured him.

Columbus shook himself from the latest stupor and stared at me. "How do you know they'll be fine? Have you been to this land and lived to tell the tale?"

"Many times...unfortunately," I groaned.

"What do they call this infernal land, then?"

It was Dad who beat me to it: "Pound...*land*!" he whooped.[14]

Columbus never responded, though I didn't expect him to. Still giggling, I lifted the bowl of potato chips his way again, but with the same result. He hadn't finished his tale and continued to bemoan his fate. "Yes, it was a difficult journey. I can't tell you what we put ourselves through to get here. Our vessel was not up to the job, you see – not quite the *Santa María*. It was dirty and cramped on board, not fit for human habitation. We didn't have an inch to move. We were packed in like..."

"Sardines?" Dad submitted.

"And the men aboard smelt like sardines, I can tell you," Columbus added. "No, if the destination wasn't hell...the journey was."

I nodded in sympathy. "Yes, I've read about conditions on a ship in your day..."

"Ship?" Columbus retorted. "We travelled most of the way by something called a...*train*?"

I smiled. I wasn't expecting that.

"And it broke down," he pressed on. "We had to finish the rest of the journey on a..." He paused. "What was it called now... a bus or something? It was all a far cry from my precious *Santa María* anyway."[15]

Dad finally got up from the table and this time offered Columbus a cookie. It was accepted.

"Thank you," he said, a smile appearing on his face as he took a bite. "Good. *Very* good. Don't let my crew know sea biscuits can be as good as this. Let me tell you, the food was awful. There was nothing nutritional on board – many of us became sick."

"I assume we're still talking about the *train*!" I joked.[16]

"How about some...*candy*?" Dad beamed, pleased to be able to share more of his American lingo; now offering Columbus a plate of jelly beans. "Your America had a president in the 1980s that used to like jelly beans," Dad continued. "Ronald was his name – that's Reagan, not McDonald..." He hesitated, noticing the gormless expression on the face of our guest. "Anyway...please help yourself."

Columbus fingered the colourful beans in awe, but clearly wasn't sure what he was supposed to do with them. Instead, he stretched for a small satchel he had been carrying. "And now I have a gift for *you*," he announced, "from another country...something I picked up on the way here."

He pulled out a toothbrush and held it aloft. "It has many uses," I think. With that, he started to 'comb' his nasal hairs with it. And, yes, the nostrils on that grotesque nose of his were big enough to accommodate the toothbrush! Having not quite received the reaction he expected, Columbus proceeded to thrust the brush into his ear, twisting it around, before handing it to my sniggering father.

"Have a go!" the explorer insisted. "It works – I can hear you clearly now."

I smiled. "Actually, you're meant to clean your teeth with it," I revealed.

Columbus snorted. "That's disgusting! You're going to put that into your mouth? You don't know where it's been!"

I think we did. And I was starting to feel sick.

My still tittering father headed for the kitchen and I allowed Columbus some time to cast his eye around his new surroundings.

"We've got so much to tell you about America," I said. "You wouldn't believe how much it's changed since you were there."

"America?"

Oh no! Not again, though, of course, I soon realised that Columbus wouldn't have known it by that name either.

"What can I tell you about the...*New World*?" I mused. "Of course, it's not really new anymore. They call it the land of opportunity. It's famous for cowboys...skyscrapers...Broadway...baseball... hamburgers...the Empire State Building...guns...the Simpsons..."

Columbus wasn't listening, which was fortunate, as I was running out of American icons. He had spotted the Disney memorabilia we had found in the loft, and picked up a DVD.

"...And for Disneyland," I added. "I mustn't forget that."

"I haven't heard of that land. What sort of people inhabit it?"

I exhaled deeply. "Well, there's a high-pitched talking mouse; a wooden puppet with a nose that grows when he lies...and seven whistling dwarfs, to name but a few."

A seagull had landed on Dad's makeshift washing line. Columbus noticed it and stood upright, peering out of the window.

"It's all right," I assured him. "It's not an albatross. It won't bring you bad luck. I know what you mariners are like."

While he was still standing, Columbus took the opportunity to study our front garden. He sniffed, and I guessed what he might be thinking.

"The garden's a bit of a mess," I apologised. "The Americans call them yards – and it's probably a more appropriate name for ours. It's not quite the Garden of Eden anyway."

Columbus nodded in agreement. "I know it's not, my friend. I've been *there*."[17]

As the seagull flew away, I noticed that it had left a little something on Dad's 'flag' – the stars and stripes now sporting a dash as well!

Columbus retook his seat and started to study the cover of *The Little Mermaid*. He shook his head.

"This is nonsense," he said. "They don't look like this – real mermaids are not half as beautiful as they are painted."[18]

"Triple cheeseburger and chips!" Dad announced as he returned to the room. "Sorry, I mean...*fries*. Don't worry, this isn't the main course...this is just a starter!"

He handed us both a plate. "No need for a knife and fork," Dad went on. "You can eat the American way – just use your fingers."

Columbus tilted his head. "They are savages, then, these Americans?" he inquired. "They still eat with their hands? It's an uncivilised race, then, yes?"

I smiled, not for the first time.

"Did you want me to prepare some salad to go with it?" Dad offered. "I don't want you to get scurvy. I've got some pizza in the oven as well, super-size, of course. Was going to do a pasta dish, what with you being Italian, but then what with the American connection, I thought pizza was a good mix between the two. I do hope some of your crew have found the *hut* where you can eat pizza – it's right next to *Poundland*!"

And so Columbus and I ate with the plates on our laps, shunning the dining table. "Fries are just potatoes," I explained, as Columbus studied one closely before popping it into his mouth. "Have you heard of potatoes?"

"I introduced them to Europe, my friend," he responded.

So it wasn't Sir Walter Raleigh, after all, I considered. Oh well, Raleigh can still take the credit (or should I say blame) for bringing us tobacco. Wrong again.

"I brought back tobacco as well," Columbus went on, as though he could read my thoughts.[19]

"What else did you bring back from America?"

"I'm intrigued by this America you keep talking about," Columbus stated. "I would like to see it for myself one day."

I nodded. "You already have, only I think you were calling it the New World. Of course, it would have been a bit different – I don't suppose they were eating hotdogs and shooting each other back then." I stopped. "Actually, they probably were!"

I put my plate on the coffee table and reached for the beach ball.

"This big area here," I started to explain; "this is America – or the New World – you discovered it."

Columbus, now mirroring our earlier guest, studied the globe closely, a grin also appearing on his face as he did so. "What a strange map," he concluded with a guffaw. "Why is it in the shape of an orange?"

At least it had progressed from a snowball. I have to admit, I was surprised by his reaction, though.

"I thought you were one of those that *did* know that the Earth was round!" I exclaimed.

"Round?" Columbus roared. "It's *not* round. Why does everyone these days think that it's round?"

Columbus put down his plate and reached for our fruit bowl.

"This is more accurate," he declared, his outstretched hand dangling a pear from its stalk.

I giggled. "That's a *pear*," I pointed out. "The Earth isn't pear-shaped – it's round. I thought you, of all people, knew that."

Columbus shook his head. I concluded that he had received the same reaction many a time.[20]

"Pizza's up!" Dad announced, now with a giant plate in his hand. "It's ham and pineapple."

Columbus picked a piece of pineapple off the pizza, as Dad was still holding the plate.

"Someone's hungry," my father responded. "We haven't even said grace!"

A now-jovial Columbus – his difficult journey seemingly well behind him – put the chunk of pineapple into his mouth and assumed a look of conceit.

"I thought so," he said. "I brought those back as well."[21]

"I had no idea pineapples came from America," Dad chewed over.

Columbus shook his head. "Why do you both keep going on about this America? What is this place?"

Dad flashed me a confused look.

I tried to explain, mouthing the words to my father: "He says he *didn't* discover America."

Dad responded with a cackle. "So earlier we had a man who *didn't* discover America claiming that he *did* discover it, and now we have a man who *did* discover America claiming that he *didn't*?"

I nodded. Yes, it was something like that.

"Careful!" I shouted. Dad had unwittingly tipped the plate of pizza he was holding. He just managed to grab it before it fell to the carpet.

"That was close," he puffed. "Thanks for the shout! I'll reward you with an extra slice, son."

"It was me actually," Columbus chipped in. "I think I shouted just before your son did."

"Did you?" Dad looked puzzled. I also looked at our guest a little perplexed. I hadn't heard him shouting at all.

"Yes," Columbus insisted, "it was me who got in there first...so if there is a reward...I think it belongs to me."

I lifted my hands in submission. "OK. He can have the extra slice."

Columbus nodded in satisfaction.[22]

"I was going to get a pepperoni pizza," Dad announced, "but I thought it might be a bit spicy."

"Spicy?" Columbus chirped.

"That's right," Dad nodded. "Not sure if you liked spicy stuff."

Columbus put down his cheeseburger, his lips smeared with mayonnaise. "I *love* spices, my friend. Do you have any here?"[23]

Dad nodded nonchalantly. "In the kitchen, yes."

"In the *kitchen*?" Columbus was flabbergasted. "You keep your spices in the kitchen...but they are locked away, yes?"

"No."

Columbus smacked his forehead.

"This is madness, my friend. Are you telling me that anyone can get hold of them?"[24]

Dad scratched his chin. "I'll get them if you like."

My father left for the kitchen and returned with the spice rack.

Columbus studied it, his eyes – and mouth – wide open. Dad was pleased such a mundane item had aroused so much interest, and he delighted in unscrewing the lids of the jars and thrusting them under the nose of our mesmerised guest.

"Have a sniff of this one!"

Columbus sneezed as he did so and reached for his handkerchief. It was made of silk and a far cry from the crumpled tissue that Dad would produce when his nose ran at dinnertimes.[25]

"What do you want for these spices?" Columbus wasted no time in inquiring, as he wiped that strange nose of his. "I assume you are willing to trade? Can I tempt you with a tomato...peanuts...coffee... chocolate?"

"You can have the spices," I smiled kindly. "We don't want anything in return."

"Especially not your cold," Dad pointed out, after Columbus had sneezed again, once more not attempting to cover his nose and mouth.[26]

"I'm sorry. The spices tickle my nose, my friend," Columbus informed us.

"Your *nose* tickles me," Dad mumbled under his breath.

I offered to take the spices away.

"No!" Columbus roared. "I *must* have them! What do you want in return?"

"Nothing," I assured him again. "Besides, we probably have all the things you brought back from America anyway...you sort of gave them to us first time around, if you can get your head around that?"

"A parrot?" Columbus persisted. "Would you like a parrot?"[27]

Dad showed some interest for one moment, but then I reminded him that we already had Mum!

"How about a native?" Columbus offered me. "Everyone could do with a slave."[28]

"I've got one already," I joked, turning to my father, who

responded with a glare. "Seriously, take the spices. There's plenty more from where they came from."

"More?" Columbus cried, licking his lips. "*Plenty* more? And you can get them for me?"

I nodded. At this, he rose to his feet and shook our hands ferociously. "You are both very generous. So when I return, you'll have even *more* for me, yes?"

I shrugged my shoulders. "I suppose so. You better put spices on your shopping list, Dad!"

"So we have a deal, then?" Columbus carried on excitedly; unaware he was still shaking Dad's hand. He finally stopped and withdrew his own. "You *will* keep your word, won't you? I don't like it when people don't keep their word. I can get quite angry, if I don't get my own way, you know."

The smile had gone. He was threatening us. Christopher Columbus was offering us a glimpse of his dark side.[29]

I think he could see that we were shocked by his change of manner and he hastily contrived a smile.

"I jest, of course," he lied. "Thank you. You are both very generous. I wish I had come to this wonderful land of Wales much sooner."

"Wales?" Dad and I said simultaneously.

"That's what you call this place, isn't it?"

"No. This is England."

Columbus laughed. "You are both very funny. No, my friends, I did my calculations...I know exactly where I am. This is Wales."

"Well, if you insist, boyo," Dad said smiling; now speaking with a Welsh accent, which was even worse than his American one. "It must have been the coal mine next to the indoor shopping centre that gave it away!"

Dad continued to tease our guest. "You may have taken a wrong turning at the Tesco roundabout," my father kept going. "It's easily done. Still, it's a good job you didn't take the High Road...or you might have ended up in Scotland!"

"I think you mean the Silk Road – and it goes to India, my friend," Columbus responded, in earnest.

I could see that Columbus was becoming agitated and I attempted to placate him.

"It's all right," I said. "It's easy to get lost – and I don't suppose you have the benefit of satnav! You just probably did what you did last time."

Of course, that didn't *placate* him.

"Last time?" Columbus inquired with suspicion. "I have never been to Wales before. There was no...*last* time."

"I didn't mean that," I tried to explain; "I meant that you were attempting to get to somewhere else in...what year was it now?"

Dad intervened. "Don't forget the rhyme, son: *Columbus sailed the ocean blue...in 1492.*"

"That's it, 1492," I continued. "You tried to get to another place then...but sort of bumped into a different place, didn't you?"

Columbus now even sported a *look* of disorientation, and I felt compelled to try to dig myself out of the hole I had dug.

"So you've sort of done the same again I suppose," I cautiously suggested. "I assume you left from Spain this time?" I reached for the beach ball. "If you look, you will see that if you travel north from Spain across the sea towards Wales, the first land you will come to is...England. It's sort of in the way – just like America was in the way...last time, I mean, when you tried to get to the Indies..."

I stopped. I knew I was getting nowhere, and that my task was a fruitless one.[30]

And talking of fruit, Columbus had in the meantime reached for the pear again, now vigorously shaking his head. "Fools! That might have been the route I would have taken if the world was round, but it's not...it's the shape of a pear!" He used his finger to chart his route along the fruit. "If you knew that, you would understand that it was quicker for me to travel from Spain to Wales...via Bulgaria!"

Bulgaria? I looked to Dad in bemusement.

"Shall I tell him, or will you?" my tentative father turned to me.

"No, don't, let him think what he wants," I replied with a whisper. "If you keep up the Welsh accent, I'll find a Tom Jones CD...we don't want to start an argument."

But Columbus had *already* started an argument, and had certainly not finished.

"And what do you mean that I *tried* to get to the Indies? What are you implying?"

"Well, you didn't actually get there, did you?" I broke it to him, as gently as I could.

"Of course I did."

"You *think* you did, but the land you discovered was...America."

For one moment, I almost said 'Wales'.

Columbus was on his feet. In fact, he had been on his feet for a while now. He was a little pink in the face.

"For once and for all, I have never set foot in this America," he stubbornly insisted.[31]

I held up my hands. "OK, if you didn't set foot on the mainland, you did visit all those islands off the *coast* of America."

"Off the coast of *Asia*!" Columbus corrected me. "I found the Indies."

Dad nodded. "In a way, he's right, son. He did find the Indies... the *West* Indies."

"*West* Indies?" Columbus queried. "Why do you call them by that name? They are in the East. Surely the East Indies is a more appropriate name!"

"It is...for *those* islands," Dad went on, "I mean the ones in the East...and that's what we call them...but you visited the ones in the *West*..."

"East," Columbus returned defiantly.

"West."

"East."

This time Columbus prevented Dad from responding with his line, quickly adding: "I sailed west across the Atlantic Ocean to the *East*."

My father opened his mouth, but Columbus beat him to it again.

"Yes, East," our guest concluded (at least he meant it to be the conclusion to the argument).

I hoped it would also be, glancing at my father, with appealing eyes.

"Anyway, it doesn't really matter," Dad muttered to me. "Most people still think he discovered *America.*"[32]

I think Dad had intended it to be a harmless observation, but any mention of *that* word now seemed to be a red rag to the bullish explorer before us.

"*America*!" Columbus raged, "I tell you, I have never set eyes on a place called America. Why do you keep going on about this America? If I had been the man to discover it, wouldn't it be named after me? My name is Columbus. Not America!"

Actually, he had a point.

"Who *is* America named after?" I contemplated, turning towards my father, even though I knew it was unlikely he would have the answer in his head.

"Captain America?" Dad offered in return, with a grin. Yes, I was right: Dad *didn't* have the answer in his head. Of course, his Smartphone would have the answer and he reached for it, whipping it out of his pocket like a gunfighter at high noon.

"Hold on a minute," Dad stopped, averting his gaze from the screen, a look of alarm on his face. "Am...*eric*...a," he said slowly. "Do you get it? It must be named after someone called Eric. Remember Leif the Lucky? He said his name was *Eric*...son!"

I shook my head. "No, Dad. I don't think so."

I snatched the Smartphone from him in an attempt to offer a more plausible explanation.

"It says here," I stated, "that it's named after some Italian." Dad pointed at Columbus, who was now tucking into a slice of pizza, content to let us get on with it. "No, not him," I continued. "Another Italian...though it also says here that it might be named after a man from...you're not going to believe this... Wales!"[33]

We both assumed a look of bewilderment.

Columbus seemed a little happier and now had a smirk on his face – and some tomato puree. "Told you," he said. "If I had set foot in this place you call America...it would be named after me, wouldn't it."

"Hold on!" I interrupted. "Officially, you discovered the *Americas*, didn't you? There's a North, a Central and a...South. Yes, we've forgotten...*Colombia*!"

Dad had reached for the beach ball. This time he wasted no time in *pretending* that he knew where Colombia was located and handed the globe to me. "You show him, son," he commanded.

And so I did. "That's where it is!" I pointed out to Columbus. "That's Colombia...and it's named after *you*."[34]

"But I didn't go to this land you keep pointing to," Columbus insisted. "Your strange map is incorrect – there is *no* land there, I tell you. I found the Indies – the islands of East Asia. The *East* Indies, if you want to call them that!" he reiterated, glaring at my father as he did so.

"West," Dad corrected him again.

"East..."

I sighed. To be honest, so defiant was our guest; I was starting to think that he might be right. And then another place popped into my head for some reason, just to add to the confusion.

"What about Colombo in Sri Lanka?" I threw into the mix. "Is that named after him as well? That's *near* India, isn't it?"

Columbus looked interested, until Dad intervened.

"No, that's named after the detective – the one with the beige raincoat," he quipped.

Of course, Columbus did not know how to respond to a joke he didn't understand. It resulted in a somewhat awkward silence. In truth, I think we had all just about stopped caring *who* discovered America.

Columbus, who was still standing, picked up his plate and looked at the fries. "I would like a fork, after all," he said firmly.

Dad shrugged his shoulders and went to the kitchen.

Columbus calmly turned to me. "I am an experienced traveller, my friend, and yet I am ridiculed by fools everywhere I go, men who *still* think the world is round..."

Dad returned and offered the fork to Columbus. To my surprise, the explorer put his plate of fries on the coffee table before taking the fork from my father.

"Let me assure you," he went on, holding the fork aloft as though he were about to conduct an orchestra, "the Earth is shaped like a pear. That is why I travelled from Spain to Wales...via Bulgaria."

He picked up the beach ball before announcing: "And, for the final time, so that you can get it into your thick skulls, make no mistake, the Earth is not round...it's pear-shaped."

And with that, he stuck the fork into our beach ball. It immediately popped and shrivelled in size.

So that was the end of the argument. I couldn't really argue with him now anyway. It *had* all gone a bit pear-shaped...our globe and our dinner party!

And so Columbus departed; our spice rack under his arm. We watched him stride along the pavement, or should I say *sidewalk*, in his tights, his shoes still in our living room.

My father sighed.

"He's still wrong, you know," Dad insisted, a smirk slowly appearing on his face as he examined our now completely deflated beach ball. "The world isn't pear-shaped...or round...it's *flat*!"

Chapter 6
Winston Churchill

Winston Churchill was crouched under our dining table. He wanted me to join him.

"You'd better take cover, good fellow," he bullishly ordered me. "Can't you hear the siren?"

"Dad!" I shouted, for the third time. "Your car alarm has gone off again – you might want to sort it out."

I smiled and raised the tablecloth slightly, my way of informing our guest that it was safe to re-emerge from under the table.

Churchill hesitated before getting to his feet. He brushed himself down and straightened his trademark bowtie.

"Didn't think it sounded much like Moaning Minnie," he admitted.[1]

"Minnie?" I inquired. "You mean *Molly*...two doors down? Yes, she does like a good moan. Did you meet any of the other neighbours?"

Now confident that no air raid was imminent, Churchill handed me his cane and started to remove his leather gloves. He still had his coat on, having only just entered the house, 'Minnie' having rudely interrupted our introductions.

"Yes, we know all about your *neighbours*," he said sternly. "I'll have a brandy before we get down to business, though."

I knew how much Churchill liked a drink and had already prepared one of his favourite tipples. He seemed impressed. After handing me his gloves and finally his coat, he took his glass and sank into the armchair, *sank* being the right word.

He nodded approvingly before downing the brandy in one go. "Now to business," he said. I watched as his expression became grave. "I have nothing to offer," he began, "but blood, toil, tears and sweat..."[2]

"Don't worry," I replied with a smile, "a bottle of wine would have been fine, or a bunch of flowers, but you don't have to bring us *anything*." And I must admit; I would rather he had kept his sweat, in particular, to himself!

Of course, I soon realised that the hardworking Churchill was actually trying to inform me that he'd come to our house to serve us in some way. I tried to reassure him that his visit should be for pleasure and not business.

"Please, make yourself at home," I insisted, refilling his glass. "And let me say, it is a great honour to have you here, Mr Churchill."

Churchill looked up at me with alarm. "You better not use that name again; careless talk costs lives," he breathed softly, casting a suspicious eye around the room. "We don't know if this room is wired! You better call me Colonel Warden, just in case."[3]

The car alarm had been sorted and Dad entered the room.

"Mr Churchill!" he exalted. "It's a great..."

"Colonel Warden," I interrupted, "it's Colonel Warden," I repeated, with a wink.

Churchill had retrieved a trademark cigar from the breast pocket of his suit. He started to pat various pockets. "Blast it!" he cursed. "Do you have a lighter?"

Dad looked at me. I knew what he was thinking. Mum didn't allow any guest to smoke in the house, and my father wanted me to inform *even* this prestigious guest of that fact.

"I'm sorry," I stuttered, "would you mind smoking...outside?"

Churchill laughed. "Don't be so ridiculous, my good fellow. That's against the rules. It's dark outside...no-one should be lighting up out there. You might as well light a beacon for the enemy aircraft to home in on."

Dad conceded defeat and reached for a box of matches from the sideboard drawer. He handed them to Churchill.

"I noticed none of the vehicle headlights were masked either," Churchill resumed, staring at my father with accusing eyes, "and why haven't they switched off the street lights? It's all very lax here. Are you not aware of the blackout laws?"[4]

Churchill lit his cigar and started to study the box of matches, sliding open the drawer of the box on several occasions, before putting it to his eye. "Camera in here, is there?"

He tossed the box to my father, who himself bizarrely started to search for some secret compartment within it.[5]

"We got your messages," Churchill started, blowing smoke into the air.

"Messages?" I asked. "What messages would they be then?"

Churchill nodded, his eyes scanning the room once more. "You're right to be cautious. We don't know who's listening in. Is there somewhere more private we can go?" he added, his final sentence now a mere whisper.

"He's worried about bugs," I attempted to explain to Dad.

My father shook his head. "It's all right. The cold I had last week has long gone."

Churchill turned his scrutinising eyes towards my father.

"Where are you serving, sir?" he asked.

Dad shrugged his shoulders. "At the table, I suppose. I've got soup for a starter and it might be a bit tricky eating it on your lap."

"I mean, serving your country, sir. Where do you serve?"

"I don't," Dad admitted. "I'm a house husband."

Churchill clearly had no idea what that role involved and

assumed Dad was purposely talking jargon because of the possible 'bugs' throughout the room.

Our guest winked and nodded once more. "Very good, I have to say," he stated. "You're both getting the idea. You're right, we mustn't let our defences slip, though we can't keep communicating in code; we have too much business to get through. Do you have a small room...where we can do our business in private?"

"Oh!" Dad smiled. "That brandy went down quickly. Yes, it's upstairs. The lock's a bit dodgy, but no-one will disturb you."

Churchill frowned. "I mean, where we can talk safely." He stopped. "It doesn't matter. I'll get my man to give this room the once over."

I was unaware that a man had been standing on our doorstep. Churchill told us to admit him. The suited man nodded to Churchill as he entered the living room.

"Check it over, Thompson," Churchill instructed him, leaning back in his chair. "We can't be too careful."[6]

And so Thompson went about his business, examining and picking up every gadget, ornament or curio in search of 'bugs'. Most of those objects had not been picked up in years and it was safe to say that the only thing he would have found on them was dust. "As I was saying," Churchill continued, now blowing smoke from his nostrils, "we've been busy since we got your messages."

"What messages?" I repeated. "We didn't send any."

Churchill smiled. "Don't worry, you can talk freely. If there were any bugs in this room, you can be sure Thompson would have found them by now."

I tried to convince Churchill that my ignorant response had nothing to do with the fact that I feared someone might be listening in.

"Honestly, I don't know anything about any messages," I continued. "I'm not pretending that I don't know anything about any messages – I *don't* know anything about any messages!"

Dad had returned to the kitchen and was making a lot of noise with some pots and pans. Churchill pointed his head in that direction as he spoke. “Your father is a clever man,” he said, “very clever.”

I smiled. I hadn’t heard those words directed towards my father before, and I was glad that Dad hadn’t been able to hear them, or you can be sure it wouldn’t be the last time that *I* would be hearing them!

“Your father was protecting you, of course,” Churchill explained, taking a sip from his brandy and then another puff from his cigar. “He doesn’t want to put you in any danger, but we’ve gone beyond that now. Yes, your father sent us a couple of messages – to get our attention.”

“Did he?”

Churchill spotted a half-empty mug of tea and thought it would make a good ashtray.

“All in code, of course,” he continued with a wink, “so as not to alert the enemy by mistake. I’m not sure he’s up to date on his Morse, though?”

“I think he is,” I refuted. “He’s got all the DVDs. It’s one of his favourite programmes.”

I’m not sure why I made the joke. I knew only too well that Churchill wouldn’t get it. And I didn’t *get* what Churchill was driving at. Dad was no codebreaker. In fact, he had enough problems doing Sudoko!

Churchill interpreted my glazed expression and attempted to explain.

“One of our intelligence officers picked it up,” he informed me. “Yes, very clever...to pretend you’re banging in a nail when you’re really sending a message in Morse code.”

I remembered Dad trying to fix a chair in the garage last week.

“But, as I said,” Churchill grinned, “your father’s Morse was a bit suspect...or his spelling was. In the end, we sort of assumed he was trying to spell out SOS. We weren’t sure at first, but it made sense. You see, he was making such a mess of his DIY job...*that* had to be a ruse.”

I might have started to believe that Churchill had a point, if I hadn't have had experience of Dad's DIY skills!

"We still weren't totally sure," Churchill admitted, "so we released some pigeons into your garden."

"What?"

"Operation Columba! It's top secret," Churchill whispered.

"Oh, I don't think it is. We know all about *him*," I tutted, our previous guest coming to mind. "He told us he brought parrots to Europe," I added, "didn't know he brought pigeons as well!"

Churchill ignored me.

"We couldn't understand it," he said, stroking his chin; "your father kept shoeing the pigeons away...without attaching a message to them!"

I apologised and tried to explain that Dad considered pigeons to be a pest.

Churchill looked horrified. "They are heroes, my friend, every one of them – bless their fluffy feathers."[7]

I smiled politely and let Churchill continue.

"Anyway, the pigeon plan didn't work, but fortunately your father did some washing," Churchill revealed, with another wink of his eye.

I say *revealed*, but I had no idea why washing his socks had persuaded British Intelligence to conclude that Dad had a message to convey to them.

My stupefied expression was enough to assure our guest that I again needed further explanation.

"It's an old trick," Churchill went on, "using your washing to get a message across. In your father's case, he used three items of clothing – pegged them all in a line – to spell out the word 'help'. Yes, very clever: hat...leggings...and pants...HLP."

As we have already ascertained, Dad wasn't very good at spelling.

Churchill knew what I was thinking.

"Well, do you know an item of clothing beginning with the letter E?" he quizzed me.

I shrugged my shoulders. He had a point.[8]

"So, here we are," Churchill beamed, "here for the summit. Here to discuss what to do next. Here to help you in your fight against the enemy."

"Enemy? Who is the enemy?"

Churchill seemed surprised by my lack of knowledge on the subject.

"Has your father not told you anything?" Our guest paused and nodded. "Oh, yes, of course...Official Secrets Act, and all that."

I continued to shake my head in disbelief.

"Anyway," Churchill continued, "we can't hide it from you now; none of us can protect our families from it any longer. The battle has come to our doorstep and we must all confront it."

"I think I might have found something, sir," Thompson interrupted with a cough.

Thompson, who I had forgotten was even in the room, was now holding a DVD that he had succeeded in removing from the DVD player. He held it aloft, purposely turning the silver disc to catch the light, wowed by the spectrum of colour it produced.

"I've not seen anything quite like it," the bodyguard admitted in awe and perplexity.

I smiled and took it from him. "And you probably never will. Dad loves it – it's a classic film. It's called *Close Encounters of the Third Kind*."

Churchill wagged his finger. "Close Encounters of the Third *Reich*, you mean. Intelligence film, is it? I'm surprised I haven't seen it."

I smiled as Thompson went on with his search. Churchill got up and strolled towards the window. The curtains were pulled.

"Turn off the light, Thompson," he commanded, beckoning me to join him at the window. When the light was off, Churchill opened the curtain slightly and peered out into the darkness. He cleared his throat. "Our intelligence officers have been hard at work, as soon as we got your father's messages. And they've discovered where the enemy have set up base." He pointed a finger, his other digits still clasped around his glass of brandy. "Number ten," he declared, stepping back to allow me to look, even though it was too dark to pick out any numbers.

"Number ten?" I grinned. "That's appropriate. That's your house, isn't it?"

"There has been a lot of suspicious activity going on at number ten," Churchill continued, ignoring my flippant observation. "It's been under surveillance for a while now."

I started to laugh. I couldn't help myself. "I don't want to put a dampener on things," I started to explain, "but you may have been wasting your time – that's the *vicar's* house."

Churchill seemed unconcerned by my revelation.

"Audacious, isn't it?" he said, with a smirk. "You would have thought he would have gone for a more original disguise, wouldn't you? It must be a sort of double bluff. He thinks that we wouldn't possibly believe that he would be so stupid as to disguise himself in the very disguise every other spy chooses."

I exhaled deeply. "He's just a harmless old vicar – a *real* one."

Churchill smiled in response to my apparent naivety. "That's what you're supposed to think. No, we've no doubt that he's working for the enemy."

"I don't think so," I continued to protest, pointing to the ceiling. "He's working for *him* up there...and I hope *he's* on our side."

Churchill was adamant. "We know the signs and there's been a lot of suspicious behaviour. My men have been watching the house. Do you know he never flushed his toilet once yesterday? Not once – and he was in the house all day. Do you have an explanation for that?"

"A strong bladder?" I suggested. "But how does that make him a spy?"

"And then there's the moustache," Churchill said, tapping his head, but offering no further explanation, leaving me in a state of bewilderment.[9]

Suddenly, something outside made Churchill avert his eyes from me.

"Is that what I think it is?" he inquired, beckoning Thompson to join him at the window. I too peered into the darkness and caught sight of the shadowy image of a cat crossing the road, before it disappeared under Dad's car that was parked on our drive.

"Get under the table!" Churchill suddenly roared. "Now!"

And so Winston Churchill was back crouching under our dining table, for a second time. He was not a small man and, actually, there wasn't a lot of room for me to join him, but I felt the need to at least look like I was complying with his order, taking up a similar hunched position close to him, but one that would not have afforded me a lot of protection from whatever I needed protection from.

"It's going to blow!" Churchill informed me, his hands now covering his ears. Well, his wrists, actually, as he still somehow held his cigar in one hand and the glass of brandy in the other. "You better get under here as well, Thompson," he added.

I wondered how that might be accomplished, and fortunately Thompson seemed happy enough to take cover behind the armchair instead.

"What are we doing?" I felt the need to ask. "*What's* going to blow?"

"The cat," Churchill responded. "Now brace yourself!"

Suddenly, the light went on. It made me jump, as I *really* did for one moment think the cat was about to explode.

"What's going on?" Dad asked. "Are you playing murder in the dark?"

"Get down!" I called out, more than a tint of irony in my voice. "Mr Churchill, I mean Colonel Warden, thinks the vicar's cat is about to explode."

Dad shrugged his shoulders and nonchalantly made his way to the window. "Possibly?" he mused. "I told him the other day that he was feeding it too much. It is looking a bit podgy these days."

"Explosives, sir," Churchill muttered from under the table. "He's fitted the cat with explosives. The Russians used the same trick to blow up enemy tanks."

Dad shook his head.

"I don't think so," he said coolly. "Besides, it's heading down the road now."

Thompson was the first to 'emerge'. He came to the window to check for himself.

"He's right, sir. It's safe to come out. The cat's gone. It's still in training, no doubt."[10]

I got to my feet and offered Churchill some assistance. He wasn't the most agile person in the world, though it didn't help that he *still* had his cigar in one hand and glass of brandy in the other, which meant he was not able to use those hands to support himself. He had been successful in keeping the glass upright, though there was ash on our carpet.

Dad was busy behind the sofa and re-emerged with *our* cat in his hands.

"Have you met Napoleon," he teased our guest. "It's all right, I've checked for explosives."

"Napoleon?" Churchill barked, now back on his feet. "What sort of a name is that? He was the enemy, sir, I should remind you. Whose side are you on?"[11]

Thompson continued to peer out of the window and Churchill went to join him again.

"When are they going to turn off those blasted street lights?" Churchill grumbled. "It's not good enough, you know."

POP! No, it wasn't the cat, but the noise was enough to startle anyone. Churchill was on his knees again, scrambling under the dining table once more, still trying to avoid any spillages. "Get down! They're taking pot shots at us now," he cried. "And I think I've been hit!"

No-one attempted to follow him this time. Both Thompson and I looked at Dad. Now in my father's hands (our cat was long gone) was an opened bottle of Champagne, the cork having come to rest somewhere in the room, via the head of Churchill it was becoming apparent, our guest rubbing that part of his anatomy with the only three digits available to him, he adeptly resting his cigar between the remaining finger and thumb of his hand.

"Sorry," Dad smiled. "Would anyone like a glass of Champagne?"

Churchill got to his feet again and growled at my father, before this time choosing to take a seat at the dining table. I think he was hungry and it was his way of informing us that the dinner was long overdue. I took my place opposite him.

"I'm going to check outside," Thompson informed us, before leaving the living room.

"And I'm just going to check on the vegetables," an embarrassed Dad added, making his departure too.

Churchill looked a bit agitated, but his first glass of Champagne soon helped restore the norm.[12]

"Look," I started, "I appreciate what you're doing, but I don't class the Reverend Brown as one of my enemies. He's a sweet old man. In fact, he bought us a bar of chocolate the other day – Fairtrade, I should add – to thank us for watering his flowers when he was away."

"I admire your community spirit," Churchill responded, "but we know what he's up to. We already know his plans, you see."

"Plans?"

"We've seen them with our own eyes," a conceited Churchill told me, removing a hand-drawn picture from his breast pocket. "Take a look."

He pushed the piece of paper across the table and took another puff of his cigar.

"It took intelligence a lot of work to get these," Churchill pointed out.

I shook my head. "You could have just gone on to the council website. These are plans for an extension. He's extending his house, that's all."

"That's how it all starts," Churchill explained. "These megalomaniacs, they get illusions of grandeur. What they already have doesn't seem quite enough for them. They start with wanting a bit more and then they want a bit more after that – and it goes on and on. He's clearly making plans to extend his empire and he'll be after your land too, if you don't stop him. You need to nip it in the bud."

"It's OK," I tried to reassure him. "It only looks like a single-tier extension and it doesn't look like it will protrude too far."

Churchill thumped his fist on the table. He had at last put down his glass, fortunately.

"If you don't stop him now," Churchill warned, "it'll be too late. He'll know that he can get away with it...and he'll just keep doing the same thing. I tell you, my good fellow, you must stop him before it's too late."

I reached for my Smartphone. "It's already too late," I said. "Look, the council's already granted planning permission."

Churchill made no attempt to look at the screen, but I could see that his face was tight with anger.

"Fools! They think that by giving him what he wants now, it's going to satisfy him – appease him."

"I'm sure that's all he's planning to do," I pleaded on the vicar's behalf. "As I said, it's not a huge extension."

"Appeasement!" Churchill continued to moan, with increasing passion. "Why does everyone insist on this ridiculous policy of appeasement? I keep telling them all; that you have to nip it in the bud. If you give them an inch at the beginning, they'll take a mile from you in the end. No, we've got to put a stop to it...now."[13]

I found myself nodding in agreement. Of course, I wasn't sure what I was agreeing to, but felt I needed to adopt a policy of appeasement at this very moment, and just let him get on with it. I knew very well that Churchill had been likened to a bulldog and I guessed that was because he didn't lose many fights.[14]

It probably doesn't need me to point out that Churchill liked his food, and it seemed to take his mind off the 'enemy' for a while. Dad joined us as we ate our soup and, as usual, overstayed his welcome. At least Dad's insistence on reprising a song from *Oh! What a Lovely War* kept our somewhat bemused guest from pinning further charges of spying onto the local clergy. In fact, we even managed to talk about something other than war, Churchill taking particular interest in questioning us over our taste in art and literature, as he cast his eye around the walls and along our bookshelves. And it wasn't all high-brow talk – he had no qualms about going from quoting Lord Byron; to doing an impression of an ape![15]

It was all quite jovial, and all ideas of the Reverend Brown poisoning the communion wine or using mustard gas instead of incense were put aside for a time.

It was only when an unpleasant smell wafted from the kitchen (no, it wasn't mustard gas); that we remembered the 'enemy' was still across the road. Churchill started to sniff the air with suspicion.

"Can you smell something burning?" he asked.

Dad raced to the kitchen. I think Churchill thought he was going to fetch some gas masks.

Of course, I knew what the burning was – even before the smoke alarm went off. This time Churchill looked at me before deciding whether to take refuge under the table.

"It's all right," I assured him, "you can stay put. It's not an enemy attack. I just hope you like your steak well done!"

We could hear Dad still firing off obscenities long after he had succeeded (with the aid of a tea towel) in silencing the piercing shrill of the alarm.

Thompson rushed into the room.

"Everyone OK? Have we been hit?"

I assured him that everything was under control. Thompson handed Churchill a leaflet.

"I found this in the letterbox." His face was grim.

Churchill shook his head as he looked at the leaflet.

"It's a warning from our intelligence people. Operation Sea Lion...I think it's under way."[16]

I took the leaflet and looked at the picture of a seal. "It's just junk mail," I tried to convince them. "It's from the RSPCA – they're just looking for donations. Read it."

Churchill started to read, but still wasn't persuaded. "Yes, clever, it's definitely our intelligence men again. They've designed it to look like an innocuous call for help from a charitable organisation, but it's really a coded message."

"And then there was this," Thompson added, handing Churchill a screwed-up piece of paper. "Found it in the borders. Another coded message, I think, though I can't work this one out."

Churchill ran his eye down the list of items and started to read them out: "Leg of lamb...gravy granules...salmon...drinking chocolate...strawberry trifle..."

"I think that's Dad's shopping list," I smiled.

"Nonsense," Churchill responded. "He won't be able to get all this – doesn't he know that there's a war on?"[17]

Dad actually re-entered the room at that moment, with a large bowl in his hands.

"Are you ready for me to serve?" he inquired.

Churchill straightened up. "Yes, we are, sir," he responded officiously, a serious look on his face. "There is no doubt the time has come. Now is the time for us all to serve. I'm glad you're accepting your responsibilities, my good chap." Churchill glanced towards the window. His face was one of determination now. "We won't let them get away with it: we shall fight on the beaches...we shall fight on the landing grounds...we shall fight..."

"In our front gardens," I added sarcastically. "Actually, I think my dad's talking about the vegetables. Are you ready for him to serve the carrots?"

Churchill showed no embarrassment and allowed Dad to pile up his plate, but refused the peas.[18]

"You *are* ready for the fight, aren't you?" Churchill flashed me a suspicious look, as he attempted to cut his steak. "However, you're going to need sharper weapons than these!" he added, running his finger along the suspect item of cutlery he held in his hand.

"I don't think it will come to that," I said. "Honestly, our neighbours are very nice people."

Churchill shook his head. "You don't know what goes on behind the curtains, my good fellow. Trust no-one, especially those that dress like nuns or vicars." He paused. "Now, your father seems like a sensible chap."

I almost coughed out my peas.

"I want him to form the defence of this neighbourhood," Churchill declared. "I think he's the man for the job."

"I think we've already got a Neighbourhood Watch scheme," I pointed out. "In fact, it's run by..." I stopped. It was run by the vicar. I thought I'd better not reveal that information.

"The battle has come to our streets, my good fellow," Churchill continued to pronounce. "And it's about to start. We need an army here in our very own backyard. We are going to call it the Home Guard. Brave men like your father are needed to step up and defend us all. Yes, your neighbourhood needs you."[19]

Dad re-entered.

"It must be time for dessert?" he suggested.

"What?" Churchill shrieked. "Never! Have you already given up, sir? Are you already talking about throwing in the towel? No-one shall dessert on my watch, let me assure you. We will never surrender: we shall fight on the beaches...we shall fight..."

"Are you ready for dessert?" Dad repeated. "I've got a nice apple pie cooking in the oven..." He stopped: "Oh no!"

My father raced out and I waited for the smoke alarm to go off again.

"We won't have weapons to give you," Churchill admitted, turning back to me. "You'll have to provide those for yourself to start with. Do you have anything in the house?"

"I'm sure there's a couple of automatic rifles and a submachine gun somewhere in the loft," I teased him. "You just don't know what you'll find in our loft. Dad doesn't throw anything away."

Churchill frowned. "That doesn't sound so good. Make a note of that Thompson: no grenades."

I didn't realise that Churchill had cracked a joke, but Thompson, who had been standing quietly in the hallway, made a point of chuckling. "You have to throw grenades away," he said, popping his head around the door to address me, clearly feeling the need to point out that it *was* a joke, and that it was my duty to laugh at it.

Churchill downed his Champagne. Delivering his rallying call had obviously made him thirsty and he poured himself another glass.

"You better see if your father has an arsenal..."

"No, you won't find anything to do with Arsenal in this house," I was quick to interrupt him. "We're Watford fans."

I thought it was one of my better jokes, but Churchill just stared at me. He obviously didn't think it was *his* duty to laugh at mine. I left him at the table and went in search of the family armoury. My first port of call was the kitchen.

Dad seemed pleased with his new appointment in the Home Guard and was enthusiastic in his search for weapons. We had all the cupboards and drawers open.

"What about a colander?" Dad suggested, pulling a plastic one from the very depths of the cupboard underneath the kitchen sink. "It might suffice as a helmet," he smiled, placing it over his head.

Within a few minutes, we had assembled a stash of 'weapons' on the living room carpet, ready for our guest to inspect.

Churchill was encouraging and nodded approvingly as he examined our broom handle, the brush removed and a toasting fork now tied to the end in its place.[20]

Dad had retrieved his old golf clubs from the cupboard under the stairs. Churchill had left the table and was now swinging a six-iron, cigar still in his mouth, as though he were on the fairway at our local course.

"We've got a bow and arrow in the loft," Dad also pointed out, looking in my direction. "Do you remember it, son?"

I sighed. "It's made of plastic, Dad. I was eight years old!"

"You've done well," Churchill declared. "It's a good start, at any rate."

He pulled out his Breguet pocket watch and nodded.

"The Turnip says it's time for a bath and a quick nap before we reconvene, I think, Thompson. I'll leave you to go through a few drills," he added, directing the final order towards my father.[21]

I mechanically showed Churchill upstairs to the bathroom. When I returned to the living room, Dad had predictably got his electric drill out.

"I don't think he was talking about those types of drills," I informed him.

"I know," my father replied. "What do you take me for? I just thought it might make another good weapon."

And so we 'drilled'. Dad was enjoying himself, with his homemade 'pike'. I had to 'drill' with the golf club.

"Stand to attention, son," Dad kept ordering me; frequently reminding me that Churchill had put *him* in charge. "Think we'll start with some camouflage training."

"What?"

"Do you see the remote control over there?"

I strained my eyes and shook my head. "No."

Dad grinned. "That's your first lesson in camouflage completed."

I groaned.

"This is madness," I felt the need to point out, watching my Dad marching up and down the living room.

He nodded. "It's fun, though – better than playing *Trivial Pursuit*."

Churchill took longer than expected. We could hear him in the bath upstairs, sounds of machinegun fire and explosions occasionally coming from his lips, and I wondered if he was using our novelty plastic duck and a few shampoo bottles to re-enact Pearl Harbour.[22]

After his bath, Churchill retired to my bedroom and had a nap. Dad inadvertently found that out, having had the misfortune of walking past the open door and glancing at our rotund guest asleep on the bed – naked.[23]

Fortunately, Churchill had put something on by the time he came down, though it was not his normal attire.

"Is that a onesie?" I had to inquire, my eyes immediately drawn to what looked like a boiler suit. "Dad has a onesie as well...though it's fluffy and has got bear ears!"[24]

Churchill didn't answer. He was too busy refilling his glass and lighting another cigar.

I started to unpack our *Monopoly* set. I thought playing a game might take his mind off the enemy.

Churchill spotted me and nodded in appreciation. "I've seen this before," he said, picking up the tiny metal figure of the iron. "There's a minute compass hidden inside here, isn't there? Good work, chaps." [25]

"I just wondered if you wanted to play a game?" I asked innocently.

"I don't play games," Churchill returned sharply. "Anyway, we don't have time for games, my good fellow, unless..." His eye started to run down the pile of board games in the corner of the room; "unless you have some Lego?" he inquired. The mere word brought a smile to his face and he seemed excited at the prospect. "We could build something together," he suggested eagerly.

Was he talking about a barricade of some sort? I had to inform him that we didn't have any Lego, though I'm sure Dad – if he had been in the room – would have pointed out that my old foam building bricks were probably still in the loft.[26]

Churchill returned to the armchair.

"In that case," he said, "I think we better get back to business, my good fellow. There's still work to be done."

Dad entered with a lolly stick in either hand, a sticky toffee apple mounted on the end of each.

"How about this for dessert?" he proposed. "Who needs apple pie when you can have sticky toffee apples?"

Churchill rose from his chair, a look of alarm on his face.

"Be careful with those, old chap," he snapped. "You shouldn't be playing with those in here. Take them away, sir. Save your sticky bombs for when we need them most."[27]

Dad shrugged his shoulders and left for the kitchen. He was back in an instant.

"That just leaves some chocolate," he said, proceeding to pick at the purple wrapping on the bar he was holding. "You do like chocolate, don't you? It's that bar the vicar brought over..."

Dad was just about to break a piece off when Thompson charged at my father, bringing him down with a rugby tackle. I watched on incredulous.

Churchill smacked his forehead.

"I say, that was close," he uttered. "Well done, Thompson – I owe my life to you again."[28]

Dad was still on the floor and clearly in need of an explanation. Thompson obliged.

"Sorry, sir," he said in an orderly manner, helping my father to his feet. "The enemy have been prototyping exploding chocolate for a few months now."

Dad gingerly picked up the chocolate bar, holding it by his fingertips. I sighed.[29]

Suddenly, the doorbell sounded.

We were momentarily rooted to the spot. Churchill and Thompson looked towards Dad. My father shrugged his shoulders in response. They then all looked inquiringly to me.

"I don't know either," I told them. "I don't think we're expecting anyone else."

Thompson went towards the window.

"Turn off the light," he ordered. As Dad flicked the switch, Thompson pulled the curtain, just enough to see outside.

Ouch! Dad had still been holding his make-do pike and, in the darkness, had succeeded in poking me in the bottom. "Be careful with that thing," I snapped at him.[30]

"I can't see that well I'm afraid, it's a bit dark out there," Thompson murmured from the window, "but it's all right, I don't think it's *him*. I think it's a woman – looks like they're wearing a dress."

Churchill relaxed, for a mere second, at least.

"Wait a minute!" he piped, stumbling towards the window. "What colour's the dress?"

"Black, I think," Thompson answered, "but, as I said, I can't see that well."

"A nun!" Churchill exclaimed.

"This is ridiculous!" I cried. "I'm going to get the door. Do you really think that if the enemy were about to attack, they'd ring the doorbell first?"

I turned on the light. To my surprise, neither Churchill nor Thompson tried to stop me, and that actually *did* have the effect of stopping me. I looked at Churchill for an explanation. He was studying me intently, but he now had a smile on his face, and it appeared to be one of admiration, much to my confusion.

"You are right, my friend," he started to explain, nodding profusely. "That's the spirit, my good fellow. We shouldn't be cowering in here. The young one talks a lot of sense, Thompson."

Churchill came towards me and put a hand on my shoulder, his cigar still clasped in his fingers, dropping ash down my back. "It's time for us all to fight," he went on. "We shouldn't be running from our fears, but embracing them. Yes, I think the day has arrived."

"You mean it's D-Day?" Dad sniggered.

Churchill continued to look me in the eye. "My good fellow," he said, "I now know that tonight was meant to be. You are right. We must face our fears and stand up to this east wind that threatens our very way of life. If we don't, the black dog will hang over us forever."[31]

He paused and tilted his head, a sign that he was about to say something even more profound. "My friends," he began, as he made his way towards the dining table, "only this morning, I felt as if I were walking with destiny, and that all my past life had been but a preparation for this hour and for this trial." He stopped and raised his Champagne glass. "And the hour is now upon us. Yes, open the door, my good fellow," he instructed me, a look of defiance on his face. "We'll be right behind you."

And they were. Churchill had retrieved his cane and now held it aloft, gripping it tightly, in a threatening manner. He had lost the cigar, but still had the Champagne glass in his other hand. Thompson was holding the golf club and Dad had reached for his makeshift pike.

I went to the door and opened it.

I had already worked out who it was before they came into view. It *was* the vicar – in full uniform...no, not in military uniform, but in his clerical robes. Yes, anyone could have mistaken his cassock for a dress.

No-one behind me moved.

"Hello," the Reverend Brown smiled warmly. "I'm sorry to bother you, but we've started up a food bank at the church, and we're looking for donations." He paused, the strange mob behind me having finally caught his eye. "I'm sorry, is it not a good time?"

What happened next, you may wonder? Perhaps you already have an image in your head of Churchill coming forward and giving the vicar six of the best with his cane, or of Thompson taking a few swings with his six-iron, or of Dad chasing him down the garden path with his homemade pike?

That might have happened if this had been an episode of *Dad's Army*, but it wasn't like that at all. The vicar was allowed to leave unchallenged and, much to my surprise, there wasn't any further talk about the impending attack on us. However, when Churchill and Thompson took their leave later that night, we failed to notice that they had taken something with them. In fact, it was not until much later, when Dad and I were getting a bit peckish, that we realised that one of the sticky toffee apples was missing. We saw it in the daylight the next morning: stuck to the bonnet of the vicar's car – stick up. It had failed to detonate.

Of course, Churchill would not have known that fact, the previous night, when they had departed, but at least I now knew why he and Thompson had seemed to be in a rush, as I had watched them disappear down the street, their hands over their ears, presumably in anticipation of a loud bang. Only once did they briefly stop to turn around...to enable Churchill to put up two fingers to form the shape of a V. Of course, it was dark, and I couldn't rule out that it may have been his famous victory sign, though, I'm guessing, he might have been communicating a different farewell message to the enemy!

I just hoped that Winston Churchill had enjoyed his time with us. Yes, I hoped Dad and I had done him proud. And, who knows, if this book is still read a thousand years from now, men will still say of us...*this was their finest hour!*

Chapter 7
Oliver Cromwell

I like Christmas. Who doesn't?

Well, Oliver Cromwell doesn't.[1]

And I thought I'd better remind Dad of that fact, as he invited our novelty singing snowman to belt out *Winter Wonderland* by pressing its button for the umpteenth time. Needless to say, Dad *did* like Christmas.

"He'll be here soon," I added. "Do you think we better take down the Christmas cards as well?"

Dad never heard me or at least pretended he didn't, as he continued to set the table.

I repeated my question: "The cards?" I said; pointing to a line of them, each suspended from a piece of string that was fixed from wall to wall. "We should probably take them down. Don't forget, Christmas was banned when he was king."

"He was never king," Dad corrected me. "I've told you already... he was Lord Protector[2]...and, no, I'm not going to take the cards down; it took me a long time to put them up. Anyway," Dad continued, "we'll just say they're birthday cards if he notices them."

If he notices them? He couldn't miss them, and there was a good chance that he might be decapitated by the string if he were more than six feet in height.

"He's hardly going to believe they're birthday cards," I pointed out.

"Nor Christmas cards," Dad assured me. "Do you really think someone from the 17th century is going to link elves and red-nosed reindeers with Christmas? He won't have a clue that they're anything to do with yuletide."

I lifted a card from the string and studied it closely. "Unless, of course, he reads the words 'merry Christmas' on them," I replied smugly.

Dad ignored me, too preoccupied with shaking a Christmas cracker that he had previously placed on the table. "Doesn't sound like there's anything in this one!" he moaned, putting it to his ear.

It was no use arguing. As I said, Dad liked Christmas and not even a king – sorry, Lord Protector – would stop my father from celebrating it.

When he had finished laying the table, Dad turned off the main light and switched on the multi-coloured fairy lights that adorned our Christmas tree.

"How's that?" he asked.

"It's nice, very colourful, but it's a bit dark in here now," I felt the need to point out.

"That's all right, then," Dad responded, a little agitated by my negativity, "he won't notice the Christmas cards then, will he?"

I shrugged my shoulders.

"And before you mention the tree," Dad added, "Christmas trees were not popular until the 1800s – I saw it on a programme the other night – so he won't know what it is, will he? He'll just think the tree's for our pet parrot or something."

"Fair enough," I conceded, rearranging some tinsel on one of the branches. "I just hope he doesn't think that there might be a prince hiding up it."[3]

Dad didn't question what I meant, but that was because he wasn't listening.

He was now rummaging through a shoebox that contained the rest of the wooden figures from our traditional Nativity set, those that hadn't made the scene this year. He picked up one of the three kings and, for one moment, I thought he might have been contemplating hanging it on a branch.

"Anyway, what are you cooking for him?" I inquired. "That's not mince pies I can smell cooking in the oven, is it? I'm not sure that's a good idea for someone who doesn't celebrate Christmas."

"Relax," Dad attempted to reassure me. "They're for us, for tomorrow. I'm just trying to get a head start for the big day. I've got the Christmas pudding cooking in there with them. No, he's a Puritan – he won't want any of that stuff. They eat simple foods. I'm just doing something basic for his dinner...and pure...just as God intended it to be. No, he won't find any e-numbers on *his* plate this evening."

The doorbell interrupted my father. Oliver Cromwell was *here*. Well, we assumed he was here. Who else would be calling on Christmas Eve? All right, apart from the man in red and white!

"Remember," Dad turned to me, "don't talk about religion or politics."

Well, that didn't leave me much, those two subjects being what preoccupied our guest for most of his life. Still, if we found ourselves struggling for conversation, I could always turn to the singing snowman...

Oliver Cromwell, predictably, was donned mostly in black, though his protruding white collar was so sizeable, the two sides met in the middle below his chin and gave the appearance of being a baby's bib. And it may have been used for that purpose, for I noticed a huge dark stain on it. I should point out that I had plenty of time to study our guest closely before we entered the dim of the living room, the hallway light revealing warts and all. No, really, I'm not using an idiom, but making a real observation: his face *was* full of warts, one enormous beauty just below his bottom lip.[4]

"Would you like to take off the hat?" I asked him.

Cromwell returned a stern look. It appears he mistook 'the hat' for 'that'. And I think he thought I was referring to the wart when I supposedly said 'that' – though I honestly did say 'the hat'. I couldn't blame him, though, as my eyes (despite all my best efforts) did seem to be fixed on the wart, rather than on the wide-brimmed black hat that still sat on his head.

"What I mean," I attempted to clarify, "is that I was wondering whether you were allowed to remove your *hat*? I know some Puritans like to keep their heads covered in certain places."

Cromwell didn't look convinced by my explanation, but he did at least eventually remove his hat and hand it to me.

It was not a good start and I tried to make up for it as I led our guest into the living room.

"It's a pleasure to have you here – especially at Chris..." I just stopped myself in time.

And, yes, Cromwell was about six feet in height and *did* almost bring the Christmas cards down. He stooped, more than was necessary, to eventually pass under the string.

"Dad is preparing a meal fit for a king," I informed Cromwell, as he took a seat at the dining table.

He looked up sharply. "I'm not a king, my friend. And never want to be."

I apologised profusely. "It's just a phrase," I explained; "fit for a king...it's just a common saying. We have lots of them..." I tried to think of another to help with my explanation, but the only one that came into my head was...yes, you guessed it...*warts and all*. Fortunately, I didn't say it out loud, but did find my eyes drawn to the region below his bottom lip again!

"I *do* know that you're not a king," I continued to waffle, "and who would want to be?" I added, remembering that the man in our living room didn't like kings.[5]

"And don't worry," I went on with a smile, "I won't address you as...'Your Majesty'."

Cromwell was quick to reply. "No. 'Your Highness' will be adequate."[6]

I didn't know if he was serious, but the look on his face suggested that he was – and that look also persuaded me that I wouldn't be calling him 'Ollie' either.

I remembered Dad's warning: don't talk about religion or politics. And if Christmas was banned, I was beginning to think that it was going to be a long night, as Cromwell was not the most talkative person.

"What do you like to do in your spare time?" I asked, thinking that he could have an unusual hobby that might help loosen his tongue a bit. Cromwell stared at me. I felt I had to get the ball rolling myself.

"We watch a lot of television," I started, nodding at the screen. "Of course, you won't know what that is, will you? It's a bit like having a theatre in your own home. Would you like to watch something?"

Cromwell eyed me suspiciously. "You have a theatre in your home? I must remind you that the theatres have been closed down. They are banned, my friend."

Whoops! I'd better get word to Dad that the after-dinner entertainment should not involve him re-enacting a scene from *A Christmas Carol*. Dad was in the local production – playing the boy who has to buy the turkey for Scrooge (they couldn't find a young person willing to take on the role).[7]

Cromwell started to examine the Christmas cracker that was set before him. Of course, he had no idea what it was. He put it to his ear after shaking it, just like Dad had done.

And so we sat in silence, and I was relieved when my father entered the room with a jug of water and two glasses.

"Good evening, sir," he said, bowing to our guest.

"*Your Highness*," I whispered to Dad, "that's how he wants us to address him."

"But he's not a king," Dad mouthed to me in response, as he started to fill our glasses with water.

Cromwell eyed the liquid with revulsion.

"Bring me a small beer, man," he ordered.

"I didn't think Puritans drank alcohol," Dad returned smartly.[8]

Cromwell got to his feet.

"What impertinence! Do all your servants answer back?" he growled, briefly turning to me before refocussing on my father. "Your tongue does you a disservice, my fellow," he continued, eyeing Dad with disdain. "The branks will teach you to hold it. Do you have access to one?"

Cromwell had turned back to me as he put his question. I hesitated. "Most have closed down – people do internet banking these days," I said.[9]

Our guest returned a confused look to match mine. I went on to explain that my father was not a servant, and a pacified Cromwell eventually retook his seat.

Neither of us said a word after that, until Dad returned with a thimble of beer. Yes, you read it correctly – a plastic thimble! He plonked it on the table, spilling the little there was of the liquid. "Here's your *small* beer," he sneered. Cromwell stared at it, too stunned to comment.[10]

"It's a bit quiet in here," Dad observed. "Shall I put on some music? I've got an Aled Jones CD – it's got all the Chris..."

I held my hand up and fortunately Dad stopped in time.

"How about a game of charades, then?" he suggested; "I'll go first, if you like."

"He's joking, of course," I was quick to intervene, turning to Cromwell, just as Dad was about to take centre stage. "My father knows that *acting has been banned*, don't you, Dad?"

Of course, in the case of my father, I'm not sure that Cromwell would have interpreted it as acting anyway!

Cromwell remained stone-faced.

"It was just a joke," I repeated. "Dad likes a good joke."

"I don't," Cromwell responded without blinking.

"How about a different game, then?" Dad went on, still attempting to lift the gloom; "Blind man's bluff? Pin the tail on the donkey?"

He stopped there. It seemed like Cromwell didn't play games.

"What's on the TV?" Dad persisted. "Do you think he'd like to watch *Strictly Come Dancing*?"

Cromwell growled again. Yes, needless to say, he wasn't a fan of dancing either. I wasn't sure if Dad was deliberately trying to wind up our guest, or if he was just genuinely trying to get the party going.

"OK," Dad finally conceded, realising he hadn't much hope of doing at least the latter. "I'll leave you to it, then."

And so we were left to it. It meant there was more silence. Sport! That was it. If I couldn't talk about religion or politics, or any form of entertainment, I could at least talk about football. I know what you're thinking – football is entertainment as well. I have to disagree: I've watched too many Watford matches to come to that conclusion.

"Do you like sport?" I turned to the Lord Protector.

Cromwell did not respond. I took that to mean that he was at least not against it.[11]

"What's your favourite?" I went on, my spirits rising a little. "Do you like football? There was a big game last Sunday..."

"Sunday?" Cromwell stopped me. "Football on a *Sunday*? What else do you get up to on a Sunday, my friend? Next you will be telling me that you *work* on the Lord's day?"

I shook my head. "No, Mum works Monday to Friday, and Dad is a house husband, and I've never seen him clean the house on a Sunday – or any day as a matter of fact," I quipped, running my finger along the edge of the table as though I were wiping some dust from it.

Of course, it didn't bring a smile to Cromwell's face. As we have gathered, he didn't like jokes.

"So we don't do much at all on a Sunday," I felt the need to clarify. "We might just go for a walk in the country."

At least he couldn't tell me *that* was banned too. I was wrong. He was quick to inform me that walking anywhere on the Sabbath, other than to and from church, was a no-go as well.[12]

There was more silence. That was not good, as it meant that we both clearly heard the Christmas music emanating from outside. The curtains were pulled, so Cromwell could not see Santa on his sleigh – but he could now hear him.

"What is that?" he inquired. "Are there people *singing*?"

Dad returned to the room full of excitement. "Santa's here!" he cheered, wrapping a scarf around his neck, his coat already on. "Are you coming outside to see him?"

I shook my head violently. In his excitement, Dad had seemingly forgotten that we had a guest – and one that didn't like Christmas, or my father, it would seem. "What's the matter?" Dad asked me. "You used to get excited when Santa came on Chris..."

"That was when I was seven!" I interrupted him, again at the appropriate moment.

Dad still didn't take heed of my warning and turned to Cromwell. "It's Santa and his elves," he gushed. "One year they got a real reindeer to pull his sleigh, but now they just use a tractor. It's organised by the Rotary Club. If you've got a few shillings to spare... it's for charity, you see?"

Now I was sure that Dad was deliberately goading our guest.

The sleigh must have been directly outside our house. We could hear the singing clearly now...*We wish you a merry Christmas...We wish you a merry Christmas...*

I faked a coughing fit, but it was to no avail. Cromwell could not have failed to hear the words.

"Are they celebrating Christ-tide?" he inquired knowingly. "You know that my soldiers are out in force this evening – and they will show no mercy to anyone who is making preparations for tomorrow."
13

Cromwell stared at my father with accusing eyes.

"You see," he started, "some people like to put up decorations or cook a goose...or plum pudding...or mince pies." He stopped. "You wouldn't be making preparations for Christ-tide, would you?"[14]

He finished by sniffing the air.

If Dad had been brash in his celebration of Christmas, the look now on the face of our guest was enough to bash the brashness out of even the most-brashest brasher!

My father returned a sheepish smile. "You're wondering what that smell from the kitchen is, aren't you? That's not anything to do with Christmas...I mean Christ-tide...that's *your* dinner for tonight. In fact, it's probably ready."

"Then bring it in...now," Cromwell ordered, as though he were a king addressing his servant. Of course, I should again point out...he wasn't *really* a king.

Dad had no choice but to retreat to the kitchen, still adorned in bobble hat and coat. Indeed, he was not quite so cocky now.

Much to my relief, my quick-thinking father did not bring in a plate of mince pies when he returned, but a plate of...uncooked vegetables. I groaned. Yes, Dad was right – Cromwell wouldn't find many e-numbers in a raw parsnip!

I lifted my fork and started to poke at the *raw* cabbage leaves. Cromwell lifted up a *raw* carrot and held it aloft.

"Is this your meal that is fit for a king?" he snarled at me.

I was tempted to point out that it was Cromwell himself who had earlier informed me that he *wasn't* a king, but I dared not antagonise him further.

"The carrots might need a few more minutes in the oven," a sarcastic Cromwell pointed out. "No problem, though," he continued; "the *mince pies* smell like they're ready."

I looked at Dad. He didn't know what to say. Cromwell was no fool; that was clear to us both. Our guest now had a sly smile on his face, the first time he had smiled since he had entered our house, I should stress. I wondered if his wart was in danger of cracking.

"Those mince pies are not meant for tomorrow, are they?" Cromwell went on. "Because, if they were; that would mean you were preparing to celebrate Christ-tide, wouldn't it? And you know that you can't eat mince pies at Christ-tide?"[15]

Both Dad and I shook our heads vehemently. The image of Dad sitting in a pillory outside Tesco had entered my head for some reason.

"We eat mince pies most days, don't we, Dad?" I lied to Cromwell. "But definitely not at Christ-tide. Dad was cooking them for *you*, of course, for your meal *this evening*."

"That's right," Dad nodded. "Quick, finish your carrots and parsnips, and then I'll bring out the next course...mince pies."

"I think we *have* finished," I smiled nervously, pushing the untouched plate of vegetables towards my father.

And so Oliver Cromwell tucked into a mince pie – four, in fact, all with custard. He almost seemed in good spirits as he did so.

"And now I better inspect your kitchen, sir," he announced, rising to his feet, wiping the crumbs from his attire, "just to check that there isn't anything being prepared for tomorrow. It's just a formality, of course."

"Sugar!" Dad muttered under his breath, dashing out of the living room. Actually, Cromwell seemed to be *really* enjoying himself now.

"I should remind you that swearing is punishable by a fine," he remarked.[16]

"We know," I smiled. "We have a swear box for Comic Relief every year. I don't think Dad was swearing, though, he just probably wanted to know if you wanted sugar on your turnip..."

Cromwell was about to head for the kitchen. I had to stall our guest – to give Dad a chance to hide the Christmas treats. But how? The first thing my eye rested on was our display cabinet. I moved towards it, intending to show Cromwell our Lladró porcelain clown (at least it wasn't *Royal* Doulton), but I panicked as I was reaching for it. After all, our guest didn't seem to approve of fun (not that I personally have ever thought clowns were funny). So my hand instinctively reached for the item next to the clown. That was an even bigger mistake. Now in my hand was Dad's Charles and Diana commemorative wedding mug. Cromwell was quick to seize it from my grasp.

"Who is the man with the big ears?" he inquired, holding the mug in the palm of his outstretched hand.

Now I had a problem. What should I tell him? Did I admit that we possessed *royal* memorabilia? Would he accuse us of being Royalists? We were dining with the man who showed little mercy to supporters of the royal family, after all.[17]

"That man on the mug?" I stuttered. "You want to know who he is, right? Well, that man is...he's...he's a..."

He's a famous actor...no, I couldn't tell him that – the theatres were banned. He's a singer...no, Cromwell didn't approve of singing. He's a footballer...a footballer who doesn't play on Sundays; I would have to add...yes, that would do.

As I said, Cromwell was no fool, and I actually found the truth coming from my lips. "His name is Charles – and he's sort of the...*king*." I whispered the last word and continued, hoping he hadn't heard it. "It's a souvenir mug to celebrate his first marriage – it's very old now."

Cromwell looked interested, and at least I had succeeded in buying Dad a bit more time in the kitchen.

"Charles?" Cromwell mused. "King?" He stopped and started to vigorously shake his head. "No, I did away with him – and I didn't get rid of one Charles for another to replace him," he scowled. "No, his son shall never rule as he did."[18]

Our guest took a closer look at the image on the mug. "Hold on! You're lying, sir. This isn't the prince – Charles' son – *this* man on your pottery hasn't got a lot of hair! This isn't the same Charlie!"

I smiled. "Some people think he's just that – a *right* Charlie! Me too, of course, because I'm no Royalist," I felt the need to point out at this moment. "We're definitely Parliamentarians..."

Cromwell looked at me as though he were a man in need of an explanation. I felt compelled to oblige.

"I think we've got our Charlies mixed up. The man on the mug is not the son of Charles I – the prince who becomes Charles II. In fact, this Charlie is Charles III."

Cromwell shook his head. "Charles II? Charles III? I tell you, my friend, no king will sit on the throne while I'm alive. I don't know who these pretenders to the throne are that you speak of, but I didn't get rid of one king for another to take over. There will never be another king on the throne. The heir to the throne is...my son."

"Heir to the *throne*?" I boldly quizzed him. "I thought you said you weren't a king?"

Cromwell had no intention of rising to the bait. "I have already named my son, Richard, to be my heir," he stated calmly. "And he will rule for many years, for sure."[19]

Cromwell handed me the mug. He had come to the conclusion that it had nothing to do with him, and had now lost all interest in it. That meant we were spared any accusations of being Royalists, and I would not now need to search for an old election poll card to prove we really did support the other side. Of course, having lost interest, Cromwell was now marching towards the kitchen. I followed on his tail, at least confident that I had bought Dad enough time to have hidden the Christmas treats.

We found Dad leaning against the fridge. He had heard us coming and, in his attempt to act inconspicuous, was doing the opposite. His acting was so bad; I feared Cromwell would have to remind him that theatrical performances were banned.

"You seem to have put on some weight, sir," Cromwell mocked him. Even with his coat on, it was obvious my father had something hidden on his person.

Dad smiled innocently. "It must have been those mince pies – they *are* very fattening."

Cromwell scanned the kitchen with his eyes, before starting to open some cupboards. He didn't find much at first, until he extended his search to less obvious places. Within a few minutes, he had pulled out a bottle of Champagne from under clothes in the laundry basket and a chocolate cake from inside the washing machine.

"You were not intending to make merry with these tomorrow, were you?"

Dad bowed his head, now a frightened pupil being interrogated by the headmaster.

"Of course," Cromwell continued, "I'd understand it if all this was for *this evening's* meal...like the mince pies had been?"

We nodded. That, of course, was the reaction Cromwell wanted.

"Very good," he declared. "I'm satisfied that you are not making preparations to celebrate Christ-tide. That would be preposterous, wouldn't it?"

We nodded again. "How foolish of me," he smiled, his eyes settling on my father's bulging midriff. "Next I'll be wrongly thinking that you're hiding a goose or a turkey under your coat!"

I laughed and Cromwell did too. My word, that wart was really in danger of cracking now!

And so we got away with it, and Cromwell got what he wanted: our Christmas treats. Within a few moments, he was back at the table eating chocolate truffles – he had found those slipped into an almost-empty box of cornflakes.

After lighting the Christmas pudding later that evening (the pudding was retrieved from the oven), Dad brushed past me and whispered: "Your mother's going to kill me when she finds out we've eaten Christmas dinner tonight!" He looked at Cromwell and sighed. "There's going to be trouble tomorrow..."

"I hope not on account of me," Cromwell stated, and, for one moment, I thought he was apologising. "I wouldn't want to be the cause of any civil unrest," he added.

Dad looked at him with incredulity. "You should have said that in 1642!"[20]

After dinner, Cromwell spotted a packet of cigars on a shelf. They were a Christmas present for my uncle and hadn't yet been wrapped. It seems that Cromwell, like my uncle, enjoyed a smoke at Christ-tide.[21]

So there Cromwell sat, smoking cigars and regularly delving into our tub of Quality Street (he had found that under a rug in the cat basket). As he took chocolate after chocolate; he tossed the colourful wrappers over his shoulder, as though he were a king. Of course, he would have been quick to remind us that he wasn't!

"I noticed a plate of coloured beans in the kitchen," Cromwell informed us when the tub of Quality Street was empty. "I can assume they are not being saved for Christ-tide?"

Oh no! He was talking about Dad's precious M&M's. Dad never shared his M&M's, even with *us*. Cromwell may have believed he had a divine right to the rest of our Christmas treats, but my father would surely draw the line when it came to his M&M's.

Dad hesitated for a moment, but, to my surprise, seemed to relent.

"Now you want my M&M's," he groaned. "You're a hard man, sir. Your heart must be made of steel."

Cromwell seemed to take that as a compliment. "Actually, they call me Old Ironsides, you know."

"Wasn't he that detective in a wheelchair?" Dad smirked.[22]

"You would have liked Maggie Thatcher," I suggested, addressing the Lord Protector. "She was known as the Iron Lady. You have a lot in common with her."

"Is she a queen?" Cromwell queried. "Not that I'm saying that I'm a...well, you know...I will never desire to be a..."

"She was the prime minister – she ruled the country like you... with an iron fist," Dad explained. "She didn't ban Christmas – just milk for schoolchildren."

I remembered we had a Margaret Thatcher biography on our bookshelf. "Here she is," I said, passing Cromwell the book, a beaming Maggie on the cover. "I forgot we had it – told you we were Parliamentarians."

Dad reluctantly departed to get the M&M's, as Cromwell started to study some of our knick-knacks. He picked up a photograph of Mum.

"Is that make-up on her face?" he inquired. "You know make-up is banned, don't you?"

I smiled apologetically on Mum's behalf. Cromwell then picked up a framed photograph of me as a young schoolchild. He seemed to approve of my bowl haircut.[23]

Dad returned with the plate of M&M's.

"That's about it," he declared. "Kitchen is empty. I'm down to the bare bones now."

"Barebone? Is he here?" Cromwell raised his head with interest. "Praise-God Barebone?"

"Who's Barebone?" I asked. "And why should we praise God for him?"

"Barebone's Parliament," Cromwell reflected, a smug smile appearing on his face. "I handpicked them all myself, but they couldn't stop arguing and handed me the throne...I mean, handed over power to me..."

I had no idea what he was talking about. I gasped again. "Praise-God Barebone? What a name! Was that *really* his name?"

Cromwell shook his head: "Of course not."[24]

I soon discovered that it was normal for Puritans to name their children after virtues or to christen them with religious slogans.

Cromwell started to list some of his serving officers in the New Model Army: Jolly, Dust, Humiliation, Forsaken, Liberty, Freegift, Lament...

Dad had reached for his Smartphone and enjoyed joining in...Vanity, Sorry-For-Sin, Ashes, Prudence and Colin were his contributions. Well, he made the last one up!

Dad and I started to giggle, and Cromwell thought we were mocking him. He glared at us.

"Do you find it funny?"

We stopped laughing and bowed our heads.

"Charles laughed at me once as well, you know," Cromwell

added in a superior tone, "when we were children – and he wasn't laughing when I had finished with him."[25]

Cromwell popped an M&M into his mouth and I suddenly realised the coloured beans were not actually M&M's, but cat biscuits. Dad had a nerve! However, they must have been quite tasty, as Cromwell didn't complain.

"What are all those coloured boxes under that strange tree?" Cromwell questioned us suddenly.

Our Christmas presents! How could we have forgotten about them? We may have been sitting in semi-darkness, but Cromwell didn't miss a trick.

"They wouldn't be gifts wrapped up for Christ-tide by any chance?" he suggested.[26] "No, forgive me, how foolish of me to think that," he added, the smug smile reappearing.

"It's a game," Dad intervened in an attempt to save our skins, if not our presents.

"I don't play games," Cromwell hissed.

"You'll like this one, it's called pass the parcel. Put some music on, son."

I looked at Cromwell. To my surprise, he didn't object.[27]

And so we played pass the parcel with Aled Jones singing Christmas carols in the background. Of course, we had to let Cromwell win.

He removed the one sheet of wrapping paper (the game didn't last long) to reveal a pair of socks, emblazoned with snowflakes.

"Oh well," a philosophical Dad responded, "they're not a lot different to the pair your mum got me last year. He can have them."

"What about the other boxes?" Cromwell nodded towards the base of the tree. "Are they meant for more games of this...pass the parcel?"

And so Cromwell soon found himself with not only a pair of socks, but a diary, some perfume and a Watford FC annual.

Dad poured Cromwell a glass of sherry. Yes, my father had forgotten to hide that as well.[28] Our guest sipped his sherry, occasionally turning over the pages of the annual with a puzzled look on his face.

"Well," Dad turned to me, "I don't know what we're going to do tomorrow – we've got no Christmas dinner or any presents to open."

Dad was now so demoralised, he didn't even bother to lower his voice.

Cromwell looked up. "What was that? Are you making plans for Christ-tide?"

"No," Dad snapped, "don't worry; there won't be any feasting or partying in this house. You've made sure of that. You can be sure we'll be going to church and straight home again to sit and look at the walls."

Cromwell shook his head. "I don't think so, sir."

"Sorry?" Dad queried in a high-pitched voice. "Is looking at our wallpaper banned as well?"

"No," Cromwell replied calmly, "but going to church is, so I do hope you won't be partaking in that activity tomorrow, my friend. All services on December the 25th are banned."

"I thought you were a religious man," I chipped in. "Why have you banned going to church?"

"Only on the 25th day of December," Cromwell explained, "because it's not a special day, is it? It's just a normal run-of-the-mill day. That is why you won't be eating mince pies, chocolate truffles, plum pudding..."

"I think you're the reason why we won't be doing that!" Dad muttered under his breath.

I was reluctant to let go.

"If it were a normal day, why are all the shops closed?" I persisted.

"Closed?" Cromwell responded, a defiant look on his face. "No, my friend; we will be doing our utmost to ensure traders open their doors as normal."

"So you'd rather we went shopping than to church? I don't understand it!"[29]

Dad had started to clear the plates from the table, with little care.

"And don't worry," my father snarled; "we won't do anything else that will cause you consternation, like watching the King's Speech!" He stopped and turned towards our guest. "Will *you* be addressing the nation...as Lord Protector?"

Dad did well not to say 'king'.

"Will your Christmas message be before or after *The Wizard of Oz*?" he continued to mock.

Cromwell didn't know how to respond, so Dad went on. "What are *your* plans for tomorrow, anyway, not that it's a special day or anything like that, of course?"

"I will be speaking in Parliament like any other day," Cromwell said. "I have one or two speeches I must deliver."

"And what message will you be bringing to the nation?" Dad continued to probe. "Has it been an annus horribilis for you?"

Dad was past caring and not even the threat of being pilloried outside Tesco seemed to bother him now. He just wanted to see the back of the man who had ruined his Christmas.

"Well, I expect you need to get back home," Dad hinted. "It's getting late. Have you a long way to go? Can we call you a cab? Where do you live?"

"I'm residing at the Palace of Whitehall at the moment."

"Palace? Aren't palaces meant for kings?" Dad questioned him without any trepidation in his voice. Go, Dad![30]

Cromwell stared at him. "For the final time...I am not a king and have no desire to be one. If I did, I would have accepted the crown when they offered it to me, wouldn't I?"

"They offered you the crown?" I yelped.[31]

Cromwell didn't answer. He was keeping an eye on my father, who had picked up the two Christmas crackers.

"Where are you going with those?" Cromwell inquired suspiciously. "Why did you put them on the table if they weren't meant for me? Anyone would think they're Christ-tide decorations. You wouldn't be decorating your home for Christ-tide, would you?"

Dad offered an insincere apology. "No, we wouldn't dream of doing that. They are for you, of course...pull one!"

It was an order and Cromwell was shocked by Dad's abruptness. He wasn't used to someone giving orders to *him*.

Dad held one end of the cracker and offered the other to Cromwell. The Lord Protector gingerly took hold of it. And on the count of three, they pulled in unison. BANG! Cromwell wasn't expecting that. Needless to say, *he was not amused*, though he wouldn't have used those famous words, of course – he wasn't a queen...or a king!

"Is this some kind of trick?" Cromwell raged.

I managed to calm things, pointing him in the direction of a mini-pack of playing cards that had fallen from the cracker onto the carpet. I handed the gift to him.

"Look, you won, though it's not the most appropriate thing for you, I have to admit. I assume playing cards has been banned as well, hasn't it?"

A still bemused Cromwell had turned his attention to a tiny piece of paper that had also fallen from the cracker.

"There's a joke written on it," I tried to explain, "though somehow I don't think you're going to like that either."

Cromwell started to read the joke and, to my surprise, the beginnings of a grin seemed to be manifesting. Yes, *that* wart was again in danger of splitting.

"*Why was the king wet?*" he read again, this time aloud, for our benefit; "*Because he was the reigning monarch.*"

Cromwell was still smirking (he obviously did like jokes, after all) as I retrieved the orange tissue paper hat that had also fallen from the cracker.

"If you would allow me, Your Highness?" I offered.

I moved towards him and, as he sat there in his chair, I crowned him.

He had acted like a king all night and now he really looked like one as well.

"You can keep it," Cromwell said, after I had reached for his wide-brimmed hat when we were in the hallway about to see him on his way. "I like this one better," he said firmly, pointing to his head.

And so Oliver Cromwell headed into the darkness, his orange 'crown' fluttering gently in the breeze.[32]

Chapter 8
Florence Nightingale

It was foggy outside.

If this were a Gothic novel, I might have made more of an effort to be a bit more lyrical in setting the scene, but it's not, and I only need tell you that it was foggy – *really* foggy. However, I should add that it was so foggy; I couldn't actually make out the houses opposite us, only the lights from within, at least from those properties where the occupants had not chosen to close their curtains to shut out the gloom. I must stress that all that was visible to me, as I peered out of the window into the darkness, were blurry lights: the ill-defined glow from houses, street lamps and the occasional car headlight (not that many vehicles had passed this evening).

"It's a foul night," Dad informed me (as if I needed informing), as he came down the stairs. "It's a real pea-souper," he added, briefly popping his head around the living room door to see what I was doing.

I think he wanted me to respond, but I didn't.

"I'm referring to the fog," he continued to yell, as he headed towards the kitchen. "Don't worry; I wasn't talking about your dinner!"

I think he was alluding to my aversion to pea and ham soup and, if I could have seen his face, no doubt there would have been a smirk on it.

I was about to close the curtains, when my eye set upon another light from outside. It caught my attention because it was moving – bobbing up and down. And it was getting closer. But every now and then, it would stop for a few moments, before continuing its journey along the street, becoming just that bit brighter as it got closer to our house.

I could now hear Dad chopping vegetables in the kitchen, whistling merrily as he did so, but it did not distract me from the mysterious light outside. Eventually, it stopped directly opposite our house. And, after a few moments, it came towards me, becoming brighter and brighter as it got ever closer. A Torch? It must be someone holding a torch, of course. And the bearer of that torch was coming down our front garden path. The glare of the light – and not the fog – was what now prevented me from observing the figure in any detail when it finally halted on our doorstep, it being no more than a silhouette to me.

The doorbell sounded. For once, it didn't make me jump, but something else did – another noise, one that had come from the kitchen at the exact same moment.

"Sugar!" I had heard Dad howl, the chopping and whistling coming to an instant halt.

Of course, I knew Dad was not making me a cup of tea; something untoward had occurred in the kitchen.

"Are you OK?" I called to my father.

"It's all right," he was quick to respond. "Everything's under control. Was that the doorbell?"

I went to the hallway and opened the front door. I probably have no need to tell you who was standing there. Or to explain what the mysterious light was, but – just in case you are still in the dark (excuse the pun) – I will oblige: there before me was Florence Nightingale, holding aloft her famous lantern.[1]

"I think my services are needed here," she announced in a firm and officious manner.[2]

I hesitated for too long.

"Well, aren't you going to show me to the patient?" Florence went on, forcing me to step back as she made her way into the hallway. "Where are they? There's no time to lose."

She handed me the lamp as she took off her cloak. I handed it back to her as a swap for her outdoor garment, which I draped over the bannister.

"It's all right," I started to mumble, "you'll be pleased to learn that there *aren't* any patients...you can have the night off."

At that moment, Dad emerged from the kitchen. He had a tissue wrapped around his little finger.

"Better not shake hands," he said, beaming at our guest; "I had a little accident in the kitchen."

Florence flashed me a disapproving look. "What were you saying?"

I shrugged my shoulders as she turned her attention to my father.

"Quick, come in here and sit down," she ordered, taking my dad by his other hand. "Get me some hot water and towels," she added, with a sense of urgency in her voice. It took me a moment to realise that the command was directed at me. I continued to hesitate, even when I did realise that it was. Did she say hot water and towels? You see, I *had* seen all those old films, and thought for one moment that I should perhaps inform our guest that Dad was not about to go into labour!

Florence guided my bewildered father to the armchair in the living room, as I headed towards the kitchen to put the kettle on, still wondering why she needed hot water and towels. I could hear his protestations. "It's all right...it's only a graze...nothing to worry about..."

When I returned to the living room with our Mickey Mouse towel, Dad was sitting in the armchair, something thin protruding from his closed mouth. I thought he was smoking at first. Florence had a small wooden medicine chest opened on the coffee table, her lamp now beside it.[3]

She took the *thermometer* from Dad's mouth and shook it. As soon as it was removed from his lips, my father was able to continue with his protestations. "Honestly, I'm fine...it's stopped bleeding now...it doesn't even hurt...you don't need to worry...thank you, anyway."

Florence turned to me. "You better prepare a bed."

"Sorry?"

"For the patient. You do have a bed available, don't you?"

I shrugged my shoulders. I was doing a lot of shrugging just now.

"Good," she went on. "For one moment, I thought we'd have to put him on the floor."

She bent down and ran her finger along the carpet, shaking her head, "and that wouldn't have done at all," she declared.[4]

And so Dad was helped upstairs to his room, and his bed...and all before Florence Nightingale had had even a cup of tea.[5]

Of course, I did continue to attempt to assure our guest that it probably wasn't necessary to confine my father to bed, but she was a forceful woman and one that clearly didn't take no for an answer.[6] And I should also point out that Dad had rather too quickly stopped saying *no* for an answer! He seemed even happy to accept his condition, especially when Florence ordered me to make him a cup of tea.

"You have beef tea?" she inquired when we reached the kitchen.

I shook my head and produced a box of tea bags.

"Will PG tips do?"

As I made the tea, Florence started to inspect our house, now running her finger along skirting boards and opening cupboards, tutting and sighing as she did so.[7]

I was about to take the tea up to my father, when Florence stopped me at the foot of the stairs.

"Is there no milk?" she asked, peering into the cup.

"Dad prefers it black," I replied.

Florence expressed her disappointment with a shake of the head.

"The only nourishment in tea is the milk, sir. Therefore, a drop of milk is vital, especially if the patient has trouble digesting his food."

I sighed and went to the fridge to get the milk.

"I assume there is also sugar in his tea?" Florence continued.

"Mum says that Dad has too much sugar."

Florence shook her head again. "Put some in – at least five teaspoons. Sugar is pure carbon, very nutritive. And be careful that you don't spill any tea into the saucer."

I looked up with pleading eyes. She never saw me, but must have sensed my irritation.

"The bottom of the rim of the cup must remain dry and clean," she started to explain. "If every time the patient lifts the cup to his lips and has to carry the saucer with it, or is concerned he will drop any of the liquid onto his bed sheet or bed gown, he will be less inclined to drink it."

I nodded, pretending that I had comprehended her meaning, and that I was in total agreement with her, but she hadn't finished.

"And unless he is able to assimilate or derive nourishment from his food and drink, he is unlikely to make a recovery," she finally concluded.

I smiled politely and assured her that I would do my utmost to get the tea to my father without spilling even a drop into the saucer.

"Would *you* like a cuppa?" I added.

Florence shook her head. "We will worry about our welfare when we have made the patient comfortable. The patient should always be the priority."

Needless to say, I found Dad more than comfortable when I handed him his tea. He was sitting in bed, propped up by pillows, a grin on his face.

"Thank you, son. Do you think you can bring up a biscuit?"

I think Dad was going to enjoy this evening.

After I left my father sipping his tea upstairs, Florence ushered me into the living room.

"Sit down," she instructed me. She closed her medicine chest, a stern look on her face, though, in truth, there had been nothing but a stern look on her face since her arrival.

"I can see that standards have been allowed to slip here," she started, casting her eye around the living room with an air of disdain. "However, we can remedy that. It's not beyond all hope, and if we can tidy up this place, your father might have a chance."

"A chance? Beyond all hope?" I boomed. "Are you serious? Look, I'm sure Dad will be fine. I don't think we need to perform the last rites on him just yet!"

Florence put her finger to her mouth to silence me.

"Shush! He might hear you," she said quietly, but firmly. "The patient must never hear you talking about their condition. It could be catastrophic if they hear something negative. You must never be loose with your tongue in the vicinity of a patient. We must feed them only positive vibes. Do you understand?"

"But it's just his finger," I continued to protest.

Florence appeared irritated by my lack of concern for my father.

"It's not the wound that kills," she snapped, "but disease. If that finger becomes infected, he's doomed. And unless we clean up this place, it will do just that. We must devise a plan of action."

My look of dismay stopped her in her tracks.

"What's the matter?" she said, eyeing me with suspicion. "It's because I'm a woman, isn't it? I know what you're thinking. You think women aren't capable of taking charge, or dressing a wound, or putting a splint on a broken limb. You think this is no place for a woman – in all this squalor."

She made a point of focusing on a plate of half-eaten toast that was resting on the arm of our sofa, before her eyes returned to me.

"You don't think nursing is a job for women, do you?" she accused me. "When you picture a nurse, you picture a man, don't you?"

I shook my head. In fact, if Dad had been downstairs with me, he would have pictured Barbara Windsor in *Carry on Doctor*!

Florence finally took her eyes off me and tossed her head back.

"Women can do more than wash floors or serve beef tea. And, one day, I hope and pray that the occupation of nursing will be one that is considered suitable for women, and...yes, maybe...our hospital wards will have a few more women nurses on them."

I returned a rueful smile.[8]

"Well, I'm taking charge here, anyway," she informed me, "whether you like it or not. Standards have clearly not been met. Now, where do you keep your medical supplies?"

"There's a first-aid box in the bathroom cabinet, above the toilet. Shall I get it?"

Florence looked at me in horror. "Above the toilet? There are going to have to be changes here, sir...big changes."[9]

I headed upstairs to the bathroom, briefly popping my head around Dad's bedroom door.

"You all right, Dad?"

Of course he was. He was grinning profusely, the cup of tea in one hand, saucer in the other. I don't think he was too bothered about any drips smearing his bed gown!

"Any chance you can bring up that biscuit?" he inquired, with a wink.

I shook my head and trudged to the bathroom, only to discover that our first-aid box contained only a pair of tweezers and one bud of cotton wool.

When I returned to Florence, she had a large piece of paper laid out on the dining table.

"I want you to look at this coxcomb," she said.

"What?"

"It will help you to understand your father's chances of survival."

I joined her at the table and took a very brief look. It looked like a pie chart.[10]

"What do you think?" Florence questioned me. "Do you think we have a chance?"

"A good one," I nodded, though my speedy response made it quite clear that it was not the *coxcomb* that had led me to that conclusion, and Florence seemed put out that I hadn't taken a bit more time to study her findings.

"Look, I'm sorry," I admitted, "but I don't have much interest or experience in this sort of thing."

"I thought as much," Florence snarled. "You're not a nurse, are you? I should have realised. You better read these notes, then," she added, producing a manuscript from a pocket in her dress.[11]

I took the manuscript. Well, actually, it was thrust into my stomach.

"You can read it during any downtime that we might get," Florence suggested.

"Downtime?" I chirped.

"I know," Florence responded. "There won't be much; our patient will need constant observation."

I took a deep breath. "Honestly, you don't have to worry about my father. I think he'll live."

Florence looked at me with suspicion. "Is that your prognosis? I thought you said you didn't have any experience in this sort of thing?"

"He's only cut his finger," I protested. "I just have an inkling that he might recover. No need to lop it off just yet!"

Florence again put her finger to her mouth to hush me.

"Do you want him to hear us? No, I'm hoping that we can save the finger."

She was in earnest and I could only return a look of bewilderment.

Florence went on. "However, the chances of that finger becoming infected are very high in a place like this – among all this bad air and dirt. Now, do you promise to do your very best to save your father; to do anything that will help him?"

"I suppose so," I nodded dumbly. "What do you mean by *anything*?"

"Read this – aloud," she instructed me, producing a sheet of paper from her medicine chest.

It was a pledge of some sort and I found myself pledging, among other things, to 'pass my life in purity and to practise my profession faithfully', and to 'abstain from whatever is deleterious and mischievous' – whatever that meant! I ended by stating my devotion to 'the welfare of those committed to my care' – Dad, in this case.[12]

As far as Florence was concerned, I was now a nurse and ready to *pass my life in purity and to practise my profession faithfully* for the good of my father. I got the impression it was going to be a long evening!

"We will move the patient's bed closer to the window in the morning," Florence informed me. Morning? Was she staying? I was wrong, it was not going to be a long evening – but a long *night*!

"The patient should have something cheerful and interesting to focus on," she explained. "It is not healthy to stare at a bedroom wall and nothing else. We will move the bed, so that he can see out of the window – and enjoy the view."

The view? Did I need to remind her that we did not live in the Swiss Alps?

"And I noticed the sickroom had wallpaper," she continued. "The wallpaper must go, of course."

"I agree with you on that one," I replied. "It's hideous."

"When was it last changed?"

"Probably in the 1970s!" I joked.

Of course, it wasn't the pattern on the wallpaper that so alarmed Florence.

"It will have to come down tomorrow," she insisted; "there is no point dusting if you don't also remove the dirt from the walls. Wallpaper is the worst invention – attracts and holds all kinds of bacteria. And we will need to pick some flowers to put on his bedside cabinet," she added, "or if we can't find any flowers, some pictures of flowers – to go on the wall."

"I think he'd prefer a picture of Jennifer Aniston," I chipped in.

"Anything that will brighten up the room is beneficial," Florence continued at a pace. "It is not healthy for a patient to focus on the same mark or stain on the wall, day in, day out."

Day in, day out? How long would it take for Dad to recover from his ordeal?[13]

"Do you have a spare bed?" Florence questioned me.

Now I was getting really worried. Yes, she was planning to stay for *more* than one night.

I'm not sure if she interpreted my fears, but she was quick to explain that she wasn't intending to sleep in our spare room. She wanted the spare bed – for Dad.

"If we can move the patient from one bed to the other every 12 hours; that will aid his recovery," she elaborated. "While he is in one bed, you can wash the sheets from the other. It is important that the bedding is changed as much as possible. I can presume his current bed is freshly laid?"

"You can," I responded.

I wasn't lying. I just said that she could presume to believe it – I never said that was indeed the case.

"The whole house will need a thorough cleaning, of course," Florence observed, this time focusing on our tomato ketchup-stained tablecloth.

"I'd better go and look for Dad's frilly apron and feather duster, then," I quipped.

Florence looked horrified. "Feather duster? You might as well just pick up the dust with a trowel and pour it down the patient's throat. No, if you're going to merely distribute dust equally over a room, you might as well leave it where it is."

Ah! That was probably Dad's thinking as well; the reason he refrained from doing the housework.

Florence must have guessed what I was thinking. "You must dust with a damp cloth." She stopped suddenly. "The carpet could do with coming up as well. Whoever invented carpet? Wallpaper... furniture...they're all sources of impurity. They all pollute the air...as if there were a dung-heap in the basement."

I was going to assure her that we didn't have any dung-heaps, or a basement come to that, but I didn't have the chance.

"Now I need a proper inspection of your kitchen," she announced. "I presume I will find it in the same state as the rest of the house. We will need to get started on that before we can serve the patient a meal."

And so we headed to the kitchen. Florence shook her head as she placed her finger in the sink. "It's wet," she declared.

"That might be because of the water that we use to fill up the sink," I felt the need to explain.

Florence glared at me. "A sink that is permanently left wet will continuously exhale germs into the air. And what is this?" she shrieked, pointing to a sopping cloth that we used to wash the dishes. She bent down and sniffed it, before reeling back in disgust. I was now just praying that she didn't open the fridge. I couldn't imagine what was growing in there – she might have even mistaken it for a herbarium!

The cutlery was next in line for examination. She lifted up a chopping knife, gently running her finger along the blade.

"I'm sure that's clean," I insisted.

She placed it down. "It's not that," she replied, "I'm just checking to see if it will be sharp enough...just in case."

I coughed in surprise and thought it better not to mention that we also had a rusty saw in the garage.[14]

Florence turned her attention to our food cupboards.

"What did you have in mind to cook for my father?" I asked of her.

"Whatever his stomach can hold," she answered.

I shook my head. "Believe me, his stomach can hold more than you can imagine!"[15]

Florence continued with her inspection. She opened the freezer and peered inside.

"It's a question of finding something that will not only nourish, but also that the patient is willing to eat. I have seen men with the biggest appetites unable to even digest a beef tea when they are sick."

I nodded in agreement. "Yes, Dad can be a bit fussy, you're right.

We almost have to force him to eat his greens. And he hates mushrooms. Whatever you do, don't give him any mushrooms!"

To my surprise, Florence agreed that it was pointless serving patients something they found disagreeable.

"It's best to let them have what they want – better for them to eat something, than nothing," she said, fingering the many boxes and packets within the freezer. "What do *you* think he will eat?"

"Fish fingers," I replied, "that's his favourite, or you can't go wrong with chocolate."

Florence shook her head. "No, we might need the chocolate later, in case it gets a bit cold in here."

I agreed. There was nothing better than a hot chocolate to warm you up. Actually, consuming the chocolate in any form was not what she had in mind.[16]

"Chocolate isn't of much use to the sick – you might as well throw it on the fire," she moaned. "I know that people back home mean well when they send gifts to their sick and wounded loved ones...but chocolate? Honestly, who wants chocolate when they're ill? No, in my experience, sweet things are the last thing a patient wants when their tongue is furred and they've got a fever. Of course, I suppose it *is* more useful than sending bottles of Eau de Cologne. The only thing in a bottle that my patients crave is gin!"[17]

I watched in fascination as Florence started to fry the fish fingers. She had already rolled up the frilly sleeves of her trademark black dress, which was now protected by a Jamie Oliver novelty apron, which she had found hanging on the oven door. I need not tell you that she *did* wash her hands before starting – as well as almost every kitchen utensil.

I offered to finish the job of chopping the vegetables, but she said it was unlikely that someone who didn't think much of his greens when in good health; would want to eat them when not in good health.

"Make yourself useful," she barked at me, as I hovered beside her, unsure what to do. "A nurse should not pass the time in idleness.

There is always something that can be done for the benefit of the patient. If you have completed your medical duties, think of something that might bring cheer to your patient. Does your father like music? Do you play an instrument?"

I nodded, but I forgot to add the fact that I was only *learning* to play an instrument. I went to the living room and sat down at the keyboard. I turned the volume up as high as it could go and started to play. As I said (and as I should have probably warned Florence), I was only a beginner and had only got as far as playing the first few notes of *Silent Night*.

And, after a few moments, Florence rushed in, frying pan still in her hand. "Stop!" she ordered with so much force; that I thought she was going to hit me with it.

I didn't think my playing was that bad, or perhaps it was the fact that she was superstitious and objected to me reciting Christmas carols in February?

"What do you think you're doing?" she asked. "Do you want to send the patient into delirium?"

I thought she was exaggerating a little bit. As I said, I wasn't that bad.

"You must never play the pianoforte when there is a sick person in the house," she scolded me. "Only wind or stringed instruments are beneficial to the patient, they being capable of continuous sound. The pianoforte has no continuity of sound, and even the finest pianoforte playing will bring damage to the sick."

I apologised and turned off the keyboard. "Shall I put on a CD instead? Singing won't do any damage, will it? I'm not suggesting that I myself should sing (that would cause anyone pain), but Michael Bublé is pretty good. What about you?" I suggested. "You should be a good singer as well, being a Nightingale..."

For one moment, I thought Florence almost smiled; I stress...only for one moment.

"What about some gentle pursuits, something to occupy his

mind?" she proposed. "What does he enjoy doing to pass the monotony of the day?"

I shook my head. "Not a lot. He goes fishing sometimes, but that might be difficult to arrange up there."

Florence looked around the living room. "Look for some things that are pleasing to the eye – things that are brightly coloured. Colour is good for a patient."

I picked up a garish pink cushion that was resting on the sofa. "Something like this?" I inquired.[18]

Florence was already heading back to the kitchen.

"Why don't you sit with the patient?" she offered, without turning to look at me, giving the frying pan a shake. "Observation is key; sit and observe, find out all about the patient...what time of day do they like to eat...what time of day do they sleep...what time of day do they empty their bowels?"

I hoped I wouldn't have to observe *that*!

In the end, I felt more inclined to observe the television, but, fearful that I might be accused of passing the time in idleness, tuned into an episode of *Casualty* to get some tips.

It was not long before Florence hailed me from the kitchen. She had finished the cooking, and we were soon tiptoeing up the stairs, the dinner tray in my hands.

We halted outside the bedroom for a moment. Florence, her lamp in her hand, even though the lights were on, turned to me and whispered clearly: "You must enter a sickroom quickly, but not suddenly, or as if you are in a rush. Show him no sign of haste or anxiety." She stopped. "He might be sleeping. If so, we'll let him sleep. It is not good to wake a patient suddenly." She paused again, this time eyeing my clothes with suspicion. "Be careful not to rustle. I have known many a person, compelled by their dress, to shuffle or waddle so that the sickroom is left shaking."

I looked down at my T-shirt and jeans.

"A good nurse won't rattle or creak either," Florence added. I slipped off my slippers as a token gesture.

At last we both entered the bedroom. Dad wasn't asleep, but still sitting up.

"Ah, the Lady with the Lamp," he declared, as he set eyes on us. He had a mischievous smile on his face and I swear he had, in fact, *actually* said, 'the lady and the *tramp*'!

I glared at my father. I knew he was going to milk this for as long as he could.

I shoved the tray towards him and plonked myself on the edge of the bed. Florence let out a shriek.

"Never lean upon, sit or even touch the bed of the patient," she growled; "the sick feel even the slightest jar."

I reluctantly got to my feet. Dad was now giggling.

"What is above us?" Florence turned to me suddenly. "Is there another floor? Footsteps can be very trying for a patient."

"It's just the loft," I answered. "There's no-one up there, except maybe a ghost or two, but I imagine they're pretty fleet-footed."

"You wouldn't mind getting my newspaper, would you," Dad interrupted, "when you're bringing up my *biscuit*? There's not much to do up here, you see."

Florence thought that to be an excellent idea, only she suggested it might be more beneficial if I read aloud to my father.

"We don't want the patient to exert any unnecessary effort. And there isn't a lot of light in the room," she pointed out, a look of concern on her face. "The patient needs light and to feel the warmth of the sun on their cheeks."

I felt as though that might be my fault as well, though I couldn't really be responsible for the sun setting three hours ago, could I?

"It's night-time," I felt I should point out in case there was any doubt over that fact.

"Now, remember," she turned to me; "listening to someone reading can take a lot of effort on the patient's part, and can bring on delirium, so read slowly and clearly."

I was about to fetch the newspaper, but was halted by another question.

"Do you have any pets?" Florence piped, her train of thought changing track once more.

I nodded. "Don't worry; I'll keep them away from the patient."

To my surprise, Florence objected. "No, bring them up here. They are good for the patient's morale and wellbeing."

I shook my head. "Not *our* pets. Our cat is not the most sociable creature."[19]

Florence removed something from a pocket in her dress. It was a stuffed owl. She placed it on the bedside cabinet next to Dad and smiled. "This will cheer him up."

I didn't think he needed cheering up, and I'm not sure a stuffed owl would have had him *hooting* with laughter.[20]

Dad thanked her anyway.

"A live bird in a cage would be more beneficial, of course," Florence admitted. "A chattering bird can be a great companion to a sick patient."

I thought of Mum. She might fit the bill, though I think Dad would probably prefer the stuffed owl!

"Of course," Florence began, turning to me again, "a baby is something even better for improving the morale of the patient. Is there one in the house?"

"No, there isn't – and I don't think we're expecting a delivery!" I was quick to add.[21]

Florence ignored my quip and was already thinking about something else. "I think I will change the dressing after dinner," she announced.

"No need to on my behalf," Dad offered back, "you look fine in what you're wearing."

He was joking, of course, and obligingly raised his little finger, the tissue still wrapped around it. He still had a smug grin on his face.

"Thank you, Flo," he said, as she started to attend to his pillow that had slipped a bit. "Can I call you Flo? They named you after the city where you were born, didn't they?"

Florence nodded. "Yes. My sister was born in Parthenope, so my parents named her after that place as well. Did your parents name you after your birthplace?"

I had to butt in. "No," I sniggered, "Dad was born in Sandwich!" [22]

Florence didn't smile. "Would you like me to write you a letter?" she asked suddenly.

Dad shrugged his shoulders. "You can just speak to me now, if you like."

Florence sighed. "I mean, would you like me to write a letter on your behalf – to let someone you love know of your wound?"[23]

Dad thought about it. "You can put a message on Facebook; then everyone will know."

I had to object. "I really don't think a tiny graze on your little finger is the sort of thing people put on Facebook..." I stopped. Actually, it was *just* the thing.

"Are you warm enough?" Florence inquired. "I have, of course, opened the window, as it is vital that clean air reaches the sickroom."

"Well, now that you mention it," Dad felt obliged to point out, "it is a bit chilly in here. Can you get me something from the drawer, son," he said, looking to me.

I opened a drawer and retrieved what I thought was a jumper. It was actually a woolly balaclava.

Florence nodded. "That's excellent. I've seen those before," she said, "at the Battle of..."

"Balaclava!" Dad interrupted her, with a smirk on his face, and I immediately wondered if my father had himself set up the joke by deliberately moving that particular article of clothing to the top of the drawer. "There was a cardigan there as well," he added, turning to me again. I continued to rummage through the drawer, as the smirk on my father's face grew bigger. "I don't mean in *there*, son," he laughed, "I mean at the Battle of Balaclava...Lord Cardigan!"

I took hold of the balaclava and forced it over my still giggling father's head.

"There! Is that better?" I asked him. "You look a proper '*knit*' now!"[24]

Florence was not impressed by my jocular behaviour, and it was the sound of the doorbell which probably saved me from a lecture.

Dad looked at me and sighed. He clearly didn't want anything to spoil his fun. "We're not expecting anyone, are we?" he pondered, now with a mouth full of fish finger.

I headed downstairs and opened the front door.

It was a woman.

"Good evening," she announced confidently. "I think my help is required here. Please show me to the patient."

I didn't respond, but just stood rooted to the spot, a gormless expression on my face.

"I'm a nurse," she felt the need to elaborate. "You have a sick person here? I have come to assist. Now let me in, please."

I eventually stood back and the woman entered. She was of Caribbean descent and possessed a strong accent.

Florence was coming down the stairs, as the woman started to remove her cape.

"It's another nurse," I informed our original guest. "I think she wants to help you. What did you say your name was?" I added, turning to the new arrival.

"Mary Seacole," she replied.[25]

I shrugged my shoulders in response to the name.

"Of course, you don't know who I am, do you?" she said, looking at me with annoyance.

"I'm afraid not," I admitted. "Should I?"

"Yes, you should," she replied testily.[26]

I returned an apologetic smile.

"I bet you knew who *she* was," Mary scowled, nodding in the direction of Florence, who had halted on the stairs. "Yes, we all know *her*, of course," the new arrival continued, a look of contempt on her face. "Everyone knows her – the Lady with the Lamp! She gets all the credit, not me, but then she's the darling of the nation, isn't she. I expect you yourself have a picture of Miss Nightingale hanging on your bedroom wall."

I shook my head. "No, not a Nightingale...but I do have a poster of a Swift...Taylor Swift."[27]

Mary had picked up an object from a shelf below the hallway mirror.

"And is this one of those ornaments they made of her?"

I shook my head. "No...that's not a nightingale either. It's a thrush. I made it in pottery when I was at junior school."

Mary put the thrush down, as Florence descended a few more steps, before stopping again.

"Florence, this is Mary...Mary, this is Florence," I said.

Mary held up her hands. "There's no need to introduce us. Miss Nightingale and I are already acquainted," Mary added with a sneer.

"Look, it's not my fault," Florence sighed. "I don't ask for all this attention and adoration from people. In fact, it's an inconvenience – having to correspond with the public, wading through the piles of letters. I have better things to do with my time. I just want to get on with my job, that's all."[28]

"And that is all that I wish to do as well," Mary snapped, "to assist you in your work; to come to the aid of the sick. And there's a sick patient up there in need of attention – so make way and let me pass."

Mary started to ascend the stairs. Florence refused to budge.

"I don't need your help, thank you," Florence said defiantly. "I've told you that already."[29]

"That is nonsense," Mary replied. "Many hands make light work. Who is with the patient now? The patient should be under strict observation at all times."

"Look," I intervened, turning to Florence, keen to put an end to the argument, "why don't you let her help you? It might be a good idea, you know. I'm sure Dad wouldn't object to having *two* ladies fussing over him! It will give you a chance to have a rest, put your feet up and have a cup of beef tea!"

"I will not rest until I have done my duty here," Florence declared.

I shook my head. "You'll make yourself ill, you know."

I turned to Mary. "I'm sorry. I don't think she's going to budge. She likes to do things her way. Perhaps you can go and help someone else? Mr Barrett was laid up in bed last week with shingles – he could probably do with some help. It wouldn't be a wasted journey then, would it? Did you come far?"

Mary looked at me as though I should know the answer to that question.

"Yes," she answered, "and at great expense, I should add, so please show me to the patient."[30]

I looked to Florence. She was adamant that she was not going to let Mary pass.

Mary glared at her adversary. "You know why she doesn't want help from me, don't you?" she started, addressing me but not taking her accusing eye off her fellow nurse. "It's because of who I am and where I come from."[31]

"Is everything all right down there?" Dad called from the bedroom. "Just wondered if you wouldn't mind bringing up that *biscuit*?"

"I think you've both woken the patient," I observed, a smug smile on *my* face now.

Much to my surprise, Florence flashed me a look of indifference, shrugging her shoulders as she did so.

"He'll live!" she stated calmly, almost flippantly, before reconvening her dispute with Mary Seacole.

And, indeed – you will be pleased to know – Dad *did* live. And there wasn't even any need to seek out the rusty saw from the garage: the finger did *not* become infected.[32]

Mary eventually conceded defeat and went on her way; probably taking my advice to visit Mr Barrett or another of my neighbours in need.

So that just leaves Florence Nightingale – the Lady with the

Lamp. What became of her? Well, she did look a bit pale when she had finished with Mary, and I did, for one moment, fear that she was in danger of fainting.

"You're not looking too good," I suggested to her, after Mary had been seen off the premises. "I did warn you...you're not getting sick yourself, are you?"

Of course, Florence Nightingale rejected that notion and, needless to say – even though I stressed that I would change the sheets first – also refused my generous offer of a bed...and a mug of Bovril.[33]

Chapter 9
Elizabeth I

Dad had warned me that Queen Elizabeth was not the most attractive woman in her later years...but I didn't expect her to have a beard!

And that observation led me to conclude – pretty quickly, I should add (and even before the doorbell had sounded) – that it *wasn't* Elizabeth who I had watched walking down our garden path, after all.

"Can you let her in?" Dad shouted from upstairs. "I want to get this wall finished." My father was painting the spare bedroom.

"It's not her," I responded, as I made my way from living room to hallway, "unless, of course, she's a man!"[1]

Yes, as I said, I had already concluded that it wasn't Elizabeth now on our doorstep and, as I swung open the front door, I soon became quite sure of that fact.

The man on the doorstep smiled warmly. What was I to do? Should I let him in? We were expecting Elizabeth I for dinner, but perhaps she couldn't make it? Perhaps he was here in her place, or was one of her many courtiers?

The man nodded. My hesitation persuaded him to make the first move.

"Greetings to you and your family," he said.

I didn't reply. He greeted me for a second time.

This time I nodded in acknowledgement and stood back to allow him to enter. He smiled and slipped off the sandals he had been wearing. Unlike Dad, he didn't wear socks with his sandals. I glanced at his bare feet, before my eyes were drawn back to his coat. Sorry, did I not mention the coat? That is strange; because his coat was unlike anything I had ever seen before, or anything I would dare be *seen* in! It was the most colourful garment I had ever set eyes on. It looked like it contained a segment of every colour of the rainbow.

"Can I take your coat?" I offered, holding out my hand.

He looked at me with suspicion. "What for?"

"I was just going to hang it up," I informed him; quick to realise that he thought I wanted it for myself.

The man started to remove the said garment. I should point out that his tunic was not as impressive as his coat.

He studied me with curiosity, as he tentatively handed the coat to me.

"I'm Joseph – you were expecting me, weren't you?" he inquired.

Joseph! Of course, Joseph and his amazing technicolour dream coat – though I'm not sure the Bible put it quite like that!

"I'm sorry," I replied. "We were expecting a queen, that's all...not a prince."

Joseph assumed a puzzled look. "A prince? Be assured, my friend, I am not a prince."

"Not yet," I smiled, "but you will be. I saw it in a dream."

That was not strictly true. In fact, I had seen it on stage. Dad was in the local production of the classic musical, in one of the dream sequences, playing a stalk of grain with seven heads, or something like that.

"The numbers of the houses are difficult to make out," Joseph informed me. "I'm expected at number 23. This is number 23, isn't it?"

I shook my head and pointed. "No. That's further down the road – you want the house of Jacob, I think."

Joseph looked at me strangely. "No, my friend, he's my father and that is where I have come from."

I shrugged my shoulders.

Joseph sighed and started to put on his sandals.

"Please forgive me, my friend, and accept my humble apologies," he said.

And he was off down the garden path.

"Wait!" I bellowed. "Haven't you forgotten something?" His coat was still in my hand.

Joseph returned and smiled in appreciation, or it might have been in embarrassment.

"You want to be careful with a nice coat like that," I said, as I watched him sling it over his shoulder and depart.

Dad was coming down the stairs as I closed the door, a paint-brush and tin in his hands. "That's the second coat," he announced.

I shook my head. "Really? You mean he has another even better than *that* one?"

Of course, Dad had no idea what I was talking about, having not set eyes on our unexpected visitor.

"I said, I've finished the second coat," he went on. "It looks good. Come and have a look." He stopped. "Wasn't that the doorbell? Where is she?"

"It wasn't her," I started to explain. "It was...oh, it doesn't matter. I'll come and have a look. Is it a coat of many colours?" I added, with a grin.

Dad sported a baffled look as I followed him up the stairs. "No, son, it's just white."

Elizabeth had still not turned up a further two hours later. Dad had decided that the spare bedroom needed a *third* coat, and I eventually went up to keep him company, as watching paint dry was only a little less riveting than sitting alone downstairs, gazing at the garden path in the forlorn hope that our guest might arrive sooner if I were looking out for her.

"Where is she?" I questioned my father. "She was due ages ago."

"Relax," Dad attempted to calm me. "She's a queen and a woman. I've told you before; it's the prerogative of both to keep men waiting. They all do it."

"Dinner is all under control, isn't it?" I continued to quiz my father. "You seem unusually laid back. I thought you'd be in the kitchen going frantic, like normal, not spending the afternoon painting the spare bedroom. You know she is known for her temper, don't you?"

"So is your mother...and if I don't finish this room by today, I'll know even more about it!"

I chuckled. "Mum is hardly going to have you hanged, drawn and quartered," I felt the need to point out.

Dad looked at me. "Don't give her ideas, son...don't give her ideas."

And so we started to debate as to who was to be feared more – the Virgin Queen or Mum. Dad argued that Elizabeth was a much more forgiving queen. I mean, more forgiving than most other monarchs, not necessarily more forgiving than my mother!

"You're thinking of Elizabeth's half-sister," Dad started to explain, as he attempted to wipe off some paint that had inadvertently dripped onto the carpet. "She was the fiery one – the one to be feared. She was the one who ordered more executions than I've ordered Chinese takeaways. They were dropping like flies under her reign."

"Bloody Mary," I responded.

"Don't swear, son," Dad snapped, but with a smirk on his face. "Yes, though her real name was Mary Tudor. Elizabeth took the throne when Mary died, but Elizabeth ruled by adopting a policy of moderation. She was a far more tolerant queen."

I was not convinced and warned Dad that she was *still* a queen, and that queens were probably not in the habit of waiting for their dinner.

"Be it on your head," I declared. "And I mean that literally!"

I gazed out of the bedroom window. The postman was further down the street and he immediately caught my eye.

"That's not her – unless she's in disguise," I said.[2]

It never occurred to me to look down into our front garden, but, as I unintentionally moved closer to the window, the garden came into view – as did the person standing on our path.

"It's her!" I yelled. "She's in our garden!"

Dad went to the window and pressed his nose against the glass to get a better look from our high vantage point.

"She doesn't look very happy, son. You'd better not keep her hanging around – or *you'll* be the one to be hung."

"It's *hanged*," I corrected him, as I raced down the stairs, two at a time.

I flung open the front door.

"Your Majesty," I bowed. "Please accept my apologies. I didn't know that you were waiting. I hope you haven't been waiting for long."

Elizabeth stared at me. Dad was right – she was not amused, to pinch a phrase from one of her descendants.[3]

The queen stood her ground and nodded at the path in front of her. It had been raining most of the morning and a puddle had formed on the concrete. Of course, now I knew what she was waiting for. Sir Walter Raleigh had used his cloak, hadn't he? I reached for a coat hanging on the bannister and laid it over the puddle.[4]

Elizabeth waited until I had stepped aside, and then proceeded to head further down the path towards me. She stopped when she reached the coat and made a point of placing both feet upon it. She looked up at me, keen to make sure that my eyes were upon her, before she started to do what I can only describe as 'The Twist'; wriggling her body, her shoes pressed together, her knees bent (not that her shoes or knees were visible under her huge dress). And all to be sure that her full weight had been dispensed on our poor coat. I cringed and thought it was a good job that Joseph had not left that nice coat of his, after all.

"Please enter, Your Majesty," I offered, pretending to be unmoved by her vindictive behaviour. "I must say that Your Majesty looks particularly *radiant* today."

That was indeed the right word to use. Her face was white. No, I mean really *white*. Dad had warned me that she used white make-up to hide her many facial blemishes. However, she looked like Dad did when he went to the beach – it was as though she had plastered her face with the highest-factor sun cream and had forgotten to rub it in. She seemed pleased with my compliment, and she may have even blushed, but, of course, I would never have known if her cheeks had turned crimson, under all that make-up.[5]

Elizabeth was dressed just how I expected her to be.[6] Her jewel and gold-encrusted dress, as I have already pointed out, was enormous and she had difficulty getting it through the door.[7] When she had succeeded in doing so, she looked at me sternly and uttered her first words since arriving. Sadly, I had no idea what those words were. It was not a question of they being in a foreign tongue and me not being able to translate them (Dad had told me that Elizabeth was fluent in a number of languages), but because she had mumbled them.

She spoke again when I returned a look of confusion, but it didn't help. I soon realised why my guest couldn't speak properly: it looked like she had two giant gobstoppers in her mouth, her cheeks puffed out like those of a greedy hamster. Only they were not gobstoppers; that I found out when Elizabeth removed two pieces of cloth from her mouth. Her cheeks immediately 'deflated' to reveal a gaunt face full of lines, though I wasn't sure if those lines were wrinkles, or whether it was just her white make-up cracking, now that her cheeks had 'popped'.[8]

The queen spoke again, and this time I concluded that she was inquiring whether we had cakes. Well, that is what I *concluded*. To be honest, it was still difficult to understand her, even though she was now able to fully open her mouth. I should perhaps also point out, at this moment, that I wished that she *wasn't* able to fully open her mouth. Yes, Dad had warned me that she liked her sweets (and obviously her cakes too), with the result that her teeth (those that she still possessed) would be black. And, make no mistake, they were – but he hadn't mentioned the bad breath. It almost blew me off my feet.

Elizabeth repeated her question. I assured her that we had plenty of cakes, so I was somewhat surprised when she put the question for a third (or it might have been fourth or fifth) time – though I knew from the tone of her voice that this was going to be the *last* time!

I hesitated before opening my mouth – not because I had bad breath like her, but because I didn't know how to respond to a question I still hadn't comprehended. I was fearful she might think I was making fun of her, or, in genuinely not being able to decipher her words, might be implying that she had a speech impediment of some sort.[9]

Surprisingly, it was Dad who came to my rescue.

He must have been listening at the top of the stairs. He started to descend.

"Welcome, Your Majesty," he said, rubbing his paint-stained hands on his overalls. "Better not shake hands, not that I would even dare to presume I was worthy to do so." He looked down at me in a superior fashion, having stopped halfway down the stairs: "I think Her Majesty said she would like the *jakes*, not the cakes."

Elizabeth smiled.

"Well, you tell her one," I snapped at my condescending father; "you're the crackpot around here!"

And, at first, I really did think that Dad was '*jaking*' when he informed me that jakes was an Elizabethan euphemism for the toilet, not that Dad put it to me that gracefully.

I felt embarrassed, but Elizabeth just looked relieved. I mean, relieved that she had finally got her message across – not the other 'relieved', as she hadn't actually done her business yet!

"Will you follow me, Your Majesty?" my father beckoned, from his position halfway up the stairs. "The jakes is just up here," he added, another smug smile directed at me.

Elizabeth did not wait for Dad to lead the way, but tried to brush past him. She appeared to be in a hurry. It would have been difficult ascending the stairs with *that* dress, even without another person in the way, and the queen and my father became wedged between wall and bannister on the seventh step.

"I beg your pardon, Your Majesty," my shuffling dad apologised. "I'm just trying to free myself from your dress..."

At that point, Elizabeth gave Dad a shove and he tumbled down the stairs.

"What the..." Dad moaned, as he lay sprawled over the bottom steps, forgetting who he was addressing for one moment. "You could have killed me! A stairway can be a dangerous place. You can't just go pushing people down the stairs like that!"

Elizabeth turned and glared at my father. Unknown to me, the glare was not in response to my dad's insolence, but because his comment had struck a nerve, a very raw one, it would seem.[10]

Elizabeth carried on up the stairs, a number of obscenities coming from her mouth. Her speech seemed a lot clearer now – and I had no trouble deciphering *these* particular words![11]

Dad picked himself up and brushed himself down, as Elizabeth found the bathroom for herself, slamming the door shut behind her.

"You're right – she does have a temper," Dad said calmly. "And, good grief...is she ugly!"

The front door was still open and Dad spotted the somewhat dishevelled coat lying on the path. I explained my chivalrous act to him.

"That's very gallant of you, son, well done," he said.

I smiled. "It was nothing...it's *your* coat!"

Elizabeth seemed to be in a better mood when she finally joined us in the living room.

Dad winked at me and whispered: "She probably needed that!"

"I have two observations to make," the queen started, as my father pulled a chair from under the dining table, beckoning her to sit down. The chair had to come out quite far in order to accommodate her dress. "The towel hanging up in your jakes will have to go," Elizabeth said firmly. "There is an image of something quite hideous on it – an image of one of those frightening creatures. I hope it was not a practical joke directed at me?"

She was talking about our Mickey Mouse towel.[12]

"My second observation," she continued, "is that I must compliment you on your jakes. Yes, I am very impressed and somewhat surprised that you have a water closet. Therefore, so long as you remove the offending item I have hitherto mentioned, I would be pleased to reside in your dwelling until they have finished cleaning the palace jakes. I will get word to my court that I will be staying."[13]

Staying? Both Dad and I flashed each other a look of alarm. How long would she be *staying*? Was it rude to ask someone (especially a queen) just how long they intended to accept our hospitality? Dad attempted to explain – politely and sensitively – that there might not be room to accommodate all of her ladies-in-waiting or her many courtiers, but Elizabeth waved away our protestations, assuring us it was not a problem – and that *she* would not be inconvenienced too much.

"It's a good job that I've nearly finished the spare room, then," Dad said wistfully.

"My servants can have *your* rooms," Elizabeth declared. "I will just have to make do. I only need two or three rooms for myself."

Yes, the servants *could* have our rooms – as they would indeed be free. You see, we soon discovered that we ourselves were expected to find *alternative* accommodation. In other words, move out of our own home. "There might be a tent up in the loft?" Dad suggested to me.

"Now I am ready to be entertained," Elizabeth smiled, leaning back in her chair.[14]

Dad looked at me with a glint in his eye.

"Do you think she'd like me to recite a bit of Shakespeare? My bet is that she's a bit of a *drama queen*," he added under his breath, accompanied by a wink.

"I think Her Majesty might like a drink first?" I suggested to the queen, keen to spare her – and me.

Dad reluctantly left for the kitchen. Elizabeth cast her eye around the room. Her chair was close to the bookcase and, by turning her head; she was able to read the spines of the books. One particular book had caught her eye and she removed it.

"This is interesting," she said, a sly look on her face, carefully turning the pages. I gulped. It was a Spanish phrase book.

"It belongs to Dad," I quickly informed her.

Knowing that the English and Spanish were not the best of friends during the reign of Elizabeth, I feared she was going to arrest us for treason, a charge of collaborating with the enemy being pinned upon us.

"Dad likes to learn a bit of the local lingo when we go to the Costa Blanca..." I stopped. I think I had given her a little bit too much information.

"You know the Spanish coast well, then?" she mused.

Was it a trick question? I hesitated and she continued to interrogate me. "And how exactly do you get there? Do you charter a ship?"

"Not exactly, we go with Brittany Ferries," I replied sheepishly.

Elizabeth started to playfully twist a finger through her famous auburn locks.

"You might be able to do something for me," she smiled, revealing those revolting teeth. "I might be in need of your services."

"What, again, you've only just been?"

Of course, I soon realised that she was not talking about those kind of services; I mean, our bathroom (or should I say jakes).

"I'm always on the lookout for those willing to travel to Spain...on sort of business trips," she said calmly. "One particular businessman, who I once held in high regard, tried my patience too much in his later years. He seemed to be more interested in playing bowls, so I lost faith in my pirate..."

She stopped and smiled. "I mean, privateer. He wasn't *really* a pirate – that was just a silly name for him."[15]

She paused again and continued to survey the room.

"Do you have many treasures from your trips to Spain?"

I nodded. "There's a fridge magnet from Alicante and Dad bought a sombrero on our last visit."

I'm not sure Elizabeth was all that impressed. "My pirate – I mean, privateer – brought me back gold, among other things. How about you? Could you get your hands on some bars of gold for me?"

I nodded again, without hesitation. "I can bring back some Toblerone bars," I gushed; "I can get lots of those from the on-board duty-free shop."

That seemed to satisfy Elizabeth. "I like the sound of those," she admitted.

And so, apparently, Dad and I had been recruited into her service as pirates...I mean, privateers.

Elizabeth was in good spirits now. "What can I call you both?" She paused. "I need a name for all those that are dear to me. I've got 'my eyes', 'my pygmy' and even 'my frog'. You can be a double-act. Have you any suggestions?"

"Ant and Dec?" I offered, they being the first names that came to mind.[16]

Dad returned to the living room with a glass of tomato juice.

"Try this," he smiled, placing it on the table in front of Elizabeth. "I bet you don't know what it's called. It's named after your half-sister – the one you took over from."

"Bloody Mary!" Elizabeth cursed.

"That's right," Dad grinned. "That's what it's called. How did you know that?"

I sighed. I bet Dad had been planning that little charade for ages, knowing full well that Elizabeth seemed to have difficulty in 'minding' her language. I should at this point inform you that I have already omitted the odd swearword uttered from her red-pasted lips, for the sake of any younger or sensitive readers.

Dad bowed before making his exit again.

"Do you play cards?" I inquired. "We can have a game?"

Elizabeth licked her lips. "I played Lord North a lot, you know. He was hopeless. I won all the time, of course."

I didn't doubt that, and got the impression that letting Elizabeth win was among the rules of the game.

"Poor Lord North," Elizabeth smiled smugly. "He lost a lot of money playing cards with me. He wasn't very good with money. He became our treasurer..."

She stopped and pondered that final statement, seemingly giving it thought for the first time. I smiled.[17]

Something in the corner of the room had now caught Elizabeth's eye. Mum collected novelty pin cushions, and one of them was sitting on top of her sewing box, with some pins sticking out of it. Elizabeth looked horrified.

"What is *that*?"

"It's just a pin cushion," I replied, lifting it up to show her. She reeled back in horror. I should point out that the cushion, in fact, took the form of a person – a clown, to be precise.

"What evil is going on here?" Elizabeth grilled me. "Is that supposed to be an image of...me?"

I shook my head vehemently. To be fair, I could see that it was an easy mistake to make. There was a resemblance: the white face...the curly red hair...the ruff round the neck of the clown. It took me several minutes to persuade the queen that we were not having fun at her expense, or up to even worse mischief.[18]

Fortunately, Dad returned to the room at just the right time, with two bowls of soup.

"Be careful it's not too hot," he warned us. "Help yourself to condiments."

I handed Elizabeth the salt cellar, it being the only condiment available to us. "You first, Your Majesty," I smiled politely.

I would like to tell you that Elizabeth *sprinkled* some salt onto her soup, but that would have been an understatement. No, she *doused* her soup with salt.

"You want to watch your blood pressure," Dad muttered under his breath.

And that blood pressure presumably went up a bit, after Elizabeth had put the spoon to her mouth.

"How dare you serve me this!" she shrieked, throwing the spoon at my father.[19] It hit him on the head. "This tastes like the Atlantic Ocean!" she gasped, coughing and spluttering.

I looked at my father – he was rubbing his head. "If I can be so bold," I stuttered, picking up the salt cellar, "it was Your Majesty who *herself* put the salt on her food, not Dad."

Elizabeth looked at me in astonishment. "Salt? I don't want salt! What would I want with salt? Why is there salt on the table? I thought it was sugar...bring me sugar!"

Not another one! Dad rushed to the kitchen, still rubbing his head, before returning with a bowl of sugar. Elizabeth took the spoon from it. Dad braced himself, just in case it was going to be heading in his direction again, but she merely placed it on the table and lifted up the bowl, pouring the entire contents into her soup. Yes, I need not remind you that Elizabeth had a sweet tooth.[20]

Next to come was a mixed salad: lettuce, tomatoes, cucumber and...sugar.

The main course was roast chicken with broccoli and potatoes. Elizabeth prodded a boiled potato with her fork.

"I see you have these dreadful things that Sir 'Water' brought back from his travels," she observed.[21]

I smiled. "I think they go quite nicely with some...sugar."

Elizabeth agreed and Dad was forced to bring in another bowl.

I expect you're wondering what the queen had for dessert? A bowl of sugar? No, well, not quite. Yes, it was a bowl of sugar...but with a slice of apple crumble placed within it...all washed down with a glass of wine, with...sugar.

Elizabeth finished her meal with another bowl of sugar, but this time she used it to clean her teeth.[22]

As she rubbed the sugar into her black molars, she let out a sudden yelp.

"Are you all right?" I asked. "Haven't got toothache, have you?"

Elizabeth returned a look of horror. "No," she was quick to lie. "I have no pain."

"We know a good dentist, if you do," I continued, turning to Dad, who was loitering in the room as normal. "Don't we, Dad?"

"How about some paracetamol?" my father suggested, producing a packet from the sideboard draw. "It should ease the pain a bit."

Elizabeth looked at it with suspicion.

"Does it hurt?"

"No. It's just a tablet – you swallow it," I assured her. "Look, it's even coated with *sugar*!"

Dad flashed me an unconvincing look.

"*You* take one first," Elizabeth ordered me.

"I don't have any pain," I responded.

"I'll have one," Dad intervened. "I've got a bit of a headache, anyway," he whispered to me. "Don't know why?" he added, rubbing his head once more.

My father swallowed a tablet and offered one to Elizabeth, but she still refused. "I'll see what effect it has on you first," she said stubbornly.[23]

Dad shrugged his shoulders.

"Now, is Your Majesty ready for her after-dinner entertainment?" Dad inquired with more than a hint of anticipation in his voice.

Elizabeth held up her hand. "Not yet, sir," she commanded. "There is something I must proclaim. You see, I have, up to now, overlooked your dress, because I was hungry, but I would like to inquire whether you think your attire is suitable in the presence of a queen."

Dad looked down at his paint-covered overalls. "I'm so sorry, Your Majesty..."

"Not you!" Elizabeth snapped, turning her head towards me. "Him!"

At this point, I need to inform you that I had, that morning – in view of the fact that we were to receive a royal visitor – ditched my jeans and sweatshirt for my best shirt and trousers, so I was somewhat surprised that she took offence at *my* clothes.

"I can put a tie on?" I offered gingerly.

Elizabeth stared at me as I shifted in my seat.

"Isn't it obvious?" she barked. "Are you mocking me, sir?"

I looked down at my clothes again and then nervously touched my hair – perhaps Dad had plonked a bright red wig on my head without me noticing?[24]

Elizabeth rose from her chair. I wasn't sure what she was going to do next, but what followed would not have been my first guess: she spat at me. Yes, without being too graphic (well, I'm going to be a little bit), the liquid projectile from her mouth – yes, from that disgusting mouth, full of rotten teeth, which also emitted the most-foul stench you could imagine – landed on my shoulder. I tentatively turned my head to look at it. Fortunately, Dad had spared no expense and had provided paper serviettes for our meal. Needless to say, I was forced to use mine to remove the sugary substance.[25]

"Your shirt," Elizabeth snarled; "it's purple, sir!"

I looked down, even though, of course, I had no need to. Purple was my favourite colour.

"How dare you wear that colour in my presence?" Elizabeth went on. "You have no right to wear apparel of that colour...unless you are an earl or a duke?"

I shook my head. "I'm sorry if my shirt has caused you offence, Your Majesty. Is there a colour more preferable to you?"

"Black," she said, "or white...like what he's wearing," she added, pointing at my father.

In fact, Dad's overalls were not black, but navy blue. However, they were adorned with so much white paint; I wondered how there had been any left to paint the walls.

"Now go and put something else on, and I will overlook the matter on this occasion," Elizabeth ordered me.[26]

I rose as the queen retook her seat. I felt like a disgraced child banished from the table for having the temerity to question why they needed to eat vegetables *every* night.

"Wait!" Elizabeth yelled, as I made my way to the door. She had been attracted by something else on my attire. "Roll up your trousers."

Of course, I couldn't refuse, though I immediately guessed that she was not going to like what I was about to reveal: football socks – and they stretched right up to my knees. They were all I could find that were clean.

"I thought so," Elizabeth tutted; "netherstocks! I presume you are not a knight of the realm either, sir? Change them now!"[27]

Dad had a smirk on his face as I left the room.

I found a white sweatshirt, but had to retrieve a smelly pair of socks from the laundry basket. Don't worry – they were not as smelly as her breath!

Fortunately, I was not inspected when I returned to the living room. Elizabeth was too captivated by my father. Dad had opened his newspaper and was reading the horoscopes.[28]

"It says here that you are feeling isolated and that you have been cooped up for too long..." Dad stopped. "Sorry, I'm reading the wrong one. That one's probably for Mary, Queen of Scots!"

Elizabeth did not appreciate the joke.[29]

Dad apologised. "Virgo...here we go...this is your one. It says that you are going to meet a tall, dark stranger..."

Elizabeth held up her hand. "Stop! If you are going to tell me that I need to get married, forget it. I am married to my country and am happy with that...no king is ever going to boss me about," she added, a determined smile on her face.[30]

Dad nodded in agreement and turned to me. "I was just thinking of your mother, son. Maybe I should have married the country as well!"

Dad returned to the newspaper and continued to read. "It says her lucky colour today is purple," he smiled, winking at me.

My father eventually put down the newspaper. Elizabeth was now studying him closely.

"Is that ceruse on your hands?" she asked.

Dad instinctively held up his hands and looked at them. "It's paint, actually. I've been painting the spare bedroom."

Elizabeth looked interested. "You are a painter? Excellent, but why would you want to paint the spare chamber? Can you not find a more interesting subject to produce a picture of – some flowers...a horse...a person?"

Dad smiled. "I see what you mean, but it's not that sort of painting."

Elizabeth wasn't listening. "You are good at this painting, yes?"

I looked at Dad's paint-stained overalls, but didn't have time to remark.

"It is settled, then," Elizabeth declared; "you will paint *my* portrait this very afternoon."

Dad looked at me with horror.

"I don't think you understand, Your Majesty," my flustered father attempted to explain; "I'm not *that* sort of painter."

"He's just being modest," I interrupted, a cheeky grin on my face. "I'm sure Dad will make a great job of it."

"Indeed," Elizabeth nodded. "I hope so, for his sake."

Dad glared at me. I have to admit, I was still smiling at the prospect.

Elizabeth remained seated. "You will find my ladies-in-waiting where I left them...at the establishment of Mr Marks and Mr Spencer, I think it is. Tell them to come here at once to attend to me. I will need this room to prepare myself for the sitting."

We got word to her attendants, as she asked us to. The store manager came to the telephone in person, and it seemed he didn't have any trouble identifying them among the other shoppers. Four ladies – all dressed in white – eventually arrived at our house, and we showed them into the living room.

"You can leave us now," Elizabeth directed. "I will need plenty of time to get ready."[31]

"What are we going to do?" a now frantic Dad questioned me when we had retreated to the kitchen. "I can't paint to save my life."

"You might have to!" I smiled.

"It's not funny," Dad responded. "Can't you do it instead? You're good at art, aren't you?"

"Wait! I've got an idea," I chirped. "We can take her photograph. She won't know what a camera is, will she? Then we can print it off. It will be a perfect likeness."

It seemed a good idea, but my father started to shake his head.

"That's the problem," he said; "it will be a *perfect likeness*."

"That's good, isn't it?" I suggested.

"Look at her, son!" Dad groaned. "She's got a face that's bumpier than the moon and her teeth are like pieces of charcoal..."

"You can use them for drawing your picture, then," I quipped.

Dad continued to shake his head. "What I'm trying to say is that the Tonga rugby team is better looking than her! I think she'll want us to come up with something that is a bit more flattering than a *true* likeness of her."

I now realised what Dad was getting at.

"We can use Photoshop," I put forward. "We can remove all the warts and lines from her face."

Dad was still shaking his head. "Or we could just replace her entire head with Angelina Jolie's!"

"This is not good," I stated, now starting to share my father's concern. "We're going to have to come up with something...or she's going to remove *our* heads!"[32]

Dad stroked his chin. "How about we print off a *picture* of her? There must be loads on the internet."

At first I thought Dad was talking about Angelina Jolie, but then I realised he was talking about Elizabeth herself. Yes, we could print a picture of the queen and then present it to the...queen?

"You see," Dad explained, "all the pictures in our history books of Queen Elizabeth flattered her, didn't they?"

It was my turn to shake my head. "That won't work, because she'll already have *that* picture, won't she? She'll know it's not you that has painted it...if it's already hanging on her wall! Who would want a picture of a picture that they have already got? She won't want another one exactly the same, will she?"[33]

"Then we're doomed," Dad said.

I shrugged my shoulders. "Shall I get some paper? There might be some crayons in the loft!"

We had a long time to agonise over what to do. The living room door remained closed, which might have been to our advantage, if we had not long given up *agonising* over what to do. Now we were just resigned to our fate and wanted to get it over with as quickly as possible.

"This is torture," Dad groaned, as we continued to wait.

I shook my head. "No, I don't think that bit has actually started yet!"[34]

Dad sighed. "It's no good. I'm just going to have to tell her that I can't do it. It's not treason, is it? Besides, what can she actually do to us?"

I didn't think Dad wanted me to actually answer that question.

My father went to the living room door and took a deep breath before opening it.

"Wish me luck," he said, as he entered.

I heard a scream, and I wasn't immediately sure whether it came from Dad, or from Elizabeth. In fact, I think it might have been a joint effort. As I followed Dad into the room, I half expected to see Elizabeth in the bath (if there had been one in the living room[35]), but, to my relief, she was fully clothed...except for her auburn *wig*! And no matter how hard we tried, it was difficult to take our eyes off her *bald* head.[36]

"Get out!" Elizabeth stormed. "How dare you enter without knocking? Get out!"

She was up on her feet in an instant, kicking and punching at us wildly.

Needless to say, we got out, and quickly. "We're so sorry," Dad called from the other side of the door. "We didn't see anything, honest." He wasn't lying. It was true; we didn't see any hair on her head, at least![37]

We could hear Elizabeth uttering more obscenities from the other side of the door. She really wasn't *amused* now.

Things eventually calmed down, but I probably do not need to tell you that Elizabeth no longer wished to stay overnight, despite the fact that we had a water closet. However, before taking her leave, she stubbornly insisted that she would not do so until Dad had painted her.

So he did. Well, I don't mean that he eventually painted her *portrait*...I mean, that he eventually painted *her* – literally.

"You'll love it," Dad assured the suspicious queen, tin of matt white in one hand and brush in the other. "Just close your eyes and mouth."

And so Dad not only painted the spare bedroom that day, but the Queen of England too.

A placated Elizabeth I left the house with our exaggerated compliments ringing in her ears, indeed convinced that white emulsion made her face look more *radiant* than ever. She and her lady attendants even took the leftover paint, the tin clutched tightly in the hand of the queen, as she glided majestically down the street, almost phantom-like in the twilight.

Notes

1. Henry VIII

1. Henry VIII was about 6ft 2in in height and some 28 stone (178kg) when he died in 1547. In his youth, he was fit and active, quite the sportsman. His waist was a little more than 30 inches as a young man, but grew to about 52 inches in his final years.
2. Henry was a germophobe and spent most of his life trying to avoid getting ill. He was paranoid about contracting diseases.
3. Hampton Court Palace – one of Henry's 50-plus homes – was (and still is) huge, with more than 1,000 rooms.
4. Henry had hundreds of people to attend to his needs. His royal court at Hampton Court Palace (his favourite place of residence) consisted of about 1,000 courtiers and servants.
5. Henry spent most of his time sitting down in later life, as he found walking and even standing difficult. His legs were plagued by ulcers.
6. Henry would consume about 70 pints of ale per week.
7. Henry himself introduced 'Your Majesty' as a form of addressing a king. Before his reign, monarchs were usually addressed as 'Your Grace' or 'Your Highness'.
8. Henry owned about 2,000 tapestries, thought to be the largest collection at the time.
9. In 1513, Catherine of Aragon – the first wife of Henry – was left in charge of the country while her husband headed off to France to sort out the French (the chief enemy at the time). And Catherine did, indeed, do fine in the absence of her husband; her army seeing off the Scots after they had dared cross the border into England. The Battle of Flodden was a great victory for the country (and Catherine), with the King of Scotland among the dead.
10. Not only did Henry have six wives, but it is thought that he had at least ten mistresses over the course of those six marriages, though historians differ on the exact number.
11. Yes, Henry really did throw the leftover bones over his shoulder, so that the servants could collect them to feed the dogs.
12. Henry had his marriage with Anne of Cleves annulled after just a few months. It was his shortest marriage.
13. Chief minister Thomas Cromwell fell out of favour and Henry ordered his execution in 1540. Cromwell had endorsed the marriage to Anne of Cleves for political and diplomatic reasons.
14. Henry reputedly referred to Anne of Cleves as his 'Flanders mare'. He had only seen a picture of her and was not impressed when he met her in the flesh for the

first time – shortly before their wedding. He was unsuccessful in postponing the wedding, but wasted no time in setting the wheels in motion to dispense with her.

15. Jane Seymour – the third wife of Henry – gave him a much-wanted son and heir to the throne (Edward VI). Henry believed Jane to be his first true wife after his first two unhappy marriages. Jane died less than two weeks after giving birth to Edward. Henry was truly heartbroken and she is considered to have been his favourite wife; Jane is buried with the king and was the only one to receive a queen's funeral.
16. It is thought that Henry may have been one of the first people to benefit from a stairlift. When he was unable to ascend the stairs at Whitehall, a device was installed, with servants supposedly pulling on ropes to lift the chair. Walking also became a problem in later life and it is believed he had several 'thrones' on wheels.
17. Henry was not the only monarch to benefit from a 'groom of the stool' – the name given to bathroom attendants. The job involved helping remove the multiple layers of fine garments that the king would be wearing and to also swiftly remove the waste itself, there being no flushing toilets. The groom of the stool was seen as a prestigious position, one of status.
18. Henry had a legendary appetite. It is estimated from his meat-rich diet that he would have consumed about 5,000 calories a day, double the recommended intake. Lunch could last for about four hours.
19. Henry wrote lots of music. He may not have composed *Greensleeves*, as once supposed, but he did write *Helas Madame* and *Pastime with Good Company*, the latter song covered by many in recent times, including Jethro Tull.
20. Henry was a fine musician and played many instruments: keyboard, string and wind.
21. Skevington's Daughter, or The Scavenger's Daughter (as it became known), was a form of torture invented during the reign of Henry. It got its name from its inventor, the then Lieutenant of the Tower of London. The A-frame metal rack, to which the prisoner was attached, forced the knees up into a sitting position, compressing the body, eventually forcing blood from the nose and ears. Henry was not averse to torture and going further than that: historians reckon up to 72,000 executions may have taken place during his reign.
22. Primero is a card game similar to poker.
23. Contrary to popular belief, people didn't always let Henry win. He loved playing cards and dice, but was not very good at it. Records show that he lost hundreds of pounds a day and some suggest that – between the years 1529-32 – he may have gambled away an equivalent of more than £1million in today's money. Indeed, Henry was a gambling addict.
24. Towards the end of Henry's reign, funds became so low that he was forced to decrease the percentage of silver used to make coins. However, the silver coating used to cover the new mostly copper coins rubbed off after a while. The image of the king on the coin would also start to wear away, beginning with the nose; hence the fact people gave Henry the nickname 'Old Coppernose'.
25. It is believed that Henry may have been the first person to own a pair of boots made specifically for playing football.

26. Henry loved jousting in his younger days. It is said he was so fit as a youth; he could jump onto his horse while wearing his armour. However, in 1536, Henry was thrown from his horse and suffered a serious leg injury, which plagued him for the rest of his life and also contributed to his mobility problems in his final years. He had to be *lifted* onto his horse in the end!
27. It is said that Henry *really* did lay a bet that he could eat a whole cow!
28. Henry loved to party, a far cry from his father (Henry VII) who was austere and some say boring. Henry VIII's parties were wild, extravagant affairs and Henry would relish the chance to flaunt his wealth and magnificence. Often under the influence of alcohol, he would also delight in sometimes showing off his fighting skills during the festivities. He supposedly fought a wrestling match with Francis I of France in 1520 (when the two countries were on friendlier terms) – but lost.
29. Boiling someone alive became a standard punishment under the reign of Henry.
30. Henry was paranoid about being assassinated and went through a whole host of bedtime security procedures before retiring for the night. Yes, at one stage he did order for his door to be bricked up. Other precautions included ordering his servants to stab his mattress in case an assailant was hiding under it, and sprinkling Holy Water onto his bedding to help him survive the night.
31. Henry would take flight if disease was rife. Whenever there was an outbreak of some infectious sickness, he would isolate himself until it had passed. He famously left London when a severe wave of sweating sickness struck in 1528. As well as trying to avoid getting ill, Henry came up with his own remedies for treatment (he didn't trust doctors), going so far as to writing his own book of prescriptions.

2. Napoleon

1. It is widely believed that Napoleon suffered from ailurophobia, a fear of cats.
2. Napoleon has a reputation for being short and was indeed nicknamed the 'little corporal'. During the Napoleonic Wars, English propagandists depicted him as comically diminutive in cartoons, and the idea that he was very small has stuck. However, Napoleon was actually about 5ft 6in, which was probably about the average for a European of that time. His bodyguards would have probably been tall, and that would have made him also appear short. In fact, Napoleon was taller than Lord Nelson.
3. Napoleon was fond of art. He stole many paintings from countries he conquered, believing them to be spoils of war. Looting was widespread following battles, but Napoleon reached new heights, with paintings from all over Europe finding their way onto the walls of the Louvre in Paris.
4. The French army wore blue and it appears that Napoleon was not very fond of black, particularly black clothes. Pons de l'Hérault, the French revolutionary whose memoirs give an account of Napoleon's exile on Elba, wrote of Napoleon's revulsion towards the fact that the wife of Pons appeared for dinner on one occasion wearing mourning clothes, sending Napoleon into a sulk for the rest of the evening.

5. Napoleon gave conquered countries as gifts to members of his family.
6. Napoleon had a habit of pinching people.
7. Lord Nelson's famous victory at the Battle of Trafalgar put an end to Napoleon's plans to invade Britain.
8. Napoleon was considered a military genius – perhaps history's greatest conqueror. He fought more than 60 battles, losing just one-tenth of those. The defeat of the Russo-Austrian army at Austerlitz in 1805 is considered his finest victory.
9. A number of people, including his own mother, remarked on the fact that Napoleon cheated at cards and other games. Napoleon was not a good loser.
10. Napoleon liked his soup to be very hot. In fact, he was very sensitive to the cold and had fires lit in his rooms nearly all year round. He complained of the fact that the British did not allow him enough fuel during his final exile on St Helena.
11. Napoleon pastry is *not* actually named after the infamous emperor. The name is believed to be a corruption of the word 'Neapolitan', meaning from Naples, Italy. Ironically, the pastry in question is generally known as mille-feuille in France and only sometimes as Napoleon pastry outside it.
12. Napoleon loved liquorice and always kept a supply of it in his waistcoat pocket. His valet would refill his little shell box with aniseed-flavoured liquorice every morning. When he was dying, Napoleon requested that liquorice-flavoured water be the only beverage served to him.
13. Napoleon was a simple eater and ate quickly, in silence, the meal not usually taking more than 15 minutes.
14. The Duke of Wellington commanded the forces that defeated Napoleon at Waterloo.
15. Napoleon carried a 'pill' full of poison on his travels – just in case. And he had chosen to commit suicide in 1814 after losing his empire, in preference to having to live a life in exile on Elba. However, the pill had been in his possession for so long, it had lost its potency and only made him ill when he took it.
16. Napoleon *did* suffer from stomach problems and was often prescribed arsenic to help. It is also thought a stomach condition led to his death. However, the idea that he regularly held his hand on his stomach because he was in pain is a fanciful one. The reason he is captured in many paintings holding his hand within his waistcoat is simply because this was a common pose adopted by those having their portrait painted, it being seen as a sign of stateliness.
17. The Siege of Toulon in 1793 – though not the most significant or noteworthy battle in history – was, in fact, Napoleon's first great military success. Fighting for the republicans during the French Revolutionary Wars, Napoleon succeeded in forcing the British out of Toulon. He became a national hero and was given command of the French army in Italy as a result.
18. Napoleon did not have a musical ear. He loved music, but, according to his valet, would 'murder' *La Marseillaise* (the national anthem of France) when he hummed it. He also liked to dance, but wasn't good at that either.
19. Napoleon was outnumbered at the Battle of Waterloo. His French army of some 72,000 came up against two coalition armies, one consisting of about 68,000 men under the command of Wellington and another consisting of some 45,000 Prus-

sians. And Napoleon was indeed fighting against most of Europe, as Wellington led a multi-national force, with the majority being made up from Germany, Holland and Belgium. In fact, 'British' troops made up only about one-third of the total and the majority of these men were Irish, Welsh and Scottish. Wellington was himself born in Ireland and was of Anglo-Irish ancestry.

20. The weather is believed to have been one of the reasons why Napoleon was defeated at Waterloo. Heavy rain had made the ground boggy and Napoleon feared his men, horses and heavy artillery would become bogged down in the mud. He made the decision to delay the attack until the ground was drier, but that delay proved costly, as it allowed the Prussian army the time it needed to join the battle, and to help swing it even more in favour of the coalition forces.
21. The battle did not actually take place at Waterloo, but at Mont-Saint-Jean, some three miles to the south. The battle probably earned its name from the fact that Wellington had his headquarters in Waterloo, though the French referred to the clash as the Battle of Mont-Saint-Jean.
22. Napoleon is often credited as being the 'inventor' of canned food. In truth, the part he played was in offering a reward to anyone who could come up with a way of making food last longer – and someone eventually did.
23. It has been suggested that Napoleon introduced right-hand traffic to Europe, or at least endorsed the practice. Theories abound as to the reason why. Some say Napoleon merely wished to display his power following the French Revolutionary Wars – the defeated aristocracy having traditionally travelled on the left side. Other historians suggest it was to deter sword-fighting on horseback, as most would wield a sword in their right hand. Because Britain was never conquered by Napoleon, it continued to drive on the left.
24. Locals removed the front teeth from dead soldiers as they lay on the battlefield at Waterloo. Dentists would make dentures from them and unashamedly advertised them as 'Waterloo teeth'.
25. Napoleon's ill-fated invasion of Russia in 1812 was one of the greatest disasters in military history, and the beginning of the end for Napoleon himself. The French army was decimated, not only through battle, but by the harsh Russian winter. Thousands of soldiers died as a result of the cold, ill-equipped to cope with the elements. It proved to be a major turning point in the Napoleonic Wars and, some claim, the reason why the European allies eventually triumphed, with Napoleon's army (and his own reputation as a military genius) severely diminished.
26. The famous Rosetta Stone, which helped experts decipher Ancient Egyptian hieroglyphs, was discovered in 1799 while Napoleon and his army were in Egypt. Some of his soldiers found it by accident.
27. This is indeed a myth: the nose of the Great Sphinx of Giza – which has a body of a lion – was broken long before Napoleon arrived in Egypt.
28. Napoleon was exiled to two islands. He escaped from Elba, but died on St Helena.
29. Napoleon was not actually French, but Corsican. He spoke French with a Corsican accent and was often teased over it.

30. It appears Napoleon didn't like dogs much either. Joséphine, his wife, had a pug named Fortune who was possessive towards his mistress and did not like men getting too close to her. Napoleon remarked that on their wedding night, the clingy Fortune was in their bed and Napoleon was told that he would either have to get used to it...or sleep elsewhere!
31. The idea that it is illegal in France to name a pig Napoleon persists even to this day. However, the law in question actually made no reference to the name Napoleon but merely related to the insulting of *any* head of state. Novelist George Orwell used the name Napoleon for one of his pigs in *Animal Farm*. The pig in question was, in fact, an allegory of Joseph Stalin. In the French version of the book, the name Napoleon was indeed changed for a spell, but this was an editorial decision and the publisher was not forced to do so by an act of law.
32. Napoleon considered December 2 to be his lucky day. That was the day of his coronation and the day he triumphed at Austerlitz. Napoleon was very superstitious: he disliked Fridays and the number 13.
33. Napoleon's apparent fear of cats may have come from an alleged incident in which he was found in his room with sword drawn after discovering a cat hidden behind a tapestry.
34. There is actually no evidence to prove Napoleon was definitely scared of cats...or spiders!

3. William Shakespeare

1. Some suggest that Shakespeare 'invented' the knock-knock joke, or was at least responsible for introducing it to the masses. His play *Macbeth*, first performed in 1606, contains a scene that follows the familiar pattern of the modern knock-knock joke (Act 2, Scene 3).
2. Shakespeare is considered responsible for introducing hundreds of phrases and sayings into the English language – more than any other individual. Even if he himself did not actually invent all of them, his work certainly popularised them, and most are still in daily use. It is also believed that Shakespeare was responsible for introducing possibly up to 3,000 single words to the English language. His vocabulary is thought to have been greater than any other writer.
3. The word 'honorificabilitudinitatibus' is thought to be the longest in the English language that has alternating consonants and vowels. It derives from a Medieval Latin word that can be translated as 'the state of being able to achieve honours'.
4. Few would dare drink water, especially in London, where Shakespeare spent most of his life. The main source of water for Londoners was, of course, the River Thames. It was severely polluted and contaminated, the main problem being that most human waste ended up in it. With no sewage system, residents would empty their chamber pots in the streets and the waste would be washed straight into the river. It meant almost everyone drank ale or beer (or wine if you could afford it) but not water.
5. Shakespeare's father was actually an ale-taster in Stratford-upon-Avon. It was a role of great importance and status. The ale-taster had a number of jobs,

including monitoring ingredients, weights and measures used by professional brewers, and ensuring that taverns sold their ale at prices regulated by the Crown.

6. Because ale or beer was the staple drink, a mini-brewery in the home was not considered a luxury, and most people of modest means would brew their own, it usually being the job of a maid or the woman of the house. Ale consisted of water, malted barley and sometimes herbs and spices. The alcohol would kill off any germs in the water. The alcohol volume would not have been as strong as it is today, which was just as well, as even children had to drink it.
7. It is quite possible – in fact, probable – that Shakespeare wrote many more plays than those that have survived. *Cardenio* and *Love's Labour's Won* are known as the 'lost plays'. It is widely accepted that both were penned by Shakespeare. *Cardenio*, based on a character in *Don Quixote*, was listed in a 17th-century register of stationers as being the work of Shakespeare and fellow playwright John Fletcher. It is known to have been performed by the King's Men (the London theatre company of which Shakespeare was a member) in 1613. *Love's Labour's Won* was included in a list of Shakespeare's works compiled by English author Francis Meres at the end of the 16th century. However, some argue that it could have been an alternative title for one of Shakespeare's other plays.
8. While many believe Shakespeare may have penned other plays which have been lost, there are many who believe he was not the author of all of those that have been accredited to him...or any of them! Doubts over the authorship of his plays started to surface some 200 years after Shakespeare's death and persist to this day.
9. Shakespeare never went to university. The only formal education he received appears to have been from the local grammar school in Stratford-upon-Avon, though there are no records available to even confirm this. It is also believed that his parents – his father was a glover by trade – were both illiterate.
10. Christopher Marlowe – he was educated at Cambridge – was the leading playwright of the time (before Shakespeare burst on the scene) and seemingly a great influence on the Bard (both were born in 1564). However, Marlowe is one of a number of writers singled out as possibly being the author of some (or all) of the plays accredited to Shakespeare. Sir Francis Bacon and Edward de Vere, 17th Earl of Oxford, are among other names suggested by those who refuse to believe the 'uneducated' Shakespeare was the author.
11. It is believed that Christopher Marlowe was stabbed to death during a tavern brawl in 1593, aged just 29.
12. Anne Hathaway was eight years older than Shakespeare and already pregnant when they got married. It appears she lived all her life in or around Stratford-upon-Avon, even when her husband lived and worked in London. The couple had three children. Famously, Shakespeare left only the 'second-best bed' of the house (plus linen) to Anne in his will, leading many to suggest that their marriage was a loveless one.
13. William Shakespeare's name was never consistently spelt any single way throughout his life, or even after his death; at least not until the 20th century when the current spelling became fixed. Even Shakespeare himself used different spellings for his name when signing documents, most being abbreviated versions

of the name, a common practice at the time. It must be remembered that during Shakespeare's day there was not really a standard spelling rule – it was a case of spelling words from how they sounded. There were some dictionaries, but they were incomplete and unreliable. It was not until the 18th century – with the publication of Samuel Johnson's dictionary – that the meanings and spellings of words became properly standardised, though even then Johnson had his own interpretations for words.

14. Little is known about the life of Shakespeare, but nothing is known of his life between the years of 1585-92. This period, beginning after the baptism of his twins, is referred to as the 'lost years'. Shakespeare 'reappeared' again in London, now as an actor and playwright.
15. There is no evidence to suggest that Shakespeare had a hand in translating the Bible or left his mark in this novel way, other than the fact that he was in the service of King James while the Bible was being prepared. Others – who do not think it is just a coincidence – believe it may have been the work of one of the translators, or the king himself, keen to commemorate the Bard's 46th birthday. Ironically, however, another anagram of William Shakespeare's name is...here was I, like a psalm!
16. Many forget that Shakespeare was an actor as well as a playwright. He spent most of his acting career with the Lord Chamberlain's Men, renamed the King's Men when James took to the throne in 1603 and became its patron.
17. It was illegal for women to appear on the stage. Boys, until their voices broke, usually played all the female roles, or sometimes men would do so, often gargling with lemon juice to produce a more feminine voice.
18. Interaction between the audience and actors on stage was expected. The audience cheered and booed at appropriate moments, and also let the actors know what they thought of them through heckling and the throwing of rotten fruit.
19. The Globe Theatre was built in 1599 from timber belonging to another theatre (The Theatre) that stood on the other side of the River Thames. After a dispute with the landlord of the land on which The Theatre stood, a carpenter and players from the Lord Chamberlain's Men – the theatre company to which Shakespeare belonged – dismantled their theatre beam by beam while the landlord was celebrating Christmas. When the weather was better, the materials from the old theatre were used to build a new one (the Globe Theatre), its construction believed to have taken just a few months.
20. Theatregoers would put their admission money in a box at the start of each play. The boxes would then be taken to a room backstage – which, some suggest, became known as the 'box office'.
21. Elizabethan audiences loved special effects, especially the gory and bloody ones! A trip to the theatre was a full-body experience. And while there were no stage lights (most theatres like the Globe Theatre were outdoors with performances during daylight hours) and little scenery, the theatregoer would still be treated to a visual feast: pyrotechnics were used to create storms; actors would use ropes and wires to 'fly' on and off stage; trapdoors would send actors to 'hell' and bags of animal blood and intestines would be concealed under costumes, to be pierced at the appropriate moment.

22. The Globe Theatre went up in flames during a performance of *Henry VIII* in 1613, after a theatrical cannon misfired. No-one was hurt, apart from a man whose burning trousers were put out using a bottle of ale. The theatre was rebuilt in the following year, but closed in 1642 when all London theatres were forced to shut their doors at the order of the governing Puritans. A modern reconstruction of the theatre (known today as Shakespeare's Globe) opened in 1997, the innovation of American Sam Wanamaker.
23. Groundlings was the name given to theatregoers who paid a penny to stand in the pit in front of the stage. They were usually commoners who could not afford to pay for a seat.
24. The two most popular forms of entertainment for Elizabethans were the theatre and blood sports. Many of the same people who flocked to the Globe Theatre would also have patronised the nearby Bear Garden to watch animals being baited or fighting to the death. Bear-baiting was by far the most popular 'sport' of the day. It is said Queen Elizabeth was among those who enjoyed the spectacle. Barking dogs would be unleashed into the arena to torment and attack a bear, which would be chained to a stake. The show would go on until the bear had been bitten into submission or had killed the dogs.
25. It took a while before acting was deemed to be a respectable profession, or for actors to make good money out of it. In the early days, travelling theatre companies were looked upon with suspicion, the actors viewed as being vagabonds and rogues. Purpose-built theatres brought more respectability to the profession, but generally still had to be built outside city walls, as aldermen did not approve of playacting. Places like the Globe, and royal approval of the theatre (Queen Elizabeth was a fan), did help to change things, and some actors, including Shakespeare, became rich and famous. However, the majority of actors were hardly looked upon in awe or treated with any respect by theatregoers. It was considered fair game for actors to be abused on stage, with audiences hurling insults as well as rotten fruit at them.
26. Some people would attend the theatre every day and so expected to see a *new* play every day!
27. No copies of the entire script were made, to prevent rival theatre companies getting their hands on them. Even the actors would only receive their specific lines, so that the play would only be 'complete' when all the actors came together to perform it. Shakespeare did not own his plays – they belonged to the theatre company, and only some were 'published' during his lifetime. The first edition of his collected plays (First Folio) did not appear until 1623, some seven years after Shakespeare's death. It was prepared by two actors who had worked with him.
28. Mystery plays and miracle plays were overtly religious, retelling stories from the Bible. They were often performed in cycles and could last for days. *The Acts of the Apostles*, a mystery play from 15th-century France, took 40 days to perform for a reason: it contained 61,908 lines of speech, there being almost 500 speaking parts. On the whole, the Elizabethan dramatists – including Shakespeare – produced very different works, religion less prevalent in their plays, as they wrote after the Reformation, during a time of religious instability. It was wise to steer clear of the subject of religion, as expressing a view could get you arrested.

29. Fellow playwright and critic Robert Greene famously called Shakespeare an 'upstart crow' when the Bard started to make a name for himself.

4. Cleopatra

1. Cleopatra famously smuggled herself into the palace of Roman leader Julius Caesar by wrapping herself in a carpet.
2. Cleopatra's colourful and heavy eye make-up has become legendary. It was not only aesthetically pleasing, but Egyptians believed the various ingredients used in the make-up protected the eyes against the rays of the sun, infections and diseases, while also repelling flies (and evil spirits). Egyptians wanted to look their best after death as well, and make-up and other beauty aids were buried with the deceased for use in the afterlife.
3. Legend has it that Cleopatra bathed in the milk of donkeys, believing it kept her skin looking young and healthy. She may have also bathed in wine for the same reason.
4. It has been said that 1,000 litres of milk was required to fill her bath, and that 700 donkeys would have been needed for the purpose.
5. Cleopatra would have had many people attending her, but Charmion and Iras served her to the end and died with their queen, having both supposedly taken their own lives after Cleopatra had committed suicide. Of course, the Egyptians believed that servants were still expected to serve in the afterlife – and many were buried alive with their master for that purpose.
6. The Romans used urine as a mouth rinse, believing it helped whiten teeth. Urine decomposes into ammonia, which is a good cleaning product, able to remove stains. Urine was used by the Ancient Egyptians and Romans – in particular – for a variety of other purposes, from cleaning clothes to growing fruit. It became a precious commodity. The Roman emperor Vespasian levied a tax on the sale of urine collected from public urinals.
7. It was just as normal for men to wear make-up, for the same reasons as women did.
8. Cleopatra liked to party. Fortunately, so did her Roman husbands – Caesar and Mark Antony. She lived a life of leisure and excess, with lavish feasts and much drunken merriment.
9. Royal marriages between members of the same family were not unusual in Ancient Egypt, the idea being to preserve quality of lineage. Cleopatra married two brothers, firstly Ptolemy XIII and then Ptolemy XIV, sharing the throne with both. As well as these ceremonial marriages, Cleopatra 'married' Roman leader Julius Caesar (while still married to Ptolemy XIV) and, after Caesar's death, went on to marry Mark Antony, another Roman leader. Both of these were political marriages; Cleopatra wooing both men because she needed Roman support at crucial times.
10. Cleopatra is said to have owned her own perfume factory near the Dead Sea.
11. The Cleopatra family tree is a complicated one. Due to marriage within the family being the norm, scholars have struggled to conclude exactly how members

were related to each other. Even the identity of Cleopatra's mother remains inconclusive. It is suggested that following the death of his wife (who was possibly his half-sister), Ptolemy XII named their daughter Cleopatra his joint ruler and effectively she became her father's ceremonial 'wife'. Following his death, both Cleopatra and her little brother Ptolemy XIII then became joint rulers.

12. The power struggle between Pompey the Great and Caesar, once allies, led to civil war in Rome. Pompey was defeated at the Battle of Pharsalus and sought refuge in Egypt. However, Ptolemy XIII had him killed and (in order to win favour from the victorious Caesar) sent the head of Pompey to him as a gift, though that gesture backfired and Caesar took sides with Cleopatra, rather than with her brother.
13. The 'marriage' of Cleopatra and Caesar was not *officially* recognised by Rome, as Caesar already had a wife of his own.
14. Ptolemy XIII, still himself a teenager, was defeated by his sister Cleopatra and Caesar at the Battle of the Nile. He was forced to flee and it is believed he drowned while attempting to cross the river.
15. After the death of Ptolemy XIII, Cleopatra married brother Ptolemy XIV and became co-ruler with him. Also being only about 12, it is said he reigned in name only, with Cleopatra still pulling the strings. However, Cleopatra still wanted rid of her sibling and supposedly poisoned him with aconite.
16. Following the defeat of Ptolemy XIII, Arsinoe IV was taken to Rome as a prisoner, before being exiled to the Temple of Artemis at Ephesus. It is said Mark Antony ordered her execution at the request of her sister Cleopatra.
17. It was once widely believed that the surgical procedure sometimes carried out to deliver babies was named after Caesar, because it was suggested he too was born in this manner. However, most historians now doubt the truth of this, as there is no evidence to prove that even one mother ever survived a caesarean section during Roman times, and Caesar's mother did not die in childbirth.
18. Following the death of her brother Ptolemy XIV, Cleopatra named her son Caesarion as co-ruler, making him the last pharaoh of Ancient Egypt, as he outlived his mother by at least a few days. Following the death of Cleopatra, triumphant Roman leader Octavian ordered the death of Caesarion as well. It is said Caesarion may have been betrayed by his own tutor.
19. Servants would be smeared with honey so that the flies would be attracted to *them* and leave the pharaohs in peace.
20. It is believed that Cleopatra committed suicide by allowing a venomous asp (Egyptian cobra) to bite her. According to popular belief, Cleopatra took her own life after husband Mark Antony had done likewise, fearing that Octavian would bring her back to Rome to be paraded as a prisoner. She was just 39. However, there are many other theories surrounding her death and no definitive conclusion.
21. Cleopatra would have worshipped the Egyptian gods, and actually identified herself as one of them – Isis. She styled herself as the new Isis and dressed like the goddess. Women throughout Egypt (and Rome) wanted to look like Cleopatra and she became a fashion icon.
22. Horus was an Ancient Egyptian god who had his left eye ripped out during a power struggle with another god. In one of many versions of the tale, the eye was

replaced, but it was never as good as his right eye. Being god of the sky, the eyes of Horus now float over the Earth: the right eye being the sun and the left eye being the moon. The Eye of Horus became a symbol of protection to Ancient Egyptians. Amulets were made depicting the symbol and people would decorate their own eyes, believing the symbol had the power to ward off evil spirits.

23. The Society of Inimitable Livers was a club formed by Cleopatra and Mark Antony to honour Dionysus, the god of wine. And while the group was supposed to have a religious purpose (people believed drinking alcohol could bring them closer to the gods); it was probably little more than an extravagant drinking club, just an excuse for members to have a few beers and to behave like college students! According to legend, Osiris, the god of the afterlife, taught the Ancient Egyptians how to brew beer, and alcohol was very popular. It was used for both medicinal and religious purposes, though, needless to say, it was also consumed for enjoyment. Its popularity prompted Cleopatra to introduce a tax on beer – possibly the first in the world – as a way to raise funds and reduce drunkenness.
24. Ancient Egyptians shaved their heads for a number of reasons, mostly because of the heat, while lice and fleas would have been a problem as well. Women also shaved their heads (and Cleopatra probably did too) but they would usually wear wigs in public.
25. Cleopatra set out to seduce Mark Antony by famously sailing up the river in a luxurious barge, dressed as Aphrodite. According to legend, she doused the sails of the royal vessel with so much perfume; he could smell her coming even before she was in view!
26. Cleopatra reputedly wore a fake beard for ceremonial duties, as pharaohs were supposed to be men.
27. When Cleopatra refused to share the throne with her little brother following the death of their father, she had all newly-minted coins stamped only with her face upon them.
28. Cleopatra supposedly had a bet with Mark Antony, in which she said she could consume a fortune on one single meal. She won the bet by dissolving a very expensive pearl in a vinegar-based cocktail, before drinking it.
29. Cleopatra is said to have given the idea of a leap year (an extra day every four years) to Caesar, who then made it a fixture of the Roman calendar. Traditionally, women are allowed to propose to men on February 29.

5. Christopher Columbus

1. Columbus Day – a national holiday in most parts of America – is held every October to celebrate the anniversary of Christopher Columbus' arrival in the Americas. It is also celebrated in other countries – particularly in Latin America – where it is known by other names. However, it is observed in different ways, and some US states no longer even recognise the day, with many viewing the European colonisation of the Americas and its treatment of indigenous populations with shame.
2. The New World was the name given to what we now call the Americas.

3. Some of the crew did not return home with Columbus during the first voyage in 1492, instead staying to establish the 'first' European settlement in the New World. The Spanish may have begun the colonisation of the Americas (Columbus sailed under a Spanish flag), but other European countries also went on to form colonies in the years to follow. Colonisation came at a cost, however, with a huge number of indigenous people wiped out in the process.
4. Even though Cristoforo Colombo (Italian spelling) sailed under a Spanish flag, he was, of course, born in Genoa, now part of Italy. He also lived in Portugal before moving to Spain. He approached both Portugal and Italy for funding for his expeditions (he even sent his brother to England to see if Henry VII would sponsor him), but all to no avail. It was the Catholic Spanish who eventually backed his four voyages to the New World, and Columbus spent the rest of his life in Spain.
5. Viking helmets did *not* have horns on them.
6. The Vikings would have probably believed that the world was flat, or at least not spherical, though this is an assumption and cannot be proved.
7. Ask someone the question 'who discovered America' and most will say Christopher Columbus. However, Leif Erikson is believed to have been the first European explorer to reach the Americas – at the beginning of the 11th century. His Vinland is thought to be an area of North America, though its exact whereabouts has been much debated.
8. Leif Erikson spent at least a winter in Vinland before returning home. It is thought he never went back to the land he discovered. However, other Norse explorers were encouraged to make the journey. It is thought the natives attacked the adventurers, and the hostilities may be the reason why no permanent settlements were established. If some were, it is thought that none had survived by the time Columbus and others came to the New World.
9. Most historians agree that Vinland or 'wine land' was so named because of the grapes that Leif Erikson found there and brought home with him.
10. Erik the Red was exiled from Iceland. He landed on a place covered with snow and ice. However, to encourage others to settle there with him, he called it 'Greenland'. His ploy worked, and hundreds followed him to establish a new colony there. According to legend, Leif Erikson invited his father to join him on his own voyage (to Vinland), but Erik supposedly fell off his horse on the way to the ship and took that to be a bad omen. He stayed behind, only to die from an epidemic that swept the Greenland colony not long after.
11. Leif Erikson is not really the forgotten man in the history of America. Some now choose to observe Leif Erikson Day, rather than Columbus Day, and there are statues throughout the country commemorating his achievements.
12. The personal appearance of Columbus remains a mystery. Unusually – despite it being normal at the time to capture important people on canvas – not one of the portraits we have of Columbus was painted during his lifetime, and those that we do have are mostly conflicting. However, from written descriptions, Columbus appears to have been well above the average height of the time and most agreed that he had an aquiline nose.
13. Columbus made four voyages to the New World, between 1492-1504. All had their difficulties. He encountered terrifying storms, and even the lull before those

storms brought problems, the lack of wind prolonging journeys and prompting fears that there would not be enough drinking water. Not all of the natives they encountered were peaceful. They came across cannibals and were themselves mistaken for pirates.

14. In truth, none of the crew abandoned Columbus, at least not on the first voyage. However, there were threats of mutiny. The voyage took longer than anticipated and supplies were dwindling. Fearing they would never sight land, the crews of the three ships threatened to turn back, and Columbus supposedly made a promise to do so if land was not spotted within two or three days (though there is no reference in his journal to suggest this was ever his intention). However, fortunately for Columbus, land *was* spotted. Not all of the crew did return home with Columbus after landing, a few dozen men being left behind to establish the 'first' European settlement in the New World.
15. Actually, the *Santa María* – Columbus' famous flagship – was not in the best of shape. There were reports of it falling apart and it had to be patched up on occasions. It never made it home from the first voyage of 1492, running aground off the coast of Hispaniola. It was partially dismantled, with some of its timber being used to build a fort on the island. Columbus found this almost providential: the first settlement in the New World being constructed from the ship that got him there.
16. Scurvy at sea was not the only problem. In his journal, Columbus remarked that their 'biscuit' was a powder that smelt like rats and was swarming with worms.
17. Columbus was a very religious man. He believed he had found the site of the Garden of Eden when he set eyes on the lush, tropical landscape of Venezuela.
18. Those were the very words penned by Columbus himself. The belief in mermaids was rife and Columbus was convinced he had spotted some on one occasion. However, it is most likely he had seen manatees, hence their 'ugly' appearance. Sailors mistook manatees or dugongs for mermaids because of their long tails. Being a deeply religious man, Columbus is not thought to have been as superstitious as many other mariners.
19. If Sir Walter Raleigh *did* introduce both the potato and tobacco to England as children were once taught at school (though even that claim is disputed now), both products were in mainland Europe well before then. Columbus himself brought back many different items even from his first voyage of 1492, including possibly potatoes and tobacco. The widespread transfer of 'things' (including food, plants, animals and even diseases) from the New World to the Old World (and vice-versa) became known as the Columbian Exchange, so named in honour of Columbus himself. One story suggests that two of his crew members – Rodrigo de Jerez and Luis de Torres – were sent to explore what is now known to have been inland Cuba. They supposedly found the natives inhaling the smoke from leaves they were burning in cane pipes. It is said that Jerez continued smoking when he returned to his home town in Spain, but the smoke scared people and Jerez was imprisoned (probably accused of some form of witchcraft or 'devilish' behaviour) and not released until smoking had become more widely accepted.
20. Contrary to popular belief, most people at the time of Columbus had already accepted that the world was not flat. In fact, even before Christ, philosophers had

put forward the idea of the world being spherical. However, while most people in the late 15th-century accepted that the Earth was round; Columbus did indeed believe it was shaped like a pear.

21. Our diets today have much to do with Columbus and his early followers. They introduced a variety of food to Europe following trips to the New World; from pineapples and peppers, to tomatoes and turkeys. And it wasn't just food that Columbus brought back. Among his more unusual introductions to Europe was the hammock and parrots.
22. Rodrigo de Triana, a sailor aboard the *Pinta* (one of the three ships commanded by Columbus), is credited as being the first man to have sighted land (a small island in the present-day Bahamas) during the first voyage. However, Columbus claimed that he had himself seen what he believed was land the night before, but had not alerted anyone as he could not be sure the indistinct light was indeed land. As there was a monetary reward promised to the first person to spot land, it was a big deal. And, needless to say, when they got home, Columbus claimed the prize!
23. Everyone loved spices in the 15th century. They were used not only to flavour food, but also to preserve it, and to make perfume and medicine. Explorers would travel far to satisfy this craving for spices. The reason Columbus set out on that first voyage in 1492 was to find an alternative and easier route to the spice lands of Asia, and any expedition that returned home without any spices would be deemed an unsuccessful one.
24. Spices were not as common as they are today. They were valuable and so people kept them locked away. To have spices was a sign of luxury and nobility. A small number of spices, including cinnamon, were once deemed to be more valuable than gold.
25. Silk was another lucrative commodity brought home from Asia by European explorers. The network of trade routes that connected the West to the East was known as the Silk Road.
26. Goods were not the only things 'traded' between the New World and the Old World. The transmission of disease became a major problem. Both the natives and Columbus' first settlers caught serious diseases from each other.
27. Among the items from the New World that Columbus presented to Queen Isabella of Spain was a pair of Cuban Amazon parrots. Livestock and horses from Europe went in the other direction.
28. It was not just food, plants and birds that Columbus brought back to Spain following his first voyage. Some captured natives were among the 'prizes' he presented to the queen.
29. Columbus returned home from his first voyage a hero, but his reputation started to suffer even during his own lifetime. Columbus was arrested during his third voyage for his treatment of both the settlers and the natives. He was forced to return home and lost his various posts before being allowed to embark on a fourth voyage. Today, his character remains in question. His brutal and tyrannous treatment of people has cast a dark shadow over his achievements. There are many accounts of him using torture and mutilation on those who opposed him. It

appears he was a man who showed little mercy to those who failed to meet his high expectations.

30. Believing the world to be circular (or at least pear-shaped), Columbus headed west from Europe in the belief that he could reach Asia via the Atlantic Ocean. Of course, he had not reckoned on there being another mass of land (the Americas) in the way. He simply believed he had found the Indies of East Asia and even called the natives 'Indians'.
31. Columbus never actually set foot on mainland North America. An island in what is now the Bahamas was the first place sighted by the explorers during the first voyage and they later landed on what is now Cuba. The first settlement was established on the island of Hispaniola. Columbus did explore other islands, as well as the coasts of both South America and Central America during later voyages, but it is thought that he never personally travelled as far north as America (United States) itself.
32. Some say Columbus went to his death *still* believing he had discovered islands off the east coast of Asia and not islands off the east coast of America.
33. It is generally accepted that America was named after Italian explorer Amerigo Vespucci, who explored the New World in the ensuing years after Columbus. However, the name was at first only applied to what we now call South America. Another theory is that both continents were named in honour of Richard Amerike, an Anglo-Welsh merchant who funded John Cabot's successful exploration of the New World.
34. Yes, the country Colombia does derive its name from Columbus – but he never personally set foot in it, or in many of the other US districts, cities and towns that have got their name from him. Of course, the name 'Columbia' is also the female personification of the United States.

6. Winston Churchill

1. Moaning Minnie was a nickname given to the air-raid siren.
2. Churchill's inspiring wartime speeches and sayings have become legendary. This particular line is significant because it was part of his first speech to the House of Commons after he had replaced Neville Chamberlain as prime minister in 1940. It was a rallying call to the House, to get its members to support his government.
3. Colonel Warden was the wartime codename assigned to Churchill. He would use it when he needed to travel incognito.
4. Heavy fines could be imposed on people who did not observe the blackout regulations, the idea being to prevent German aircraft being guided by lights. All outside lights were turned off and people were required to cover their windows with dark material. Some glass roofs had to be painted black. However, the darkness brought new problems. There was a big increase in car accidents, and it became common to paint white lines on the roads to help drivers steer clear of each other. Some farmers even painted white stripes on their black cattle to prevent cars hitting any stray cows in the darkness!

5. Some incredible spy gadgets were produced during World War Two; from cameras small enough to fit into matchboxes, to biscuit-tin radios. Secret compartments were made in ordinary objects such as shoes, baseballs and shaving brushes. One ingenious idea (it never made it past the prototype stage) was for a pipe that not only could be used to smoke tobacco, but could also fire real bullets at the same time.
6. Walter H. Thompson was one of Churchill's bodyguards. He served him for 18 years over two spells: one before the war and another during its entirety. Thompson was very close to Churchill and always by his side. His memoirs, published after the war, made him famous.
7. From Morse code to the use of carrier pigeons, there were various ways to send messages during World War Two. Columba (the scientific name for a genus of pigeon) was the codename for a secret intelligence gathering operation that used homing pigeons to relay messages. The birds were dropped into occupied Europe in small containers that were attached to parachutes. Locals who found the birds would then attach a message and the pigeons would fly home. Some pigeons flew hundreds of miles and became famous, with some even awarded medals for bravery. Not only had they to brave predators and poor weather, German soldiers would sometimes shoot them, fully aware of what was going on.
8. Semaphore, a system of sending visual messages, usually involves using flags, though an unremarkable clothesline was one ingenious way of serving the same purpose with less risk of the message being intercepted by those it was not meant for.
9. Suspicious residents would sometimes accuse their neighbours of being spies. Anything that wasn't considered 'normal' behaviour might have aroused suspicion. A lodger who never flushed the toilet and a man with a moustache similar to that of Hitler were two innocent individuals who were bizarrely accused of spying for the enemy.
10. All kinds of animals were used by both sides to try to gain an advantage. The Russians actually strapped explosives to dogs (rather than cats) and trained them to run under enemy tanks. But even more unusual creatures were used or considered for action. Dead rats, with explosives put inside them, were placed in strategic places, such as factories, in the knowledge that when discovered most people would simply chuck the body into the fire...bang! Bat bombs and pigeon-guided missiles were among the stranger ideas put forward, as was releasing poisonous snakes or infectious flies into enemy territory. At one stage, both the Germans and British also feared the other side might try to drop the Colorado potato beetle from their planes in a bid to destroy crops and bring about starvation.
11. Churchill actually had a cat called Nelson, named after the admiral who defeated Napoleon's forces at Trafalgar. In fact, Churchill loved cats and always had them. Churchill said himself that his pet Nelson helped the war effort, saving fuel and power by acting as a hot-water bottle.
12. Churchill not only liked his spirits (he would think nothing of drinking them in the morning as well); he also loved Champagne. It has been suggested that he

may have got through 42,000 bottles of Pol Roger during his lifetime, though most feel that is a rather fanciful estimate.

13. Neville Chamberlain, the man Churchill replaced as prime minister, adopted a policy of appeasement towards Hitler. In a bid to keep the peace, Chamberlain signed the Munich Agreement in 1938 relinquishing Sudetenland (a German-speaking part of Czechoslovakia) to the ever-advancing Germans in the hope that it would be enough for them. However, Hitler was not satisfied and, when the Germans invaded Poland in 1939, Chamberlain was finally forced to go to war. Churchill was among those who opposed Chamberlain's policy of appeasement.
14. To the world, Churchill may have been known as the 'British Bulldog' – but his wife actually called him 'Pug'.
15. Churchill loved the arts. He was both a talented artist and writer. He painted some 500 paintings and even won the Nobel Prize in Literature in 1953. His other talents apparently included being able to entertain all with a fine impression of a gorilla!
16. Operation Sea Lion was the codename the Germans gave to their plan to invade Britain.
17. Food rationing in Britain during World War Two was first introduced at the start of 1940, with bacon, butter and sugar among the first items to be controlled. Many turned to a thriving black market to get what they wanted. Rationing continued long after the war had ended; only officially coming to an end in 1954.
18. The Germans supposedly came up with a plot to bomb the British royal family... using peas! Tins of peas packed with explosives were discovered on agents apprehended in Ireland in 1940, their target reputedly being Buckingham Palace.
19. Churchill formed the Home Guard shortly after becoming prime minister. The initial aim was to recruit about 500,000 volunteers to help protect Britain in the event of a German invasion. However, 250,000 signed up within a week and some 1,500,000 were eventually recruited.
20. Members of the Home Guard had to provide their own weapons at first, earning it the nickname, the 'Broomstick Army'.
21. Churchill called his pocket watch 'The Turnip'.
22. The hardworking Churchill would sometimes continue to work in the bath, often dictating speeches to his secretary who would be stationed outside the bathroom, typewriter on her lap. He also worked long hours from his bed.
23. During a stay at the White House, President Roosevelt is said to have caught Churchill naked after inadvertently bursting into his room, the British prime minister having just stepped out of the bath. The quick-witted and unflustered Churchill supposedly responded by declaring that he had nothing to hide from the president of America!
24. Churchill did wear a 'onesie'. Its proper name was a siren suit. The idea was that the one-piece garment, similar to a boiler suit, could be put on quickly in the event of an air raid. It could be worn over night clothes, keeping the wearer warm and also protecting their modesty. Churchill actually invented it.
25. Special *Monopoly* sets were created to help prisoners of war escape. The Germans allowed the Red Cross and other charitable organisations to send packages of 'compassion' to prisoners, which sometimes included board games. Tiny

compasses, silk maps detailing the prison location and other useful items to aid escape were hidden among the *Monopoly* play pieces, while a file could be hidden within the board itself. Real local currency would be mixed among the *Monopoly* money for use after the prisoner had escaped.

26. Churchill could list building as a hobby. He enjoyed bricklaying and built several walls at Chartwell, the family home. He even joined the union for bricklayers.
27. The sticky bombs of World War Two *did* look a bit like sticky toffee apples on sticks. They were effectively hand grenades that could be held by the 'stick' before being attached to enemy tanks via their sticky spheres. Needless to say, carelessness led to one or two accidents!
28. It is said that Walter Thompson saved the life of Churchill numerous times; from assassination attempts, to occasions when Churchill himself put his life at risk through his own foolhardiness and reckless behaviour (he was also very accident prone). Thompson received the British Empire Medal for his services to both Churchill and his country.
29. Chocolate bombs became a real concern. It was feared that German agents were plotting to smuggle exploding chocolate into the British War Cabinet dining room. Breaking or biting into the chocolate would trigger a timer and, within a few seconds, the chocolate bar would explode. The British took the threat seriously and got as far as employing an artist to design a poster to warn the public.
30. The image we have of the Home Guard is of an organisation full of bumbling idiots, as depicted in the BBC comedy *Dad's Army*. It has been stated more than once that the Home Guard never killed anyone except each other (the Germans never invaded Britain in the end). Indeed, some suggest about 50 innocent Brits died (and many more were injured) at the hands of the over-zealous Home Guard; from misuse of weapons, to mistaking parachuting British pilots for German ones.
31. The expression 'black dog' has become synonymous with Churchill. He is believed to have used the expression – a metaphor for melancholy – when alluding to his own bouts of depression.

7. Oliver Cromwell

1. As a Puritan, Cromwell did not like Christmas because it was considered to be a pagan or popish festival. The Puritans opposed both the secular and religious celebrations associated with it. The festival had become an excuse for people to indulge in excess, and the Puritans – keen to rid the country of all Roman Catholic practices – also declared there to be no biblical justification for it. Famously, Christmas was 'banned' while Cromwell and his fellow Puritans ruled the country.
2. Cromwell, a Parliamentarian, was given the title 'Lord Protector of the Commonwealth of England, Scotland and Ireland' when he came to power. The Parliamentarians saw off the Royalists during the English Civil War, King Charles I executed in the process. Throughout the rule of Cromwell, the country did not have a monarch. However, most accept that Cromwell was a king in all but name.

3. Prince Charles (the son of Charles I) was forced to flee after the Royalists were defeated at the Battle of Worcester in 1651. Before escaping to Europe, the future king famously had to hide within the branches of an oak tree. He became Charles II at the Restoration in 1660, when the monarchy was reinstated.
4. Cromwell did have warts on his face, including a big one between his mouth and chin, just below his bottom lip. It is said that he turned up for Parliament on one occasion with blood on his collar, having cut one of them. The phrase 'warts and all' has been attributed to Cromwell, who allegedly instructed an artist painting his portrait to produce a true picture, even if it meant including his many facial blemishes.
5. Cromwell was among the Parliamentarians who signed the death warrant of Charles I, the first English monarch to be tried and executed for treason.
6. Cromwell did not want to be addressed as a king would be addressed (he wasn't a king), but he was still treated like one...and most argue that he clearly *wanted* to be treated like one!
7. The governing Puritans banned many forms of entertainment. Theatres were closed in the 1640s and did not reopen until the Restoration in 1660. Bear-baiting, cockfighting, boxing and wrestling were outlawed, as was playing cards and gambling. Even dancing was forbidden, with maypoles being cut down to help villagers resist the temptation to strut their stuff.
8. Cromwell was actually more tolerant than most Puritans. Contrary to popular belief, many Puritans drank alcohol for pleasure and it is said that Cromwell himself enjoyed a private beer.
9. The 'branks' was a nickname given to an iron contraption used for torture or public humiliation. It consisted of a metal frame that fitted over the head, and a sharp bit or gag to restrain the tongue. The wearer would find it difficult or painful to speak. It was mostly used to silence gossiping women or to punish insolence.
10. A small beer was not so named as a reference to the amount of liquid in it, but to the alcohol content. It just meant it had a lower amount of alcohol by volume than a normal beer. Because water was not safe to drink, everyone – including Puritans – would have had to drink beer or ale. The small amount of alcohol in a small beer was just enough to kill the germs in the water.
11. Cromwell was a fine horseman. He loved riding and enjoyed hunting by horse. Even when the sport of horseracing was banned (because the Puritans believed it encouraged wicked behaviour, such as gambling), Cromwell is said to have still kept a personal stud for racing. Cromwell also enjoyed a game of bowls.
12. Failure to observe the Sabbath was an offence. Working or playing sport on a Sunday could result in a fine or a spell in prison, or at least the indignity of being humiliated in the stocks. Many would fall foul of the rules; from a barber trimming a beard on a Sunday, to sweethearts ditching morning worship in favour of a ramble in the country.
13. The Puritans tried to change the word 'Christmas' to 'Christ-tide', as the former incorporated the word 'mass' – a Catholic practice.
14. Soldiers patrolled the streets to ensure nothing was being prepared for Christmas celebrations, the festival being banned. 'Christmas' food would be seized and the

perpetrators could be punished. People were encouraged to spy on their neighbours and report anyone getting into the festive mood!

15. There has been much debate as to whether it was actually illegal to eat mince pies on Christmas Day during the rule of Cromwell. However, they were certainly disapproved of, deemed to be symbols of gluttony and excess associated with the festive season. It was therefore a further sign that you were celebrating Christmas if you consumed one.
16. Swearing was a punishable offence and offenders were often fined on the spot.
17. Not only did Cromwell oppose the Royalists in Parliament, but he also personally fought them on the battlefield. At the start of the English Civil War in 1642, Cromwell had had little military experience, but he went on to become commander of the parliamentary forces. As a soldier, Cromwell enjoyed significant victories over the Royalists. Cromwell showed little mercy to any Royalist supporters, particularly the Catholic Irish. His conquest of Ireland was achieved using much brutality, and many innocent civilians lost their lives.
18. Of course, the son of Charles I *did* take to the throne, becoming Charles II when the monarchy was restored in 1660. A coronation mug was produced to mark the occasion; it believed to be among the first commemorative royal souvenirs ever sold in England.
19. Oliver Cromwell died in 1658. He had already proposed that his son Richard should follow him as leader of the country. However, Richard Cromwell was a meek and unambitious man who lacked authority. Richard renounced power just nine months after replacing his father, paving the way for the return of the monarchy (Charles II) in 1660.
20. The English Civil War began in 1642 because Charles I and Parliament were unable to settle their religious and political differences. Many Parliamentarians were Puritans who called for religious reform, but Charles had a Catholic wife and appeared to be leaning even closer to the Catholic faith. When Charles forced his way into the House of Commons in a failed attempt to arrest five vociferous MPs, it was the last straw for both sides, and war followed soon after. Technically, the English Civil War was a series of civil wars, which did not come to an end until 1651.
21. Cromwell did smoke tobacco. In fact, it was not one of the pastimes banned by the Puritans. Smoking was not viewed as the evil it is now deemed to be. In fact, many believed it had health benefits and children were encouraged to take clay pipes to school.
22. There are various theories as to how Cromwell gained the nickname 'Old Ironsides' or simply 'Ironsides'. Some say the name was given to him by his Royalist foe Prince Rupert in recognition of the fortitude Cromwell and his army showed during the Battle of Marston Moor in 1644. At some point, the name 'Ironsides' had come to represent the entire Parliamentarian cavalry under Cromwell's command, and it may even be that his troopers were actually first to get the nickname, with Cromwell earning his from them.
23. The Parliamentarians were nicknamed 'Roundheads' because of their haircuts. They had a habit of cropping their hair, all the way round their heads. It was no bigger contrast to the Royalists (who were known as 'Cavaliers'), as they tended to

wear their hair in long ringlets, that style being fashionable in the court of Charles I.

24. In fact, some have suggested that the full name of Praise-God Barebone was actually Praise-God Unless-Jesus-Christ-Had-Died-For-Thee-Thou-Hadst-Been-Damned Barebone! A son of Praise-God Barebone supposedly also 'inherited' a variant of his father's strange full name. In truth, there is much confusion (perhaps not surprisingly) surrounding the name and to which, if any, member of the Barebone family *really* was christened with it. However, the name (at least the shorter version) lives on because it was used as a nickname for the Little Parliament, Praise-God Barebone being one of its prominent members. The Little Parliament (or Barebone's Parliament) was the last parliament of the English Commonwealth. Members – unable to sort out religious differences and put an end to the constant infighting – eventually voted for its dissolution, handing power to Cromwell, who was sworn in as Lord Protector at the end of 1653 – becoming the first person who was not a member of the royal family to be the head of state in Britain.
25. It is said that Cromwell and Charles I met as children and ended up fighting each other, Cromwell giving the future king a bloody nose in the process.
26. The exchanging of gifts – another sign you were celebrating Christmas – was also forbidden and punishable by a fine.
27. Actually, Cromwell enjoyed music. When the organ at Magdalen College, Oxford, was removed (the Puritans were against music in church), Cromwell had the organ transferred to Hampton Court, one of his homes. He employed composer John Hingston as his court organist and music tutor to his daughters. Even though many forms of entertainment were frowned upon by stricter Puritans, Cromwell liked to entertain and was known for his hospitality towards visiting ambassadors. He would stage lavish feasts, which were often complemented by entertainment.
28. As well as enjoying his beer, Cromwell is said to have enjoyed a glass of sherry as well.
29. Owners of shops could be fined for *not* opening their doors on December 25, Parliament – in its attempt to stop people celebrating Christmas – being eager to remind the public that it was a normal day and not a special festival. And going to church on that day was also forbidden for the same reason. However, many were willing to suffer the consequences, determined to celebrate Christmas the old way. The Plum Pudding Riots of 1647 involved pro-Christmas rebels in Canterbury decorating churches and demanding that December 25 be restored as a special day. Keen to do something *special* to mark the occasion, they also played football in the streets...before rioting. Diarist John Evelyn was among those who attended an 'underground' Christmas Day service in London in 1657. Soldiers surrounded the building and the worshippers were interrogated.
30. Cromwell indeed took up residence in the Palace of Whitehall, the home of former monarchs, including Charles I. Cromwell also died there, just before his 60th birthday.
31. In 1657, Parliament offered Cromwell (who was already head of state and head of government) the crown itself. For a man so opposed to the monarchy and the

idea of a ruling king, you would have thought that he would have immediately declined the offer, but he agonised over his decision for five weeks before finally rejecting the idea.

32. Oliver Cromwell is a hero and liberator to many, but others view him as being a hypocritical and tyrannical dictator – a man who got rid of a king, but proceeded to rule just like one!

8. Florence Nightingale

1. Florence Nightingale gained her famous nickname – The Lady with the Lamp – because she carried a lantern as she walked among the hospital beds at night, inspecting her patients. A newspaper report first described Florence making her solitary rounds, with a little lamp in her hand. However, it is thought the tag really took off in 1857 with the publication of *Santa Filomena*, a poem by Henry Wadsworth Longfellow, written to honour the work of Florence: *Lo! In that house of misery, a lady with a lamp I see.*
2. Florence believed from an early age that God had called her to be a nurse. She was running a hospital for women in London when she received another call, this time from close friend and politician Sidney Herbert. He wanted Florence and a team of volunteer nurses to travel to Scutari in Turkey to help soldiers wounded in the Crimean War. She arrived there in 1854.
3. Florence took a small wooden medicine chest with her to the Crimean War. Most of the medicines within it were used to treat various diseases, such as malaria and dysentery. Even before arriving at Scutari, it is clear Florence was aware of the fact that more soldiers were dying because of disease, rather than from their wounds.
4. With very few beds available, most injured soldiers at Scutari had to lie on the floor. In the absence of blankets and pillows, they were covered by their coats and rested their heads on their boots. And that floor would have rarely been washed; consisting of blood, human waste, vermin and insects.
5. Actually, Florence could not immediately ring the changes when she arrived at Scutari. It took her a while to make her mark and to start to improve the horrific conditions she encountered. Being a woman and only a nurse, she had to convince the doctors that she could do more than simply hand out food and mop floors. Gradually, the overstretched doctors gave her more responsibility and she was allowed to dress wounds or fit splints on broken limbs.
6. The determined Florence became a nurse, despite fierce opposition from her family, who did not approve of her choice of career.
7. Conditions at Scutari were horrendous when Florence first arrived there. The 'hospital' was filthy, rife with disease. One visiting priest reported that the premises were covered in lice. Soldiers were sometimes left lying on the floor in their own blood and urine for weeks until being seen by a doctor. There were hundreds of patients crowded together and, until Florence and her team of nurses arrived, few people able to care for them.

8. One of Florence's biggest achievements was making nursing a respectable profession for women. In Victorian Britain, affluent young women like Florence were not expected to work, but become a wife and mother. And nursing was certainly not seen as a job for those women that did choose to work. It was not a respected profession, with low wages and low status. A dirty hospital was the last place a woman should be seen in! Ironically, today, it is male nurses that are in the minority.
9. Once Florence had earned the trust and respect of the male doctors, she took control and made big changes at Scutari. Germs were the biggest problem, and she knew that unless the poor sanitation was improved, the mortality rate would continue to rise. She implemented strict hygiene rules and a regimented cleaning programme. One of the biggest problems was the malfunctioning sewer system and lack of ventilation. She ordered that the drains be unblocked and cleaned, and this was a major factor in reducing the death rate.
10. Florence loved mathematics and left a mark on the world of statistics. Some claim she invented pie charts. In truth, she only really popularised them, and her own coxcombs or coxcomb plots (as they became known) were actually polar area diagrams, to be more precise. She used them to present health statistics, such as outlining the causes of death at Scutari, the hospital she managed. They helped get her message across when lengthy technical medical reports may have failed. Florence was a trailblazer in the presentation of visual information and became the first woman to be appointed a member of the Royal Statistical Society.
11. Florence wrote numerous books, pamphlets and articles on her profession, but none more famous than *Notes on Nursing*, which was first published in 1859. The book is full of practical advice for those entrusted with the health and care of the sick. It was a revolutionary book, changing the way people viewed nursing; covering subjects such as food preparation, personal cleanliness, ventilation of the sickroom, observation of the patient and even their mental wellbeing. The book became an international bestseller and is still popular today.
12. Many nurses still recite the Nightingale Pledge (or at least an updated version) at the end of their training. It was created in America in 1893 and named after Florence – the founder of modern nursing. A few years after returning from the Crimean War, Florence set up the first official training school for nurses – at St Thomas' Hospital, London, in 1860. Florence spent almost the rest of her long life preoccupied with the promotion and organisation of the nursing profession.
13. Florence may not have been able to provide her Scutari patients with a sunset view, or able to hang up oil-paintings, but she did introduce screens to at least afford soldiers some privacy – and prevent them from having to view the sometimes grisly fate of a patient in the bed next to them!
14. The amputation of limbs would have been common at Scutari, due to a lack of suitable alternative medical treatments. It would have been a terrifying and risky procedure, with usually only a blunt (and probably infected) saw to hand. It is said prior to the arrival of Florence; the amputated limbs were simply thrown outside for the dogs to feed on!
15. Florence believed poor nutrition was among the reasons why many patients never recovered. As well as there being very little medical equipment at Scutari, there

was also no means to adequately process and preserve food. Florence set about ensuring patients ate fresh food that had nutritional benefit.

16. Soldiers fighting in the Crimean War did not always eat any chocolate that was sent to them. They had a more practical use for it. On discovering that it burnt well, the freezing soldiers would use it as fuel for their fire in order to keep warm.
17. Florence did complain about the inappropriate gifts sent to sick soldiers by well-meaning people back home. It is said Queen Victoria herself offered to send some perfume, but Florence responded by saying that the soldiers would probably prefer gin.
18. In even thinking about the mental health of her patients, Florence was ahead of most. She believed that the physical recovery of a patient could be aided by the improvement of their state of mind. Even something seemingly trivial as surrounding the patient with bright colours or filling the sickroom with music could make a difference, according to Florence.
19. Florence did advocate the use of animals to improve the wellbeing of patients. Soldiers at Scutari were allowed to keep pets. One of the soldiers had a tortoise called Jimmy. Florence herself loved animals and believed wholeheartedly in their therapeutic qualities. She was particularly fond of cats and owned dozens of them during her lifetime, reputedly 17 at one time.
20. Florence hand-reared an owlet that she rescued while in Athens. She named it Athena and carried it in her pocket. She had it stuffed after it died.
21. Florence never had children herself. In fact, she never married, even though there were proposals of marriage from admirers, choosing instead to devote her life to her career.
22. Florence and her sister were both born in Italy and named after places there. They were born into a wealthy family and enjoyed a privileged upbringing, with servants to tend to the needs of the household. Florence was born in 1820 and her birthday (May 12) is now celebrated as International Nurses Day.
23. Florence was often the bearer of bad news. She wrote letters home on behalf of dying or dead soldiers to inform their loved ones of their fate and to convey their final goodbyes.
24. The balaclava did indeed get its name from the Battle of Balaclava, one of the major skirmishes of the Crimean War. Knitted headgear was sent to the British and allied troops to help them keep warm. And, yes, there was a Lord Cardigan as well: he was the man who famously led the ill-fated Charge of the Light Brigade during the Battle of Balaclava.
25. Mary Seacole was a British-Jamaican nurse who, like Florence Nightingale, travelled to the Crimean War to help tend to the sick and injured soldiers. Mary set up her own hospital/hotel close to the front line (in contrast to Florence who was hundreds of miles away from the fighting), and Mary is said to have actually ventured onto the battlefield itself to treat wounded soldiers.
26. Mary Seacole has always dwelt in the shadow of the much more famous Florence Nightingale. Even so, Mary was actually also very well known in Victorian society. It was only after her death that she became largely forgotten. And her posthumous fame has grown in recent years, with many now accepting her role as a pioneering nurse. The statue of Mary erected at St Thomas' Hospital, London, in

2016 is believed to have been the first in the country to honour a named black woman.

27. Florence returned home from the Crimean War in 1856 a celebrity. She received thousands of fan letters, and sister Parthenope acted as her unofficial manager. Florence Nightingale ornaments and pictures appeared in homes throughout the country. Queen Victoria was among her fans; presenting Florence with a special brooch to thank her for all that she had done for British soldiers.
28. Florence did not like being famous and couldn't understand all 'the fuzbuz about my name'.
29. Mary Seacole tried on several occasions to join Florence's team of nurses at Scutari, but was rebuffed each time. Still keen to serve, she established her hospital/hotel at her own expense.
30. The determined Mary, a daring adventurer and prolific traveller, was in Panama when she decided she wanted to go to the Crimean War. It meant travelling hundreds of miles to get there, and she had to borrow money to do so.
31. Prejudice and racism was common in Victorian Britain, and most believe that is the reason why Mary – a penniless black woman – was prevented from joining the nurses at Scutari. However, Florence did reportedly on one occasion cite a different reason: that she feared drunkenness and improper conduct might become a problem among patients, presumably being of the opinion that Mary was a little too liberal in the distribution of alcohol. Mary did meet Florence at Scutari while she was on her way to Crimea and it is thought that the visit was amicable enough.
32. There is no doubt that the lives of many wounded soldiers at Scutari were saved thanks to Florence. In 1855, over a period of just a few months, the mortality rate for patients dropped from almost half, to just a couple of percent. And as the founder of modern nursing, Florence Nightingale perhaps did more than anyone to transform healthcare, not only in Britain, but throughout the world.
33. Florence was 90 when she died. However, she did suffer from illness for most of her long life and spent much of her final 50 years bedridden.

9. Elizabeth I

1. Incredibly, rumours abounded that Elizabeth I was actually a man; that being the reason why she never got married, or wanted to get married and have children, something that all women were expected to do in the 16th century. Known as The Bisley Boy theory, some historians have suggested that the real Elizabeth (daughter of Henry VIII and Anne Boleyn) died as a child while under the care of a governess in the village of Bisley. Fearing the wrath of Henry, the governess successfully hid the fact by finding a child of similar age and fooling the king into believing it was his daughter. However, the only child with a head of red hair similar to Elizabeth, that was available to the panic-stricken governess at the time, just happened to be a boy! Bram Stoker, author of *Dracula*, was among those to present the fanciful theory in later times.

2. Elizabeth would sometimes disguise herself as an ordinary citizen to avoid attraction.
3. Queen Victoria is famous for the phrase: "We are not amused." However, there is now much doubt as to whether she actually ever said it.
4. Sir Walter Raleigh supposedly laid his cloak over a puddle to prevent Elizabeth from getting her shoes wet.
5. Paleness was considered beautiful at the time. Elizabeth reputedly painted her face, neck and hands with ceruse (white lead) to also cover up scars caused by smallpox, a disease which almost killed her in 1562. However, the make-up was highly poisonous and many say it may have even attributed to her death. It is said that Maria Coventry, Countess of Coventry, died at 27 from excessive use of lead make-up.
6. Elizabeth was a fashion icon. She owned hundreds of dresses, many with detachable parts, meaning that she could detach the sleeves or bodice from one and attach them to another. This mixing and matching meant she was rarely seen in the same outfit twice. She also owned hundreds of pairs of gloves.
7. Elizabeth wore an enormous petticoat called a farthingale.
8. Because Elizabeth had so many teeth missing, her face appeared gaunt, so she would stuff her cheeks with perfumed cloth to make them look plumper, the perfume also helping to disguise the fact that she had bad breath.
9. Foreign ambassadors claimed that Elizabeth was difficult to understand, the gaps between her remaining teeth affecting her speech.
10. Amy Robsart, wife of Robert Dudley, Earl of Leicester, died after falling down the stairs. Dudley was a favourite of Elizabeth and some claim the two were secret lovers, leading to the suggestion that Elizabeth may have been involved in the suspicious death of Amy.
11. Elizabeth was well known for her colourful language, just like her father.
12. It is said that Elizabeth was terrified of mice.
13. Before there was running water or a sewer system, the palace toilets were cesspits, which needed to be cleaned out – a smelly job that often took weeks. Elizabeth would move out of the palace, sometimes into the homes of others, until the work was completed. It is believed that Elizabeth eventually became one of the first people in England to benefit from a water closet (flushing toilet), it being the invention of her godson John Harington.
14. Elizabeth enjoyed court masques, being particularly fond of singing, dancing and poetry.
15. Elizabeth affectionately referred to Sir Francis Drake as 'my pirate'. Drake – hero of England and scourge of the Spanish – would attack Spanish vessels and raid Spanish ports, encouraged by the queen herself. He famously insisted on finishing his game of bowls before seeing off the Spanish Armada.
16. Elizabeth gave nicknames to many of her friends and acquaintances, including her favourite Robert Dudley ('my eyes'); the short Robert Cecil ('my pygmy') and her French suitor Francis, Duke of Anjou ('my frog').
17. It is believed Roger North lost hundreds of pounds playing cards with Elizabeth. He was appointed Treasurer of the Household towards the end of the 16th century.

18. When a wax doll made in the image of Elizabeth was found in London, with pins stuck through it, the queen became convinced that it was the work of witches, and that it was responsible for her poor health. Her personal adviser on mystical matters – the renowned alchemist John Dee – had to be called to lift the curse.
19. Elizabeth had a temper and reputedly threw objects at people in her rage. Sir Francis Walsingham – her 'spymaster' – was hit by a slipper on one occasion. She would also allegedly hit out at people. Elizabeth stands accused of breaking the finger of a maid and, famously, is said to have boxed the ears of the Earl of Essex when he turned his back on her.
20. Elizabeth was addicted to sugar, putting it on her food and in her wine. Her favourite sweets were candied violets.
21. 'Water' (as opposed to 'Walter') was the nickname Elizabeth gave to Sir Walter Raleigh, the court favourite supposedly not being able to pronounce the letter 'L' very well due to his strong Devon accent.
22. Elizabeth also cleaned her teeth with honey, before a sugar paste became available.
23. Elizabeth was so scared of the idea of having a rotten tooth pulled out on one occasion, John Aylmer (the Bishop of London) gallantly volunteered to have one of his healthy teeth extracted in her presence, to prove that the pain was tolerable!
24. Actually, Elizabeth made red hair fashionable and women would colour their hair red for this reason, and not to mock the queen. Some of her courtiers even dyed their beards to match her colour.
25. Indeed, Elizabeth supposedly once spat at a courtier who was inappropriately dressed.
26. Purple was considered the colour of royalty (and still is). Only members of the royal family or those of a high-ranking status were allowed to wear it. There was a strict dress code, according to rank and status, with fines for those who did not dress accordingly. Elizabeth also ordered her ladies-in-waiting to dress in either white or black, so that they did not draw any attention away from her.
27. Netherstocks were long stockings – no-one below the rank of a knight was supposed to wear silk netherstocks.
28. Royal adviser and astrologer John Dee would read Elizabeth her horoscope and foretell the future. In the planning of upcoming royal events and engagements, Dee would consult the stars to ensure the day chosen was likely to be a favourable one. Elizabeth was very superstitious.
29. Elizabeth feared that the Catholic Mary, Queen of Scots was plotting to take over the throne, so she had her cousin put under house arrest for some 19 years, before ordering her execution.
30. Parliament tried to persuade Elizabeth to get married, in order to produce a Protestant heir and stave off the Catholic threat to the throne. At one point, she was told that she would not be granted any further funds until she found herself a husband. Elizabeth never yielded, claiming she was already bound to a husband – namely the kingdom of England. Throughout her life, she turned down numerous proposals.
31. Elizabeth would supposedly take between two and four hours to dress.

32. Elizabeth was very vain and loved to be complimented. Artists commissioned to paint her portrait were encouraged to produce flattering depictions, and each portrait was carefully inspected to ensure this was the case. Some artists even depicted her as a goddess.
33. Yes, Elizabeth really did have 'copies' made of earlier portraits that she particularly liked.
34. It has been claimed that torture was used more freely under the reign of Elizabeth than any other monarch.
35. Elizabeth often took a portable bath with her when she travelled from place to place.
36. In truth, the long-held belief that Elizabeth was bald is probably a myth. Some claim that the queen started to lose her hair after her bout of smallpox and hid the fact by wearing a wig. However, it is more likely she chose to wear a wig to hide any grey hairs!
37. The hot-headed Earl of Essex, Robert Devereux, burst into Elizabeth's chamber on one occasion, before she was dressed or had applied her make-up. Shocked by her haggard appearance; he later made reference to her 'crooked carcass'. Essex eventually led a rebellion against the monarch, but it failed to draw any meaningful support and he was executed for treason.

www.ingramcontent.com/pod-product-compliance
Lightning Source LLC
Chambersburg PA
CBHW030426310726
48979CB00009B/1633/J
9781916556201